The Quiet Child

Merry Christmas
' 01

Love,

The Quiet Child

John McKenna

Writers Club Press
San Jose New York Lincoln Shanghai

The Quiet Child

Writers Club Press
an imprint of iUniverse.com, Inc.

For information address:
iUniverse.com, Inc.
5220 S 16th, Ste. 200
Lincoln, NE 68512
www.iuniverse.com

ISBN: 0-595-19871-6

Printed in the United States of America

To Eleanor.

a picture worth a thousand lies
the memory and the mirror...
something that was left behind
something in a child's mind

bury my lovely, hide in your room
bury my lovely, forget me soon
forget me
forget me now
forget me not

—Julie Flanders, Emil Adler
October Project, "Bury My Lovely"

Chapter 1

She's with Julia at the cemetery. Julia is wearing her little coat of green velvet, and her matching hat, and she is pointing at a gravestone. In the dream, Julia is only four. "What does it say, Mommy?"

"The name of the person," Anne answers.

"What is it?" Julia's voice, like a mourning dove's, seems out of place amidst the caws of graveyard crows. "What name is it?" she asks again.

But how do you tell a child such a thing? Her own mother?

"It says Anne." Her own name sounds thin, like the lettering in cold granite. "Like Raggedy Anne," she says.

"Is it you, mommy?"

"It just says Anne," she replies. "Someone will take care of you."

"Is it you? Mommy?"

In the middle of the night, nightmare-shaken, Anne McGilvary hurries down the hall to her child's bedroom—to make certain all is well. Julia slumbers in serene child-rhythms. But the window is open again. Lately Julia swears she can't sleep without it. She needs the fresh air, she says. She needs the ocean sound to help her sleep. Why does an eight year old need help sleeping?

Anne supposes Julia won't be stopped having her way about this. She supposes her daughter is entitled to some choice in the matter. Still, she closes it three-quarters. There's enough drafty air for the compromise.

Safe, Anne thinks. In bed, at home. The portrait of security. But what about Julia's dreams? Anything could come to her there, and Anne would be a million miles away.

No, Julia is safe. Anne leans close to her and kisses her cheek once more.

"Night, night sweetheart," she whispers.

✶　✶　✶　✶　✶　✶　✶　✶　✶　✶

Much later, Julia awakens, startled. Her eyes open to the sight of the window. The sash is blocking the waves. That's not how she left it. Someone moved it again.

"*Julia…*"

With Summer over, there are no more singing crickets at night. It's colder. And the ocean's sleepy breath tells of scary dreams.

The voice comes again from up above, as if whispered through her ceiling. "*Julia! Come see!*"

She pushes away the down comforter, tucks her Marianne doll on the pillow, and steps barefooted onto the loop stitched rug by her bed.

There's a night light in the hall. Her mother put it there when Julia was three, so she could find her way to the bathroom at night, and it's been there ever since, even though Julia doesn't need it anymore.

She doesn't have to go to the bathroom now. Instead, she walks toward her parents' room, but stops half way down the hall. At the far end, her mother and father are asleep in bed. She hears daddy snoring.

She turns toward the upstairs stairwell.

Up here, Julia! Hurry!

The sixth stair creaks, like always, and the stairway is dark. When she reaches the first landing, where the stairs turn, she can see into the upstairs hall, because in her playroom, someone has turned on the little lamp. She climbs farther. There's no nightlight in the upstairs hall. Crossing it is like crossing a dark river.

And the playroom is like a wilderness. One wall has the ocean painted on it. Another, jungles. One has deserts and another— forests. As she enters the room, Julia sees the familiar faces of illustrated animals all around, watching her with steady eyes.

The other child sits at the small table, facing away.

Julia draws near. The other child does not turn to face her, but continues with the private game. When Julia is close enough, she sees something on the table.

A blue baby.

The infant's head is twisted, its mouth open in a silent scream, its eyes sealed up tight by death. Poor little arms and legs are missing.

Julia holds her breath.

The child at the table turns, grins, and tips a tiny baby arm like a tea cup. Red dribbles down.

There's a setting prepared for Julia. Another baby arm, brimming with blood at the shoulder socket, has been carefully placed on one of Julia's toy saucers, and a linen napkin is folded beside it. She knows she is expected to take her seat and join in the "tea" party.

But it's bad!

It's a bad thing. A bad game.

And yet… she doesn't want to seem impolite.

CHAPTER 2

The channel below the street was damp, as it always was first thing in the morning. Willie peered through the steamed lens of his viewfinder at the young girl on the grate in the sidewalk above him. It was no easy trick, trying to make himself come while holding the camera steady.

She was talking to someone. Maybe someone leaning out of an apartment window, above. But she was having a goddamn conversation! Which was why she stood there so long, shifting from leg to leg, letting him record her.

Keep talking, honey!

Her summery skirt really let the light through, and she couldn't have been older than twelve. Her panties had daisies on them—little girl undies!—and not only did they ride into the crack of her ass, but they had a hole in front, about the size of a quarter.

Willie zoomed right in there. Unbelievable! He was getting her snatch! The shot of a lifetime!

The greaseballs who paid him for odd jobs were hooked into shit like this, internet shit, and this kind of shot was worth plenty, because it could lure thousands of cyber-voyeurs into charging a website membership on their credit cards. The audio he was getting added credibility—the girl's young voice, and her natural way of speaking, demonstrated how candid the shot was.

4

Yeah, this was pay day. He'd known his patience would pay off. All the long waiting, in this damp pit. All the time it took to carve the hole in his apartment wall. It was a long struggle. A long climb to the top. Yeah. And he'd suffered for his art.

Looking back, he'd have to say that the hole he'd carved in the wall was a window of opportunity. Through the long, dreary Winter, the gentle clink of hammer on chisel, one inch chunks of concrete rendered into dust. Always patient with his work, never rushing toward completion. Meticulously removing one spoonful of concrete dust at a time. And, naturally, treating his nose to a different sort of dust.

Whistling.

Alone for hours in his one room apartment, like a tortured prisoner, in some old movie, with a masterful escape plan. He chose different hours of the day for his work, so that no one would become curious about the *clink! clink! clink!*

And when the passage was functionally ready, did he stop? No. He continued his work. He prolonged his agony, and heightened his anticipated pleasure, pursuing the perfect aesthetic. The shape of the hole had to be just right.

The project was what he was meant for, the true reason he had rented the damp, smelly apartment… although he didn't know it at the time. When he rented the room, his only thought was of the window, high up on the front wall, at sidewalk level.

Women in their prime. Old ladies. Little girls. In skirts, walking by all day, everyday.

What a perfect apartment! What an ideal studio! What an awesome, fifteen square foot, piss damp, concrete pit! What paradise!

To lie in bed, naked under one crusty sheet ripe with his own bodily smells, to lie there, perfectly within the bounds of legality (except, of course, for the hypodermic by the bed), his digital camera on its tripod, the video monitor before him, two views of the passing thighs, and him, maddeningly teasing his angry hard-on with delicate strokes, while summer ladies strolled by in swirls of fabric, with hems above the knee…

God, those first months were blissful.

Sometimes he would whip the sheet away, exposing himself completely, and he would jerk furiously toward climax. The only possible witnesses, whose shoulders weren't cut off by the framing of the window, were the little ones. And he didn't mind giving *them* a show. What the hell were they gonna say?

But, like everything else, in time the view through the window lost its kick. The angle was less than perfect. It was so close to what he needed that it threatened to drive him over the edge.

Then, one afternoon he noticed the grate in the sidewalk, about a half block from where he lived. It was about three feet long by two feet wide, and there was some sort of channel below, for drainage or something.

Did it run the length of the sidewalk? It had to run at least as far as his building. And if it did, what a hiding spot!

Willie Prager did what he liked in this life. He was a secret, slippery man with powerful visual appetites. He'd be the watcher below, the troll under the bridge, with his sturdy, gnarly stick.

There was something so sexy in the shape of the wall aperture, once he'd finished carving it. So inviting, with its chick-like curves. On the other side of it lay a ready made addition to his apartment: a new playroom, a "lower deck" that awaited his use, whenever he wanted it. And as it turned out, it was the best place in the world to shoot up.

Shoot up, he thought. *Like I'm doing now. Heh heh.*

The girl above him shifted her weight, creating a hot delight in his viewfinder.

Come on, come on…

Seconds before he was ready, she called out, "Bye-ee!"

And she was gone. *Fucking bitch!*

It pissed him off.

He closed his eyes and imagined driving his blade into a neck. Not hers, necessarily. But somebody's. Anybody's. Just to show how pissed he was.

Huhh!!! Plunge it in. Then, *huhh!!! huhh!!!*, again and again.

Like that bitch in Connecticut. And that prosecution witness in Portland, Oregon, who never did testify. It was like being a star, getting paid for shit like that.

His anger, and the violent acts he visualized, enabled him to gratify himself. He finished the job at hand, and went inside to watch the instant replay.

CHAPTER 3

Where was her mind?

Anne worked at a manic pace all morning in her studio, then saw the time and scampered for the door, throwing on a wrinkled raincoat even though the sky seemed to be clearing. Her hair was unwashed and wild. Underneath the jacket, her baggy man's shirt was smeared with oil paint. This was not how people showed up at school conferences. Would the teacher think she was a horrible parent?

Good naturedly, she chided herself. *Chill out!* for God's sake.

As she entered the school, she remembered a habit she had when she was little. She used to pretend the reflection in the glass doors was a window into a dark, parallel universe, and she would avoid the glance of the bad little girl in there.

The odor of the school brought her back in time as well—back to when her nose was forced into a warm yellow puddle by Sister Bernadette. Elementary schools always smelled of urine after that. Now she was sending her own daughter to one.

Maybe. This was a trial period. That means you try it, with an open mind. So lighten up, for crying out loud.

Hurrying down the corridor to the room at the end, she finger-combed her hair. She could only imagine what an unholy mess it must be. Why hadn't she at least washed her hair?

The door was open. She poked her head in, surreptitiously scraping dried paint from behind her thumb.

"Hi—"

"Hello again, Mrs. Clausin," the teacher said cheerfully, as she stood.

Anne let the greeting slide. (Her husband's name was Clausin, not her own. She'd introduced herself as Anne McGilvary already to this woman.)

As she entered the little people's space, where drawings were clipped to strings stretched corner to corner above like clotheslines, she zeroed in on a group of finger paintings posted behind the white haired teacher. The paintings exploded with color, and freedom, and joy in expression. She pointed to a minimal, abstract rendition—a curve with two eye bulges, and a signature, spiral tongue. "Is it a frog?" she asked.

"I don't honestly know—"

"I wish I could do that," Anne said.

"Mmm, our little Picassos…"

Anne doubted the woman knew much about Picasso, except maybe that he had a "blue" period, and that his name was convenient to toss around in an elementary school. This woman, whom Anne would entrust with Julia's creativity, seemed like a church secretary with her conservative grey dress and refined speaking style. Anne was tempted to grill the teacher on her appreciation of the ingenious Spaniard.

"Well Julia's clearly done well for herself," the teacher said, when they sat face to face. "She's a bright child. Her reading is quite good—I'd say you've done wonders with her."

As if it should be so hard for a child to learn such a thing without the benefit of school education.

"Her shyness, I think," the teacher continued, "is the most important concern at this point. Of course it's expected—"

…because other third graders all knew each other—and Julia didn't have the *socialization*, etc…. Yes. Anne knew all that. She used to dismiss it as nonsense. "Why is it a concern, in the first few days?"

"Oh, it's not a *big* concern. She's not psychologically withdrawn. In fact, I'd say she's quite engaged, aware of what's around her. She's bright. Her work is terrific. She simply hasn't chosen to utter a word here, yet, that I am aware of. The other kids, in a way, aren't sure what to make of it. Selective mutism, I suppose, is the term—"

"I don't want her pressured," Anne said, sounding too severe. "I appreciate your concern. But I was shy at her age, and the pressure to be sociable was the worst part—" She shook her head.

"I've heard some of those horror stories," the teacher warmly protested. "I would never make it an issue with Julia. It's just one of those points to consider."

Anne sighed. "Of course. But if she needs to be by herself—"

"Mrs. Clausin, I would never force a third grader to do anything emotionally troubling."

Anne smiled, demurely. "McGilvary," she said. "We have different last names, Julia and I."

"Agh, I knew that. I've learned so many names in the past week."

The teacher was consistently positive, upbeat.

"Julia likes your class," Anne said. "We are, of course, still in the process of deciding." She laughed. "I am sorry for being defensive—"

"Oh—you're a mild case. Parents are defensive by nature, and that's how it ought to be."

In the air, August heat was supplanted by September's gusty promises. The minutes of the day, which just last month seemed to number with the inches across the sky, were now more like shiny SUVs zipping kids off to soccer matches. Anne and Julia walked from their ocean-nestled neighborhood, all the way down the hilly shore road and into town.

"Take my hand, sweetheart."

"I'm okay."

"Julia—"

"Are we getting lunch?" Julia asked, taking hold of her mother's hand.

"Mmm hmm."

"Why not at home?"

"You'll see."

Among the Victorian bricks of downtown, they entered a cafe where the windowsills were painted purple, and the work of local artists hung on the walls. Julia's recognition of her mother's style in the colorful canvases was a gradual dawning, a glance followed by quick, quizzical scrutiny, then comical delight. "Mom—those are yours!"

"I know, sweetie," Anne said, hushed. "Impressed?"

Julia nodded vigorously.

A little embarrassed, Anne diverted Julia's attention to the pastry display. Two women behind the counter were talking about Hurricane Harriet, which struck the North Carolina coast that morning.

"They say we might get it, this time," one woman said. (Another hurricane earlier in the season defied prediction and danced out to sea.) "Maybe two or three days from now."

When she was younger, Anne loved hurricanes. Now, as a homeowner with waterfront property, and as a mother, the threat presented a mix of exhilaration and dread. She paid for her purchase and gave Julia the small, white bag to carry.

Outside the cafe, they sat on a bench and ate almond crescents and tea, as clouds thickened overhead. "I never had art in school," Anne said. "When I was your age."

"Why not?"

"The nuns taught the three *r*'s."

Julia searched her mind for all the "r" subjects. "Reading…—"

"Writing and 'rithmetic."

"Writing is a *w*…" Julia said.

"Yeah, and it's *a*-rithmetic. I guess to teach art they would have had to say…*rt*."

Julia giggled. "So why bother? But did they teach… *running*?"

"Only at recess."

"What about… r-stronomy?"

Anne chuckled. "No. Galileo was still in purgatory."

Julia was tickled by this.

After one pause in their chatter, a pause filled with the taste of goodies and the smell of potential autumn rain, the wide-awake, cinnamon-haired eight-year-old, equal parts professor and pixie, began spontaneously to sing the Beatles song "Good Day, Sunshine."

Anne laughed, draped an arm around her daughter and kissed her cheek. Julia was fine. Everything was going to be fine.

They sat there a few moments more, their faces each a reflection, through time, of the other. Then they walked up the block, and turned the corner. While Julia ran ahead, Anne caught herself taking mental snapshots, trying to seal the moment in memory.

Then Julia exceeded a comfortable distance.

"Sweetie!" Anne called.

Julia froze, satirically, and spun around. Her voice was a mock-musical instrument. "Yes mother?"

That's when Anne saw that the necklace had come loose. *Mary's locket!* It was precious, a family heirloom, from her great-grandmother. Valuable, in dollars, sure, but even more so in sentiment. It held a miniature wedding portrait from the 1890's, and Anne had indulged, against her best judgement, in adorning Julia with it this morning.

One end of the chain slipped downward from Julia's shoulder, while at the other end, the clasp loosely adhered to her collar.

"Oooh, honey!" Anne shouted, "the necklace!"

Julia glanced down, and her small hand reacted, too late. As the locket slid to the end of the chain, its momentum pulled the clasp free of her collar. As quick as a shooting star, it streamed through space, and fell through a grate in the sidewalk. A loop of chain folded across two steel reeds, then drained like liquid gold down into the hole.

"Oh! Julia!"

"Sorry, mommy…"

"Shit!"

"I tried to hold it, but it went through my fingers like a snake!"

There was that part, there was definitely that part of Anne that wanted to scream at Julia, and blame her for it. *God Damn It, Julia! Why Can't You Pay Attention! You're always lost in a dream world…!*

That's what Anne's own mother would have said.

But Julia's face was somber, her skin whitened. She seemed afraid she'd done wrong. But she had done nothing of the sort.

Anne sighed out the brunt of her anger.

"It's not your fault," she said softly.

It was only an object.

No, it was more. Her grandmother passed it down on Anne's fourteenth birthday. It was what she wore when she needed luck, or a blessing. When she wanted to look her best. Now, botched responsibility bit her on the hand, as if her grandmother were looking down that moment, saying, *'I entrust her with a prized keepsake—and look what she's gone and done…'*

Nonsense. Death wasn't like that. And if she never got the locket back, she still had the memories, which were what mattered.

But she wanted the locket! Why couldn't they go back twenty minutes and walk home on the other side of the street?

Julia, then, was on all fours, peering into the dark space below.

"Oh, honey, you'll muck up your clothes."

"But we can get it—"

"How? Julia, I don't think—"

It was not even in sight. It was so dark down there.

The grate was hinged on both sides, and two panels connected solidly in the middle. A pair of flat, rusted steel plates overlapped the link. The hinges were firmly embedded in concrete, and the plates had key holes in them, large enough to pass marbles through. Anne imagined enormous skeleton keys dangling from an iron ring on a medieval jailer's belt.

She tried to shake the grate, but it was fixed, solid.

Who would have access? The city? A building owner?

"Come on, honey." She took Julia by the hand.

They were before a row of three connected brick apartment houses, and she determined to march to the nearest door, and try to learn who managed the building.

She paused at the top of a set of steps, looked at the long column of buzzers and the list of names beside them, and thought it might be better to go buy a pack of gum and some string. Julia was lingering by the bottom step, playing on the iron railing. Lord knew it wasn't her fault. Anne's own vanity was responsible, wanting to adorn Julia with that elegant, country-lady look. She'd also hoped the locket would serve as a good-luck charm.

She pressed the last button and waited, and when a young woman's voice answered, Anne said she was looking for the super, or a maintenance person. She was buzzed in without further response.

She hesitated, holding the door, and pressed the button again.

"Yes?" came the voice.

"Oh—thanks," Anne said. "But do you know where I can find—"

"I don't even live here," the voice said.

Sor-ry, Anne muttered to herself. Then, "Come on, sweetie-pie."

Julia charged up the stairs.

The outer door closed behind them and muffled the outside sounds. Anne looked over the row of mailboxes in the foyer for some sign of where to knock, but the names printed there were just names. Beyond the glass of the inner door, a short corridor led to a stairway; above the first landing, concentric squares of stained glass filtered the light. It was like a dusty step back to the forties in there, accented by square, vinyl floor-tiling.

"Good grief." She felt the old nervousness again. That flutter. Those panicky waves. The impulse to drop everything and flee, to find some reason why the locket was not all that important and could be forgotten.

"Well?" Julia asked, impatient and cocky. "Are we going in?"

"Julia, for crying out loud!"

"Sor-ry!" Julia huffed.

Anne took Julia's hand. "Yes, we're going in, dear. For a minute."

They pushed through the swinging, inner door with a squeak, and were greeted by the smell of stale disinfectant.

There were two apartment doors to the right, and one, at the far end of the corridor, to the left of the stairs. Something about that one, being tucked in the corner like that (and maybe it was an association with tool closets or furnace rooms below stairwells,) told her that if a building manager lived here, that was where they would keep him.

She tried to convey an attitude of determined problem solving as she led the way, and as she rapped on the door.

At first there was only the silence of the old paint and wood of the corridor. Then, from within the apartment, she heard a thump, and a clank, and hasty shuffling around.

"Be right with you!" called a man's voice.

CHAPTER 4

All night Ed Jones had been caught in the cycle of bringing up old memories, envisioning one small thing he could have done differently, then tracing the hypothetical changes, through successive outcomes, to the land of what might have been. Around six am he took the box with his service revolver from the top shelf of the closet, and he sat at the kitchen table and cleaned and loaded it. This was a once-a-year, ritual event, usually in February or March. He prepared himself, as usual, for the possibility that when he was finished with the maintenance, he'd use the gun.

But like the time before, and the time before that, suicide wasn't an option. The biological instinct to survive, the taboo against self-murder—he had no wish to let them influence him, but they did.

He decided to obliterate consciousness with drinks. While working toward that goal, he watched the American Movie Classics channel, and wished Myrna Loy would marry him. When he started to fade, he set the television timer for an hour, and drifted off with Myrna's sweet voice still in his ears.

He dreamt that he was below decks on a cruise ship. Heavy machinery pressed down on him, and forced him under the water, over and over. Then the dream changed. He was in his apartment, and all the tenants in the building had to pass through his living room. They made comments on his drinking, and his poor housekeeping.

He woke up late, believing he'd heard a knock at the door, and he stashed his bottle and threw on a robe.

He expected one of the kids at the door—a twenty year old, with dyed green hair, who would make Ed feel old, and who would complain of broken plumbing or something.

Instead, when he opened the door, his wife and daughter stood there. They must have forgotten the keys.

Relief flooded him to see them home. They could join him for a group cuddle. He could nurse his hangover, and when he'd slept enough, his drinking would be finished for good. They could go to the park. At night—maybe a bucket of chicken for dinner in the living room, on the couch, with the cool autumn air blowing in through the windows. They'd have a blanket across all three laps, and they'd watch a movie.

But *they're dead!*

No. They were here, in front of him!

The skin on their two sweet, familiar faces suddenly turned eggshell white. Their eyes turned red, muddy. Their smiles stretched into stiff grimaces.

A fissure crackled across his wife's forehead, and a beetle crawled from it, skittered across her brow, and burrowed into her yellow hair. His daughter's lower jaw vanished, and red vomit poured from her gullet.

Ed screamed, and jumped back. Then the light in the hall dimmed as the dream window popped.

They stood there—a woman and a little girl he'd never met. He'd never met them. But now he'd frightened them.

The woman pulled her child close in a protective stance. She was frozen, with that wide-eyed look. Ready for fight or flight.

Ed clutched his heart. "Good God. I was still asleep!"

He'd known that heavy drinking would get him into trouble sooner or later, and that he'd embarrass himself. It figured that it would be with someone as lovely as this.

He felt like a disease.

Bad enough to be over fifty, scraping by fixing heaters and unplugging toilets. Bad enough to smell the way he did, and to be standing against the backdrop of his garbage-dump apartment. Did insanity make him any more attractive?

"Are you all right?" the woman said, nervously.

"Sorry," he said again. "I was asleep. I was still out of it."

Her face was as flawless as a 1940's film star. Her hair was dark, ocean-wavy, and colt red. There was something else, in her eyes. A sparkle of something warm.

He mourned the missed opportunity of an adequate first impression. He wanted to do this over—to be civil, and sociable enough that if he ran into her in town sometime he could say hello and maybe she'd smile, and not feel put upon.

As it was, she must have noticed he was still drunk. He tried not to breathe. He tried not to cloud his visitors in vodka fumes.

Warily, she told him why she was there. She'd dropped something.

— *What? Where? The sidewalk?*—

She repeated details until his brain sorted and processed them. Oh yeah. He knew the grate in the sidewalk.

He saw the smallest chance for redemption.

"Tell you what," he said, after learning her name. "If you come back tomorrow, I'll have it for you. Not to worry."

She protested. He did his best to assure her.

"I'll get it back. I promise!"

CHAPTER 5

"Strange guy."

"He's nice," Julia said.

"We'll see if he gets the locket."

They walked from downtown toward Bow Lee Point as clouds thickened overhead. They climbed the big hill past September grasses, which grew tall and yellow against the inlets and streams. Between houses, the ocean breathed as blue as Winslow Homer had said. Docks waded in it, and the coastline bowed inward, carving an indigo basin toothy with whitecaps and sailboats.

The slender lighthouse poised, three miles out, like an artist's pencil against the sky, held in the flat palm of three flesh-toned islands.

Their house was like a white-haired uncle who welcomed them home and embraced them, with a sneaky twinkle in his eye. Across from a wildlife sanctuary, it sat atop a wide slope just a quick tumble to the lapping shore. Its gables, like bony crow's wings, jutted skyward, while the widows watch between them seemed a center of perceptivity. Wide windows at overlapping levels lent a certain quirkiness to the facade, and the skyward crawling, crumbling brick chimney deepened a sense of decayed gothic. To Anne, it was a mansion fit for an errant disciple of Poe, or for the kind of old-world governess whose architectural commissions might have featured liberal delineation of the gargoyle.

Inside, Julia raced up the stairs yelling on her way to the playroom on the third floor. Anne followed, and peered lamentably into her art studio on the way. She was currently under contract with the subsidiary of a major book press who used her original paintings for the covers of eerie paperbacks—ghost books, supernatural tales, both new and classic. They needed three paintings to choose from before the end of the month.

Ah well. There was time for one story. Most likely she'd be working well into the night anyway.

The playroom was Julia's favorite place, a room all her own, but not for sleeping. The murals expressed her personality and imagination, because even as a three year old, she'd had an active role in creating the images for the walls—which animals went where, and what moods would be read on their faces. Anne's only concept, beginning the project, was to paint leafy green jungles on the south wall, to capture the heat of desert plains and red clay canyons on the west, the climb of the forest into snowy mountains to the north, and the ocean to the east, and to populate each of these milieux with authentic-looking animals. She'd done all that, but she hadn't intended to create such eerie and somber intricacy. Little girls' playrooms were supposed to have happy characters on the walls. It was in honoring Julia's impulses that a result far more dramatic than any candy-cane land of fuzzy pink and blue bears was produced.

"She's scared!" Julia, age three, had said of the fawn in the Maine forest. "She heard a gun!" So Anne captured a wide-eyed, adrenaline pumped look for the young creature. And when Julia said to make the desert coyote hungry, "but sick!" Anne obeyed, and gave it the drooping head and red saucer eyes of advanced rabies.

Other animals were not so terminal. The woodland porcupine was distinctively pleased, and the blue whale seemed self-satisfied. The moods on the faces of the monkeys in the jungle were diverse, to say the least.

What Anne liked best about the finished product was the way the east wall, when you faced it from the proper angle, gave a view in which the outside world blended with the inside one: two oceans combined, their horizons lining up like the focus line in a camera.

The south window, by contrast, peered past a Belezian waterfall, through South American vines, and through a carpeted window nook, to a view of treetops and rooftops on the Maine coast.

Miniature furniture ordered the space in Julia's playroom. Books and playthings filled every shelf and corner. And Julia tended to live there. It was her office.

Through the years, when Anne looked in on her daughter in the playroom, she observed the child's total immersion into worlds of fantasy and imagination. Many times she watched Julia gesticulate in conversation with invisible playmates, so engaged as to take no notice of Anne standing in the doorway.

When Julia was six, her fantasy play seemed appropriate. She had an especially lively imagination—a sign, perhaps, of future talent and creative ability. But in the following years Julia's fantasy world seemed to bloom into something more intense. Anne sensed a frightening edge to Julia's solitary play. On more than one occasion, Anne approached the playroom as the sound of Julia's one-sided conversation grew sharp. Then Julia abruptly halted her fervent chatter and pretended to Anne that she'd been quietly reading all along. She didn't want to talk about her imaginary friends, the way she used to.

If Anne, climbing the stairs, heard Julia's strange, airy song—*mee-I, Julia,—hello, hello, hello*—she froze for a moment and listened. Then she announced her approach with slightly louder steps, or the tap of her ring against the railing.

A creative mind was a wonderful and horrible gift. Anne wanted Julia to have all of the ecstasy and none of the anguish. The richness of vivid dreams, and artistic vision. But not the madness.

Perhaps home schooling left her too isolated. Maybe exclusive exposure to Anne as a role model was unhealthy.

She looked over the colorful volumes on the shelves. Julia still treasured her picture books, though lately she spent time with much more advanced materials. "What are we in the mood for?" she asked.

"Maybe not one of those," Julia said. "Can't we tell the one about…" She paused, and kneeled on the settee, facing the window. Staring out toward the sea, she seemed so mature for a moment, and so beautiful. Was she a siren? A sea nymph? Why was her destiny a mystery? Some adult life awaited her, and it was worlds apart from Anne, though some part of it was written, now, in some corner of Julia's dreams and desires. "Can't we tell the one about the island witch?"

This was an invitation to a familiar ritual: the collaborative invention of a tale.

"Do I know that one?" Anne said.

Julia nodded, a serene, other-worldly grin on her lips. "Let's go up to the roof."

"Ah. Top of the world, eh?"

Together they slid Julia's toy chest into the corner. Anne climbed up, reached for the ceiling, and took hold of the small, brass ring.

"Stand back, honey," she said, and tugged. The drop-away ladder unfolded.

The widow's watch was like a clear, cubby hole in the sky. They sat on the octagonal wall-bench and watched the world bathe in breezes.

"The Island Witch," Julia said.

Anne feigned recollection. "Ah, yes. Who made the weather fierce."

As if a gust of sea air met her on the prow of a mighty ship, Julia's features enlivened. "Many sailors perished in her storms," she said darkly.

"And no one knew why," Anne said, putting her arm around Julia and pulling her close. "No one knew why the weather in that part of the ocean changed so suddenly, and became so violent."

"No, mom!" her daughter chided, aghast. "It was always violent."

"That's what I meant. The weather surrounding that island, for miles around, was always violent and stormy. It was just when sailors entered the storm that they were surprised. Because it never showed up on their instruments."

"Exactly! But it was all different storms, sometimes at the same time, sometimes one after the other. Like that."

So the story began. As it unfolded, Anne did most of the telling, but Julia filled in many important parts, and she guided her mother's literary choices with giggles, nods, and explosive contradictions. It was a story about a family of religious pilgrims, zealots really, whose ship was tossed in the gale, and who wound up shipwrecked on the island of the witch. The teenage daughter left the others to see what she could find on the island, and she discovered the witch's hovel. She looked down at it from the top of a hill. The eye of the storm shrouded the dilapidated cabin in a dry, still area no wider than the shack itself—with its window boxes full of black orchids and black tulips. Clearly, this place was the source of dark magic.

"There was a large rock, delicately balanced on top of the hill," Julia said. "That gave her an idea. She shoved the rock, really hard!"

"And the massive boulder teetered on the edge…"

"And it rolled down the hill, faster and faster, toward the witch's house!" Julia said. "She was inside, and she could see it coming toward her window. Bigger and bigger! Then it crashed into the wall, and the whole wall collapsed! The ceiling crashed down, and broken boards came crashing down on her so their sharp points drove right into her eyes, and cracked her skull—"

"Julia—!"

Julia caught herself, and smiled meekly. "Well—! She was baaddd!"

Anne sighed, a little alarmed, though somewhat bemused by her daughter's bizarre edge. "Anyway— The witch was, in fact, dead," Anne said.

"Very."

"And the dark magic died with her."

"Did it?" Julia asked, all irony. "Did it really?"

"Well, I guess we'll never know for sure."

"Of course it seemed that way," Julia said. Then, in a mysterious, whispery voice—"But there are those who say…"

Anne took her cue. "That sometimes when sailors are cruising near those waters… They feel a violent wind…"

"Which their instruments never showed!"

"And for just a moment, it seems as if a sudden storm is raging but a few kilometers off their leeward bow."

"What's a leeward bow, mom?"

"Sweetheart, I have no idea. It's nautical. It sounded good."

After the story, Anne asked Julia about school. She apparently hadn't taken much notice of other children in particular, but she liked the lessons.

"We don't have to decide yet," Anne said. "We can wait until after the first full week."

They closed up the widows watch. Anne left Julia alone in her playroom, and descended to the kitchen, where she flipped through a couple of cookbooks, and pulled some meats out of the freezer to thaw. Had to prepare the man's dinner. God forbid he'd ever do it himself.

A news break on the radio briefly addressed the potentiality of Hurricane Harriet arriving within the next few days. Outside, the sky over the sea was silvery.

There was a message on the answering machine. The sight of the red light made her mad, because she assumed it was Mark leaving one of his take-care-of-something-else-for-me messages.

It wasn't Mark, though. It was Maria, calling from New York. Another painting had sold, and Anne was twenty-five hundred dollars richer.

Yes!

She brought the cordless phone out to the screened in porch, and sat, looking out at the sea as she dialed. When she learned which seascape had sold, its unique blend of sea greens and rock filled her with a familiar mixture of joy and bereavement. It was wonderful to know someone loved the piece enough to buy it, and she hoped they would enjoy it forever. Whoever they were.

After hanging up, she closed her eyes and visualized the painting once more. Her farewell ritual. She saw the smooth, rain-colored rocks and the bunches of green scrub, charged and alive. Then the water, a swimming span of deep purity; and the coastal houses, benevolent eccentrics darkly characterized, marching toward eternity. It was the last she would see of the painting, except for photographs.

Her next call was one she didn't relish, but it seemed necessary, and appropriate.

A nurse on the unit picked up, and Anne explained who she was, and asked if Mark was available.

"Well, I'm sure he'll make time for you," the nurse said cheerfully. Undoubtedly, Mark conveyed the impression, around the hospital, that his marriage was a portrait of bliss. Unless, of course, he was trying to get laid.

She listened, on hold, to some Mozart strings and watched a Blue Jay hop among some ground ivy. Then he answered. "Yes?"

"Hi. I was wondering when you'll be home tonight—or if you could try and make it before dark."

"What for?"

"We dropped Mary's locket down into some kind of storm drain, and I don't know if I trust the super to get it back—he seems nice, but a little out of it I thought. I hate leaving it out there. Not that anyone would see it, but I didn't know if it started to rain heavily, if it would get washed away to who knows where. Is it supposed to rain again?"

"Are you finished?"

"What?"

He used his controlled, put-upon voice. "I didn't understand a word you said, Anne. You call me about these trivial things, and when I've got interns waiting in the O.R.—"

"I call you?"

He sighed. "Anyway, I'll be home later. Okay?"

She studied her fingernails. "Were you going to your club, or whatever?" Have sex with Lucy, she meant.

"How should I know?! I suppose it depends, doesn't it?"

"On what?"

"On whatever!"

"Well, then, this is what I'm asking you. Would you come straight home, because there's something I need your help with."

He sighed, exasperated. "Whatever. I've got to go."

"Goodbye, dear," she said mock-pleasantly.

The click in her ear made her growl.

CHAPTER 6

This is damnation. What my world has come to. Confinement in the shadows. This is Hell.

I used to think there were reasons. That it wasn't my part to know them. I struggled to accept that.

But it's hard, I tell you.

I live among pipes and wires, and raw timber with nails left protruding. I breathe the shag of fiberglass insulation, and the last time I saw the moon, it was blood red, and turned out to be a knot in the wall interior.

I share crevices dug by termites, and was, for a time, intimately acquainted with a family of rodents, before their death by poisoning. I live in closed closets, where I smell mothballs and reach into pockets to know what was left there. The corridors I walk are narrower than most, and the last time I cried my anguish out, it was with breath stolen from a mist-silvered sky, and intonation burgled from the groans of these aged, petulant planks.

I live in obscurity. But I live.

And the lives of these trespassers, to me, at first seemed inconsequential. A new cluster of voices to disrupt my silent, emotional scream. Homely faces to observe through the scrim between dimensions. Another family to leave me cold, who cared nothing for me, who would not assist me if they could. Despised, ignorant leeches.

But I have, at times, wormed my way into the space beneath the child's bed. She believed me there! And… I lived below wire coils that spewed dust mites.

The night she cried out to her mother, when the light went on and my presence was addressed, the bedspread corner was lifted, eyes peered under to verify my absence, to prove my nonexistence. I was banished. Adults expect nothing. So they find nothing. The worthless shits!

And there was another time, once upon a time, when the child's fear alone banished me. I thought, This is what it's come to. The status of my potency. Her fear, in raging sub-conscious form, amidst the buried memories of her parents' mellow assurances, thwarted my will, and shaped the reality under her bed.

But we have overcome such contradiction. We've reached an agreement, her subconscious and I. The simple birth I achieved in her dream life carved a lasting stronghold. I will not relinquish that. One oar lowered in the flow of her imagination is all I require. Her mind, to me, is a vast ocean of possibilities. And the very young are easily maneuvered.

The woman is of the brooding, manic sort. Typical artist. She is fecund, and provocative I confess. It's better, I suppose, than if some ugly sea-hag took occupancy. But she heightens my rage and frustration.

So I am waiting.

I've waited this long, and I'll wait yet. Something is bound to effect a catalyst.

I try to remember, and to understand, that the Great Laws of the universe have called upon me, that I am marked as the New Creator. I try to remind myself that the current phase is in some way necessary. It must be!

It must be, yes?!

I have used this time to repeatedly run the algorithms of religion and science, of necromancy, astrology, voodoo and black magic. I have exhausted my wits. I am fed up.

DAMN IT TO HELL!

The time must be near. So I wait. And when my opportunity arises, I'll pounce like a wolverine on bloodied prey.

Come on, come on…

CHAPTER 7

The rain poured like the fountain of youth, and the sky rumbled like tympany drums, like horses hooves pounding across the heath. Anne called up to Julia and they hurried on with their raincoats and down to the shore to walk on the rocks. They inspected the rippling tide pools. They peered through ribbons of reflected sky into lower worlds where minnows and crabs sought sustenance among twisted seaweeds.

Anne took photographs. She thought they would make an exciting series of paintings: *Tide Pools in Rain, September.* But the effect was so abstract, in the way Truth is stranger than Fiction, that no one would believe the images were extracted from nature. *Broken Light Concealing The Underworld*, then.

"Hey mom! Come take this snail's picture!" Julia called.

Anne went over and snapped a few shots of the creature, who, in the wet sand, made its trail beneath a swirling, rusty-blue shell.

"Her name's Louise," Julia said. "And she just adores the rain. She's going to visit her mother." She pointed to another snail, on the opposite side of a hunk of rock. "Flora."

"Rain is good mother-visiting weather."

"I know," Julia said.

"Will she see her dad?"

"No. Flora, the mother, left him. And his house."

Anne felt a jolt. It was too close to home, and she worried what the kid must think. She glanced up the slope behind them, at her own, grand cottage. Its posture against the rainy sky, like a cormorant drying its wings, tickled her. "Took the house, huh? The mother must be upset about that."

Julia rolled her eyes. "Not really! She *is* a snail, after all! She takes *her* house wherever she goes!"

The little elf-witch.

"And she goes wherever she wants!" Julia concluded.

"Not lonely, then?" Anne asked.

"Well... sometimes, she is, of course, because everyone gets lonely sometimes. But the daughter comes to visit a lot. Whenever it rains."

"Ah."

Sometimes Anne suspected she was inflicting a horrible lesson on the child, by staying with the man. There used to be so many reasons to justify keeping the marriage together. For the longest time, Anne couldn't bear the thought of losing Julia, even for a weekend a month if that's all it came to. She felt Julia needed her, always.

But lately that seemed a selfish, clinging impulse. Julia was old enough now that they could all handle it.

But Anne wanted Julia's childhood home to remain more privileged than her own had been. How could she pull her away from the house she loved? And the coast?! It was nourishing. Julia's developing mind had the far reaches of the ocean to roam, and that connection engendered an inner serenity, and a strength of character. A vastness of inner self.

But, she had to wonder, were those really Julia's needs, or her own?

Sometimes she secretly enjoyed her predicament. Trapped in a loveless marriage, like a heroine in one of those gothic novels she painted covers for. Long-suffering in a lavish, hideous castle.

Oh God. That was *warped*. She looked at her poor daughter.

Together they walked up the coast a ways, along the narrow, pebbly beach, past their neighbors' elaborate mansions and past hillside growth. When they came to the sloping churchyard, Anne photographed old gravestones in the rain from a number of different angles, loving the moodiness the scene inspired.

The truth was, Anne didn't take much notice of the missing ingredient her marriage withstood. Whatever longing she felt, she accepted as a normal part of life. Everyone had emptiness somewhere. Few found passion that lasted. But Anne had her daughter, and her work. They were everything. She had her home. And Mark more or less stayed out of her way.

When she turned and looked, her daughter was charging full speed along the top of the breakwater toward its mid-ocean tip.

"Julia! No running!"

The rain got heavier, and Julia yelled and giggled, splashing with red rubber boots as a wave's foamy song gushed.

CHAPTER 8

After his embarrassment that afternoon, Ed took a couple of Tylenols and crawled back into bed, hoping to sleep away his misery. Unfortunately, his misery followed him. He dreamt of machinery again, in some kind of wire factory. Wire stretched in every direction, between coils. It zinged noisily through the air as it wound onto spools. Then the factory opened onto a desert with an oil refinery, where enormous drills wailed in their mechanical rhythms.

When he woke up, his headache was worse than ever. A hot shower and some soup helped him stop thinking about it.

In the late, grey afternoon, he worried constantly about the whole issue of Anne McGilvary and her daughter. He'd made an ass out of himself. His gut cringed when he thought about it. And sure, she was nice. Maybe the best looking woman he'd seen in years. But she'd never have anything to do with him.

So now, when he'd much rather lick his wounds and forget the whole thing, he was indebted to her. He had a job to do. It had been his drunken mind-set that told him he'd make everything better, once he was sober. That he would impress her the next day. But did he really feel like crawling down into that hole out there, and digging around in the muck? Did he feel like laboring through the night to make his place presentable? Not to mention dealing with the nervous anticipation of expecting company.

Fuck!

Why the hell should he have to impress anyone? He was who he was. An old geezer with a beer gut. And she was married, undoubtedly. So why should he bother?

Because he'd screamed at them while sleepwalking, and maybe a little self-respect was in order.

So he shaved. And he gathered all the dirty dishes from around the apartment and piled them in the sink, and he brought the garbage out. And he was feeling better, until he walked halfway down the block, and realized that the grate was cemented in place, and that he couldn't see a thing down there. That set off a burning anxiety, which seemed to pulse and grow within him, and which made him want to forget the whole thing, and go have a drink.

Sorry lady, but when you left I realized, 'this building's not connected to any underground channel.' You need to call City Hall.

Ah, cripes!

He got a flashlight from a kitchen cabinet, took it outside, and shined it down into the hole. Old, decayed leaves and litter coated some old pipes. The necklace must have fallen behind them.

He went inside for a wire coat hanger, which he used to swirl the muck. A half hour later, he was back inside, throwing the crumpled, wet hanger at a chair. "For God's sake!"

And while his body tightened in aggravated frustration, some quiet part of his mind worked on the problem. *Maybe there's a way to loosen the grate,* it said.

Yeah, if I had a jackhammer, and a permit.

You have a sledge hammer.

I can't do that.

That's true. What about those keyholes?

They're a hundred years old. The locks must be rusted through. How would I close it? You can't leave a future accident in the middle of the sidewalk!

What about string and chewing gum? A vacuum cleaner with a long hose? Where does the channel lead? Could you go down a manhole, and find a connection?

Now we're really talking about getting covered in it.

So what?

Yeah, there could be another way down there, I guess.

And, oh yeah—what about those locks?

Chapter 9

All the angels were crying today. That's why it had begun to rain so hard. Angel tears dripped down the small window at the back of the carpeted nook in the jungle wall, where Julia nestled like a snail inside its shell. She had climbed on her toy chest to get up there. Now she drew pictures on her big pad, with a box of colored pencils dumped out beside her.

It was dark inside a snail's shell, when it rained.

She drew a picture of the park, where she and her mother often went. She made all the trees, and the fountain. She made the man who sold the cinnamon buns. She even made the big garden, using every color she had. Way on the other side, she made the river, and the docks.

Then she drew lots of kids. Some of them played on the fountain. Some held their mothers' hands. One boy had a balloon.

The tall man was there. She didn't mean to draw him. Her hand just started making a mark, with the black pencil, and it turned out to be him. She'd never seen him in the park before, but there he was. He sat on a bench, holding a book. But he wasn't looking at the book. His head was turned, so he could see the big, grassy area between the bathrooms and the docks.

Julia drew Beth, climbing a tree at the edge of that grassy area.

Beth was a nice little girl. Julia just loved her pale blonde hair. It was fun playing sisters with her, or playing mommies. Sometimes they played school, too. Beth liked to visit Julia's playroom. She asked Julia to invite her every day.

Julia turned her pad to a new page. There was a certain way to invite Beth. She wasn't like other little girls. You didn't just ask your mother to call hers.

On the blank page she drew a huge circle with the black pencil. Then she tore out the page, and climbed out of the nook, onto her toy chest, and down. She went to the middle of the room, and put the circle on the floor. Then she went back to her toy chest, and opened it.

It was messy in there. She would have to clean it out sometime soon.

The toy chest was filled with different kinds of hearts: zebra hearts, gazelle hearts, goose hearts, lion hearts, human hearts, monkey hearts, porcupine hearts, crow hearts. They were all sticky, and had mostly turned brown. They didn't smell very nice, either.

She reached in, and picked among them, until she had an armload. Then she closed the toy chest. She brought the hearts to the circle in the middle of the room.

It was important to put them in places around the circle like numbers on a clock. One number pointed to the desert. She put the coyote heart there. Another number pointed to the mountains. One to the jungle. She put down the bobcat and monkey hearts. The last number was for the ocean. That's where she put the human heart.

Then she went back to the nook, and climbed in. She wiped her hands off on the blue carpet.

Like a snail who'd crawled down into a secret cave, she peered out into her playroom. It was all grey, with the rainy light from the windows. Near the circle, a dull reflection splashed across the hardwood floor like a puddle of seawater.

"Mee-I, Julia—" she sang. *"Hello—hello…!"*

Then, as if tar paper rolled over the windows, the room turned black, like a closet at night.

From each of the hearts on the floor, one by one, exploded a puff of orange sparks, blinding, then gone, leaving each lump of orbish muscle glowing dull red, and pulsating in smoke, like breathing embers.

It was Bazil, not Beth, who crawled from the circle. Julia shrank deeper into her nook.

Rising from the circle in the darkness, he looked like a puppet drawn from above by invisible strings. Dressed in black, his body merged with the dark surroundings. Only his face and hands were visible, like white plastic. And his eyes. Like someone took a doll's head, and burned holes where the eyes should be.

He stepped out of the circle, his movements jerky and mechanical.

Then the room brightened to its rainy day light. The hearts in the circle were shriveled, black lumps, still smoking. Bazil looked more like a boy, now. But Julia still hated his eyes.

Her voice sounded timid when she talked. Small, like a snails voice. "I wanted to invite Beth…"

Bazil's low voice sounded like it was made from electric wires, like an old man with a hole in his throat from too many cigarettes, and sometimes his words buzzed, like they had extra "z" sounds. "From now on," he said with spite, "Beth can't come unlezz I zay zo."

"Why not?"

"Come out of there," he commanded.

Julia turned around inside the nook, and backed out slowly. She felt with her foot for the top of the toy chest. When she touched it, she put her weight down. She immediately slipped and fell, banging her knees and elbows.

She picked herself up from the floor, made a hurt sound, clutched her arm and bobbed in place.

Bazil laughed. "You're so dumb!"

Then Julia realized why she slipped. The toy chest was different. It was longer, shinier, its surface was smooth, and rounded.

"What's that doing here?" she said.

"It's a coffin, idiot. And if you want to play with Beth ever again, you better play with me first."

Julia wanted to leave the room. She wanted to go downstairs to her mother. She wanted to sit in the tv room, and she wanted to watch *Pinky and the Brain*.

"What do we have to play?" she said.

"You know it's scary to go in a coffin," Bazil said. "But I know a way to make it all right."

"I don't want to."

"Of course you don't, dummy," he said angrily. "That's why we need to play thiz game."

He got two chairs from the child-sized table, and set them face to face by the coffin. He sat in one, and told Julia to sit in the other, facing him.

"Look at me," he said. His eyes reminded her of being sick in the middle of the night, so she stared at his black jersey.

"Don't be a baby, Julia! Look right at me!"

She looked at his forehead.

"Now," his voice dropped to a hum. "Pretend you're on the merry-go-round, Julia. On the prettiest horse. On the prettiest merry-go-round, Julia. At the seazide. On the boardwalk midway, by the ocean. At the beach. You go up and down. All around you everything goes by." His voice was like organ music.

"The sea whips by, then hurls up at you. It flies by, and flies past. The wind and the sky."

The way he talked made her feel as if foam from the beach was all around her, and even inside her too. Like she was lying in the foam from waves, and she had no skin, and the foam went through her. It was frightening, and a little like falling.

"And the music is like a piano. You feel like you're flying, and you're spinning around and around. Your horse goes up and down, and everything flies past you."

* * * * * * * * * *

When Julia opened her eyes, Beth was there, at last. Beth sat in Julia's rocking chair, cradling a doll. She smiled in a shy way.

Julia went to her, and Beth fingered the doll's hair, and fiddled with its dress.

"I remember your baby," Julia said.

"You do?"

"Yes."

Beth stared at the doll. She was so little, her fingers were like the ivory hair pins Julia's mother sometimes wore. Beth was different from anyone Julia had ever seen. Her eyes were pink, and her skin was like skim milk when it spread out on the table and you could see through it. Inside Beth's skin was a fancy map of blue veins.

Beth got out of the chair, and together they went to find Julia's Marianne doll, who was taking a nap on a pillow in the corner. They brushed their dolls' hair, and talked about the different hairstyles the dolls liked. Then Beth asked if Julia would invite her again.

"Of course," Julia said. "Whenever you want."

"Will you invite me tonight?" Beth said.

"But I'll be in bed."

"Please?"

Julia didn't want to say no to her friend. So they agreed.

CHAPTER 10

When Dr. Mark Clausin walked into his house that evening, Anne greeted him at the front door with a brief kiss. Behind her, dinner was waiting for him on the dining room table. It was all an effort to maintain outward harmony.

She called to their child. "Julia!"

"Coming!"

Julia raced down the stairs, "...Daddy!!!" and leapt from the second-to-last stair into his arms.

"OW!" he said. "Anne! Can't you control her?"

"Julia," her mother said, softly.

"Sorry, daddy."

"March back up those stairs, now," Mark said. "You're going to walk down properly, and greet me the right way."

"Mark—"

"She nearly knocked me over! Jesus. That's not how I like to be greeted, you know? You could teach her how to behave. When I'm tired—"

"She apologized, didn't she?"

"I want her to learn the right way. Julia, up." He pointed.

Julia, clearly offended, trudged back up the flight, and disappeared into the hallway above.

"Well? Are you coming down the right way?"

"Call me."

"I just did call you," he said.

"Say, '...*time for dinner!*'"

"Julia, you come down those stairs right now like a proper lady."

Her voice grew softer. "Are you going to call me, daddy?"

"I'm not calling you again! One! Two—"

"That's enough," Anne snapped. "Be glad she's happy to see you!" She brushed past him, and hustled up the stairs. "Stupid," she hissed.

When Anne turned into the hallway, Julia hammed a startled look, eyes and mouth wide open in mock shock. Anne squinted teasingly, and stooped down. "I am starving!"

Julia held out her hand. "Please to meet you."

"Oh, ha ha, I never heard that one before..." Anne took the svelte hand and kissed it. "Okay, let's go." She glanced down. "Good grief, Julia, your nails!" They were filthy. Black and grubby. "What in the world were you into?"

Julia shrugged, and giggled. "I don't know."

"Get washed up!"

When they came down to the table, Mark had begun eating.

"Hope you said grace," Anne said.

"Please." He chewed his steak and studied his gin and tonic. "Remember last year," he said to his wife," I performed on that guy Burt Philbrick—the one in the boating accident off the Vineyard? I pulled a spike out of his frontal lobe?"

"Oh yeah," she lied.

"He did PT, the whole bit. Fully recovered, back at work for a year. Found out they brought him into the E.R. today. He lost his leg."

"Oh my God!" Anne looked up from her macaroni as her stomach turned. "Was it a car accident?"

"No. He's a construction guy. This steel girder let go, a hundred feet up....*bam!*"

"Mark, that's horrible!"

"No shit. Make a hell of a lawsuit, though. Weird luck, huh? He'll be set for life."

Anne made a rattle of cutlery on china. "For God's sake!"

Mark looked at her blankly. He glanced at Julia, then back, and defensively he asked, "What?!"

Right then, Anne decided. She would ask him to leave, forever. Or maybe she'd take Julia, and go.

Anything. Just so the lie would end.

CHAPTER 11

His supper and two gin and tonics relaxed Mark enough that he felt like a walk anyway, with the rain having stopped, and crisp, early autumn smells in the air. He still protested when Anne asked if he would make the trip to town. Complaining made it seem more like a sacrifice, something he was doing reluctantly, but doing, nonetheless, because he was a family man, the man of the house. He was gallantly fulfilling that role, and maybe his wife would cut him slack in other areas.

If he could spot the necklace, he planned to ask at the news stand for the pole they used to close their awnings at night. Which proved he was smarter than his wife. Of course, only a guy would think of something so obvious. With the hook on the end of the pole, he would easily scoop up the necklace and go home a hero.

He reached downtown within half an hour, and found the grate where she'd described. Then—what a joke!—the thing was hinged. It easily opened from the middle. There was no need to borrow anyone's pole. This was a cake walk.

He'd have time for a quick visit to his sweetie pie, and still return home victorious.

But how the hell was he supposed to get down there? He saw potential footholds by missing bricks, and on pipes which ran along the inner wall. But he didn't know how sturdy any of it was.

Feeling awkward, he glanced up and down the road for a police car. He probably looked suspicious, and he figured he could use some assistance. A cop should be the one to climb down there, not a fucking brain surgeon. His taxes ought to cover something besides jelly doughnut watch.

Anyway, where was the frigging thing? There was nothing down there but a bunch of shit. Damned if he saw any necklace.

Anne might have come with him, for Christ's sake, to try and help. He'd told her not to. But still. That was simple politeness. She could have insisted.

He got on his knees and twisted around to enter the hole backwards. This was asinine! He was dressed in good clothes. It was seven feet down, at least, with no clear landing area.

Half way down, with no footing, and no view below him, at the point of transition between the push-up and chin-up positions, he panicked and flailed.

"Shit!"

He landed feet-first on the slippery pipes, and ass second, his back against the wall, in a pile of debris.

"Fucking Hell!" he yelled. "Goddamn Bullshit Christ!"

His good pants, and an inch of muck.

It was darker, then, as if the underground chamber repelled the scattered photons above.

Okay, where is the damn thing? Come on…!

It was time to grab the necklace and get out. Why wasn't it where she said it would be?

"Goddamn it, Anne!" he yelled.

CHAPTER 12

Julia stood in the doorway to the studio, after readying herself for bed. Sounding younger than she was, she phrased a request. "Can I sleep in the playroom, mommy?"

Absolutely not!

Anne turned from her easel. "What, honey?"

"I want to sleep upstairs tonight. In the playroom." Now she sounded grown up, and unusually assertive.

The way Anne felt, Julia might as well have asked to sleep on the roof, or alone in the park, or anywhere else that would be unsafe and inappropriate for an eight year old.

"What for?" Anne felt like an inquisitive parent trying to determine if her teenager was using drugs.

"It would be fun. Like a vacation."

"You have school tomorrow."

"I know."

"No, sweetheart. Not tonight."

"Pleease?"

What reason could she give? The thought of it terrifies me? I don't want you imagining things...

She remembered being Julia's age, and the excitement of altering the sleep routine. A simple pleasure. To sleep in a different room. To wake up and be confused for a moment, then be struck by a reminder.

"You need to be rested. That's part of being in school, you know. The routine—"

"But mom! I will be rested. What difference does it make if I'm upstairs?" Julia was seeking to explore a form of independence. To sleep an entire floor away.

The wheels spun in the back of Anne's mind. It was an opportunity, she had to admit. Maybe she could find out what Julia talked about, when she was up there alone. The prospect was too intriguing to ignore. Maybe she could eliminate those vague, gnawing fears for Julia's safety, for her well being, and mental health.

"How about on the weekend?"

Julia silently considered the question. She looked down suspiciously, with the transparent demeanor of a child plotting something in the shadow of that savage force, parental authority. Then she shook her head. "It's *because* of the routine, mom."

Normally, it wouldn't bother Anne that Julia should win an argument with such an insightfullly made, subtle point. But what secret was so important to defend?

She could still use the age-old, 'No-because-I-said-so' method of rebuttle, of course. She was not above that.

"Well I suppose it'll be all right," she said, instead. She said it. But it wasn't what she meant. "Should we bring up your blankets, and make a bed with the sofa cushions?"

"And Marianne?"

"Of course."

After they had made the bed by securing a fitted sheet to the cushions with safety pins, and after carrying assorted dolls and animals up from Julia's bedroom, and graham crackers, grapes and lemonade from the kitchen, Anne got a flashlight and fresh batteries from the utility room off the garage. While she was there, she spent a few minutes hunting for the box with the baby monitor.

In the playroom, Anne plugged in the monitor and arranged it behind some of Julia's books on a shelf. Julia would reject the device if it wasn't hidden—she was not a baby, and she knew it. Why take the fun out of the adventure?

When Julia returned to the room, carrying her lion pillow, Anne shifted to the next column of shelves, pretending to be searching for a book. She selected one and faced Julia, casually.

She was bugging her daughter's room. Planning—executing—willful deception. Outright invasion of privacy. Spying. Like her own mother would have done.

And she was nearly caught.

She left the monitor where it was. What choice was there, at this point? But she decided against listening in. In fact, she would return the receiver to the utility room as soon as she was downstairs.

What was I thinking?!

Julia was safe, at home, and she did not need to be monitored like a prisoner, or a lab rat. She was eight years old, not three. There was nothing up here that could harm her.

After two story books, Anne tucked her little girl in, and kissed her, and left her in the glow of the Beatrix Potter night light, which she'd taken from the downstairs hall. The flashlight was by Julia's side.

Anne left the door open a crack, and the stairway light on. From the upper hall, the murals in the playroom, illuminated only by the small, orange nightlight, looked contorted and eerie—too frightening a sight for a child to sleep by.

She considered the baby monitor once more. What if Julia awakened from a nightmare and her frightened cries went unheard? Anne recalled a time when Julia screamed like a banshee in the middle of the night because a man was under her bed. It took both parents half an hour to talk her down, like someone in the bad trip tent at Woodstock.

But that was years ago, when Julia was five.

"I'll be all right, mom," came the confident voice of her daughter.

"Of course you will, sweetie. I'll be right downstairs."

CHAPTER 13

The full-length mirror, which he bought at Wal Mart for thirteen bucks, hung on the inside of his one closet door. And Willie, covered by a black, German army blanket, spied on himself.

"Fuck, dude!" he said to his reflection, "You look like Death warmed over!"

He snickered. It was a good effect.

He had a perfect blend of smack and coke running through his bloodstream. And the blanket, like a hooded cloak, made him look like the baddest mother of all. Nobody fucked with Death.

He poked his erection through the folds, imagined frightening some poor girl that way, and laughed. Then he crawled through the hole.

Daylight was spent. There was no point in bringing his digital video camera. But sometimes it was just about being there, with no one knowing. Being near enough to smell the crotches of the women who passed.

Chapter 14

Mark plunged his fingers behind the pipes which ran along the floor of the channel. All he felt was muck, at first. Then a brain signal formed a picture of something wrong. Something sharp, maybe, or hot.

Pain!

He yelled, and pulled his fingers half way to his lips, then stopped short of gumming them. They were covered in shit.

"Fucking gross! Fuck!"

His fingers pulsed with the burn, and he wiped the muck on his pants (they were ruined anyway.) Then he pressed the hand between his arm and rib cage, hoping the pressure would numb the pain.

A hot pipe. He wondered if he had grounds to sue the city. *Children* could have been down here!

This entire venture, he decided, was useless. A waste of time. The damn necklace was nowhere in sight, and he would pursue it no further. And now he was too filthy to go visit Lucy. God damn.

From the corridor of darkness came a scraping sound. Something moved toward him.

An animal?!

Not a person, down here? Why would anyone—?

In his mind, he saw himself leap out of the hole with one jump. But his reflexes took over, and backed him deeper into the shadows of the tunnel. Then he froze.

A figure stepped into the dim space below the grate, and a sweaty prickle crawled up Mark's spine at the sight of the hulking shape. The cloaked figure, with a black oval for a face, paused, and looked above.

Mark tried not to breathe, but his trembling wanted to force loud noises from him. A squeal wriggled its way into his constricted throat. The shrouded figure—which had to be a homeless guy—seemed to hear, and turned toward Mark.

"Shit, I'm sorry, man!" Mark cried out, "I didn't mean to be here—"

The figure stood still for a moment, and said nothing. Then it turned, and hurried back the way it had come.

In a desperate, protracted process that racked his arm and back muscles, Mark hauled himself out of the hole. The effort seemed to wish injury upon him, but he accepted the trade off—acute muscle strain for immediate safety.

He crawled onto the sidewalk, lifted himself up, and slammed the grate shut beneath him.

CHAPTER 15

Willie scampered back through the hole into his apartment and his blanket fell to the floor. He slid a sheet of plywood across the opening, and grabbed his jeans off the back of a chair.

Who the fuck was that asshole? What the hell was he doing down there?

He zipped his fly and pulled on his leather jacket over bare skin. He needed a weapon. The gun? Or his blade? The knife was easier to conceal. He slipped it in his sleeve.

He slammed his apartment door behind him, ran upstairs and out to the sidewalk. Then he leaned into the stoop, and casually scanned the block.

The grate was closed. On the other side of the street, a guy walking away fast looked nervously back. When Willie finally caught up to him—in his own nonchalant way—he observed the crap smeared on the back of the asshole's pant-legs. Willie knew that substance like his own blood.

This guy should've minded his own business. Willie wasn't about to let his world be fucked with. This prick screwed with the wrong man.

CHAPTER 16

Her bare feet were cold on the hardwood floor of the playroom. Julia quickly placed four animal hearts in a diamond shape, then crawled back into her bed of cushions and quietly sang her song. She waited for a long time, commanding her eyes to stay round and open, even pretending she was swimming, so she'd be wide awake. But she got too sleepy.

In a short while, it seemed, there were voices, telling secrets not meant for her. She opened her eyes, and all four of them were there. Bazil, and pretty little Beth, over by the window. Eli, who once talked with Julia about being *boyfriend and girlfriend*. (Neither one of them said anything about it since, so she supposed they still were. He was the cutest.) He leaned against the wall by the bookshelf.

Chubby Liza was there too, standing over Julia. She was too bossy.

The moonlight from the window behind Beth made a silver outline, and Beth's face was in the shadow. Bazil stood beside her, gripping her arm, keeping her still. It scared Julia, to see Beth trapped by him.

Liza said, "Julia, you need to get up and clean up all your stuff."

"Aren't we having a sleepover?"

"No. We're going to play what Bazil showed you."

It felt like toilet flush, inside her stomach. For a minute she didn't know what to do. They were all waiting for her. Bazil was motionless. She knew he could wait forever like that, if he had to. Liza's puffy cheeks made her eyes narrow and angry-looking. As Julia stood, she saw the coffin.

She moved her bedding to the other side of the room, as the other children assembled in front of the big, wooden box. When Julia joined them, she positioned herself in the circle between handsome Eli and little Beth.

Then Bazil started talking in a language Julia didn't understand. His eyes burned, and his voice sounded like a screaming cat. Julia wished she could block her ears, but her friends held her hands. She felt sick. It felt like a squadron of sparrows flew through her belly.

Bazil saw that she was scared, and laughed. "Julia's a fraidy-cat!"

"No she isn't," Eli defended.

Liza silenced them. "Who's first?" she said.

Bazil said Beth was first, because she was the littlest.

But Beth didn't want to climb into the coffin. "You'll close me in," she said.

"That's the game, stupid," Bazil said.

Beth looked like she was going to cry.

"Don't make her, if she doesn't want," Julia said. Beth's little hand was stiff, like a dead rabbit's foot.

"Julia!" Liza complained.

But Bazil said, "Beth doesn't have to, if you take her place, Julia."

The four playmates stared at her. Little Beth's wide-eyes and pale face pleaded with her. Julia didn't want to disappoint her best friend.

But she felt as cold as an when an air conditioner switches off, and the whole window frame shudders. Could they see how cold she was?

A strange thing occurred to her. Despite her trembling, she felt strong. She could protect little Beth.

"Okay," she said.

Bazil grinned. "Good. First we'll all say the words to make you not afraid. Like we practiced. Remember?"

Julia nodded.

He told her to stand in the middle of the circle. The other children held hands around her, and started to chant, softly, in that other language. Almost immediately, Julia felt that feeling again, like foam.

Then Bazil and Liza broke the circle to let Julia through, and she walked tentatively up to the coffin.

The children sang,...*get on, get on, get on— climb into, feels for you... get on, get on, get on— let out, let come, let go, let in, let on... get on, get on, get on...*

Julia obeyed, climbing up on the firm, brass handle.

Inside, the coffin wasn't as soft as it looked. The cushions were hard, like unripe fruit, and the red cloth was rough and scratchy. She lowered herself to a seated position with her legs in front, then scooted her feet into the closed compartment.

"Lie down and play dead," Bazil said. "We're at your funeral."

This part of the game wasn't too bad. Julia tried to lie completely still. She suppressed a giggle when they all came and prayed by her. They talked about times they'd played together, and what a nice girl she'd been.

"Poor Julia. She died so young."

"She looks peaceful."

"She's in heaven."

"We'll miss her. We're so sad."

Bazil said, "Julia was special to uz. She was our beszt friend."

And he laughed.

It was time to close the coffin. Julia opened her eyes to see Bazil acting as the undertaker. He grinned as he shut her in darkness.

"Wait!" she shouted, too late. Her voice sounded weak in the dark, and she didn't want them to be mad with her for wrecking the game.

Her friends sounded far, far away, as they sang, out there in the room,...*stay in, stay in, stay in— climb into, feels for you... stay in, stay in, stay in— let out, let come, let go, let in, let on... stay in, stay in, stay in...*

She thought if she just closed her eyes and pretended to sleep, then it would be like sleeping. The foam feeling made her warm, and calm, and for a second, she wanted to giggle again. If she slept, they would open the lid before she knew it, and she could jump out and laugh and pretend it was fun.

But her courage only lasted a second.

Because the singing stopped. Had they left her all alone? She felt anxious to move around. To see. The coffin was too dark, and too small!

Something strong grabbed her feet, and started to slither over her legs and body.

"I don't like this!" she screamed. "Open! Open iiitt!"

CHAPTER 17

The road home was a black tunnel of raw wind. Mark cursed himself for not driving. The gin wore off into a headache, and he expected a menace from every shadow he passed.

The whole thing was stupid. He'd been startled by a homeless guy—who was probably more afraid than he was. Most of those types were harmless, but you could never tell for sure. They were so territorial. Don't cross that line.

To think of the guy, living in filth under the sidewalk. Mark would have to notify the police.

Finally, his house was in view. His safe haven. Lights were on upstairs, in the bedroom and in Anne's studio. She was probably working. At least he had a story to tell her, about the guy under the sidewalk. Would she think he was full of shit? Would she act all disappointed because he didn't get her damn necklace?

She already thought he was a wimp. What the fuck did she want, blood? Should he have risked his life for a scrap of metal? If he came home cut and bleeding, would that make her proud?

He decided to go in quietly, by the back door. He could stay up for a while, and watch tv on the porch. He'd find something to change into downstairs, in the laundry room. He'd give Anne time to fall asleep before he went upstairs.

The screen door in back always stuck, the swelled wood always shuddered when tugged free of its frame. But from behind closed upstairs windows at the front of the house, classical music blared in Anne's studio. He applied slow pressure to the screen door, but the wood still quivered.

Ah, fuck it. He had every right to come home, and stay downstairs for a while, without announcing his presence. Anyway, she wouldn't hear anything up there.

The porch windows were styled like venetian blinds, with glass slats in metal grooves. He turned the dial at the base of each, and closed them tight. Then he switched on the portable space heater out there.

The kitchen was up three steps, and he flipped the light switch under the china cupboard. Then he hurried downstairs, where he found clean jeans and a sweater in the dryer. Bathed in soft white light, he was suddenly tickled by the evening's combination of events. Sneaking around at home, now, was a make-believe adventure, and a hell of a lot more fun than real danger.

And the gallon jug of milk in the refrigerator, planted beside chocolate cake in a box, was the happiest sight in the world. He could have been eleven years old, the way he felt—with the ocean wind rattling the panes in the porch windows, and the mercury gradually climbing on the porch thermometer.

When he finally sat, the space heater radiated a warmth which rushed up his calves. He arranged his plate and milk on a folding table, and turned the television on with low volume.

To his joy and amazement, the tail end of a used car commercial was followed by the cheesy opening graphics of *Tales From The Darkside*. Ha! He hadn't seen that show in years! This was like when he was a kid, and used to sneak tv watching on the old portable black & white. It was the kind of moment you couldn't plan, but which arose spontaneously, and made you feel like school was canceled for a snowstorm.

It was perfect. Until he heard a man outside, laughing.

For a second he thought it was his imagination. Then he heard the screen door. Someone tugged it.

Mark stood up with a fork in his hand and the person outside succeeded in yanking open the screen door with a snap and a shudder. Then the inner door flew open and smashed against the wall.

A thin, long-haired man charged in.

Mark opened his mouth to protest—to say something like "You can't just barge in here!" But before he could swallow the bite of cake in his mouth, the intruder lunged, with a knife, and poked Mark's throat. Just a little jab.

It dawned on Mark that ordinary rules did not apply here, as the man laughed ecstatically and wiped his blade on his jeans. Was this the homeless guy? When Mark tried to scream, he gagged instead, and tasted salt. He heard something like rain, and confusedly thought the ceiling was leaking. He looked up, saw nothing, but still felt moisture pouring down on him. Then he saw his own hand, and realized he was covered in blood.

The fork landed on the floor. Mark clutched his throat. Then he was on his knees.

The man watched calmly, grinning. From the amount of blood that spurted, Mark knew his carotid artery was severed. Many things went through his mind.

Was this guy a maniac? Someone should call 911!

My God, I'm dying!

Why was he as good as dead? Why had this man killed him? It was a loss—Mark's skills were needed, didn't this bastard know? People needed him!

Although he was already having trouble keeping from falling over, the maniac knocked him to the floor with a kick.

Why wouldn't he let him up?

Why, when life was just starting—just starting to feel good—was it all over?

The segment on the tv show ended with mysterious music, and the channel went to a commercial.

CHAPTER 18

Willie loved this part of it. His latest victim was helpless, unable to lift his face from the floor, or to do anything more than twitch his fingers as blood left him in a bubbling stream. And Willie couldn't believe his good luck when he saw the plate with chocolate cake on it, and the frothy glass of milk beside. He sat down, used the dying man as a footstool, and arranged the plate on his lap. He ate with his fingers.

King of the castle.

The dying man became the dead man. Too bad. Willie wished there was a way to prolong the final phase. He wished the whole world was writhing beneath him. Alive, but just barely.

But the guy on the floor had definitely passed his sell-by date. What looked like two gallons of blood coated most of the painted floorboards and permeated the air with the smell of iron. The guy stopped breathing. He stopped twitching. He was dead.

The only part of him that moved now was his blood, which still flowed in its slow expanding shape. It seeped into cracks in the wood and followed their contours. It glistened in the light cast from the kitchen. And in a surge of intense pleasure, Willie found it hypnotic.

Lost as he was in this joy, he didn't immediately notice when the liquid movement started to behave strangely. When he did realize, when he consciously observed how the laws of nature were being defied, he froze in mute terror.

The pool of blood had stopped expanding. Now it was shrinking.

The thick fingers of red that had oozed across the floorboards began to recede. Round bubbles of blood crawled out of cracks to higher, smooth surfaces. Crimson rivulets retraced their courses and deleted all residue of their previous journey. The blood was backing up.

Willie's eye quickly traced the blood's new path, and he saw where it led. It was pouring back into its source.

From the gash he carved in the dead man's neck protruded an end of severed artery. And it was sucking blood like a vacuum hose.

"Jesus!" Willie jumped up from his seat and sent his plate and glass crashing to the dead man's side. Blood leached its way from beneath newfallen china fragments, and from clumps of chocolate cake. It wormed itself out of marbleized milky puddles, its spirals uncoiling and twisting into backward-moving strands. It sponged itself from the soaked fibers of the dead man's clothes, and funneled its way toward the hungry artery, which slurped it like a straw.

Willie leapt over the body, and backed to the door as the last red bead flowed upward into the tube of human tissue. The wound sealed itself, formed a scab, and the scab crumbled and fell away, leaving a thick, black scar. The dead man's feet jerked. His eyelids fluttered.

Willie bolted through the screen door and raced off into the dreary night.

CHAPTER 19

I initiate the transmigration, and the first thing I am aware of is sheer physical torture. It replaces my plans, this agony, and I am cognizant only of the wish to undo my last step, and to return to my solitary dungeon. My throat is locked, so that I am not permitted even the release of screaming.

Cool air comes to me from the outdoors. I lift my face to it, tear my eyes open, and gasp. There is blood in my mouth. It gurgles, and blocks the air I suck. I cough and gag and spit, and gasp again. As if in flight from the biological sting of my every molecule, I crawl. I crawl through the door and down a step. I am beneath the night sky I longed for. But the pain follows me, even as I struggle to stand, even as I stagger through the night, down to the water. After many desperate inhalations of harsh, ocean air I am still not cleansed of the pain.

I hasten toward the waves. I drop to my knees in the foam and spray. The numbness of cold offers the smallest relief. I collapse in the surf and let the cold saturate me. And to the Great Laws which have placed me here, I cry out—not with words but in the primal language of the newly born.

I lie there in exhaustion. Gradually, with each crashing wave, my discomfort ebbs. And with a steady dawning, my eyes fixed on the silvery dome above, pain is supplemented by realization, and with realization comes bliss! I am incarnate!

I roll to my side and fill my mouth with cold, salty water to rinse away the taste of blood—the blood I pursued into the world of physicality. The blood in which I swam, in which I was baptized.

What a wonderful substance. The river of life.

Life! Coursing through me! Like a child again! Alive, and energetic! Like a gathering of energetic children.

How I adore the little ones. The sheer power of their minds. An endless resource. The magical mind of the child. How many people truly realize? Hmmm? Ah, yes—only me. I'm the one who knows. The one who can tap the central creative force, and bend it to my will. My will is the will of God!

Victor Van Rensselaer stood up in the surf, stretched his neck and his arms, flexed his fingers, and took a deep breath. His joy was incalculable. To be alive, in the flesh again! To have hands! Nostrils! A cock, and balls!

The blood that had flowed back into Mark Clausin's neck now flowed in Van Rensselaer's veins. It engorged his sex organ. He smelled the sea, and felt the wind surround him, as mighty as his erection. The lighthouse blinked its repeated signal, a message to him, a beckoning. Years ago when he chose this location, that lighthouse had been the deciding factor.

At last! The waiting rewarded. The Great Laws had seen him through to the next phase. He was their chosen one. He'd passed the final trial, and had already crossed the threshold into eternal life.

But what—what?—was the purpose of the suffering? He thought for certain that upon entering this phase its meaning would be apparent.

Then a blissful shudder overtook him, the result of a flash of memory: an anaesthetized patient lay before him in the operating room, with two plates of sawed skull removed to expose the living, human brain! And Van Rensselaer understood! The Laws had given him a great gift—and there could be no better pleasure for a man of scholarly pursuits than the instant access to knowledge upon which Van Rensselaer now feasted; access to years of learning, years which he thought he'd missed!

His studies during his own lifetime had focused on many schools of Science and the Occult. But now, in addition, he was a twentieth century brain surgeon!

A brain surgeon, and a daddy. How well those two things combined. The Great Laws were masterful planners.

And he was, once again, a man respected in the community.

He was Mark Clausin, a man with a diploma on his office wall. A man who—ah yes!—had fucked his wife Anne in the grand suite at the Ritz Carleton on their wedding night. Goodness! He had fucked her whenever he wanted for years.

There was a certain disappointment accompanying this particular revelation. So many nights he had wanted to—ah, but the fulfillment of those longings was in the past. How strange, to have it over so quickly. To have the desired object, Anne, instantly reduced to something acquired long ago, something familiar.

Van Rensselaer turned from the waters to face his house in the distance. He could go back to the house and fuck her right now. Of course, she'd turned cold toward her husband in recent years. But he could easily force himself on her, justified by their spousal relationship.

No—that was not, these days, a culturally accepted policy. Things had changed.

Besides—memories flourished in his mind now which meant to alter his view of her. Could a woman really be so spurred by learning? She held passions which equaled his own! Fascination—by God!—for Science, Religion, Mythology and Magic!

He thought of her—on a weekend getaway to Lake Winnepesauke, when she'd stood her easel beside their picnic blanket and, while she worked, discussed her notions of the creative process. A flow, she'd said, from an unnameable source, channeled though universal psychic elements and tapped at the point of earliest emergence! Clausin had actually made an effort to listen. But he hadn't comprehended her. Clausin was a fool. He had no idea what an insightful creature this was.

And when she put her brushes down that day, how she had interrupted his reading with her lascivious, urging tongue! How she had guided him in pursuit of such mutual gratification!

No—she would not be approached indelicately. And much damage had been done to her impression of him. Her preconceived notions of him were well founded, and destructive, and would be difficult to work against. But he must!

She was intended for him. She was his Eve, his Hera, his Mary Magdalene. It was woven into the master plan.

Yet—how would he speak? What would he say to her? There was bound to be such resistance, especially—

No matter. She was already his, as much as the perfect existence which awaited him. Which awaited them both! For the time being, there was work to be done. He would stay focused on the matters at hand.

So in the raw night, he walked north along the water's edge, toward the cemetery, relishing the feel of mist on his skin and the pressure of breath in his lungs.

CHAPTER 20

An organ blared Bach from Anne's c.d. player as wind whipped around outside, and as brush informed canvas with shape, and with color. Her painting dealt with familiar subjects—tangled branches on weather beaten grounds, an aged house, once opulent, grown decrepit, with a mystery locked inside. She longed to seize the mood of a New England October, so she painted gnarled twigs, scattered leaves, and wrought iron. A single light burned in an upper window of the house in her painting. In a window above that, peering out from forgotten attic spaces, it seemed a pale reflection of the moon resembled facial features where it hugged the dimpled glass. And down in the blue-black grass by the brick walkway, was that small, dull shape a rounded stone, or a human skull?

Anne relished her solitude, and she gloried in a new-found future, where independence would flower. If she'd known such release would come from a simple decision, she might have made it long ago. There was still an edge of uncertainty. Mark might resist divorce, he might give her a difficult time. She prayed he wouldn't use custody issues as a means of expressing rage.

But no court would grant him full custody. Not with his schedule. Not when Anne's work allowed her to stay home. She'd practically been the sole caregiver all these years. She'd educated Julia, and nurtured her, and seen to all of her needs.

There was a good chance she'd be able to keep the house—it was half hers to begin with. Julia deserved that stability.

Alimony was unimportant.

Maybe she should get evidence of his adultery before making another move. She might have had it now, if she'd followed him tonight. Chances were he hadn't spent all this time trying to get her necklace.

These and other thoughts were soon banished as the work took over. After hours of feverish painting, she stepped back, looked at the canvas, and decided her work was done for the day. She liked it.

A couple of details caught her eye, which she never intended to put there. A formation in the tall, willowy grasses resembled a human shadow. And three marks on the stone wall looked like carved letters. J L E.

Such subconscious exhibitions were part of the creative process, and it was always fun to draw them out, and to assume they had symbolic significance. Of course, maybe they were attempts at communication, generated by resident ghosts.

Four hours had passed on the clock, as quickly clouds pass the moon.

Hadn't Mark come home *yet*? Maybe he decided to spend the night with her—his little friend, with her teenage face. But how would he explain it?

Perhaps the girlfriend was harping on him. Maybe he'd come home and hesitantly report a decision to move out. Wouldn't that be lucky. Wouldn't that just be a gift from heaven.

Anne understood that she'd viewed him through a fog of wishes, way back when. But maybe the one-time gleam in her eye had reflected off a clairvoyant glimpse of the daughter who would be. She would never regret marrying Mark.

She decided to sleep on the futon in her studio. It would be better to smell paint fumes all night, than smelling *him* when he came home.

And he did come home.

Later that night, she wasn't sure what time, she heard him climbing the stairs and shuffling around in the bedroom. His footsteps were heavy. He must have gotten drunk after getting laid.

Good.

He'd feel like shit in the morning.

CHAPTER 21

Before sun up, with her neck pressed uncomfortably into the futon frame, Anne woke with a start from a dream of falling. Her head throbbed.

Downstairs, she put coffee on and searched a kitchen drawer for a bottle of aspirin. She found instead—amidst old coupons, rubber bands, loose screws and a pair of pliers—a pack of Marlboro Light cigarettes—her old brand.

She thought back to a night when guests had come—an associate of Mark's and his wife. The woman lit her Marlboro Lights with a fancy silver lighter, and had left both the pack and the lighter behind. Anne stashed them out of sight for safe keeping. She'd informed Mark and left it up to him to tell his friend. And more than a year had passed since.

Even though it was nine years since she'd been a smoker—since before she was pregnant with Julia—there was no denying that the cigarettes still evoked a powerful urge. And it would be another hour before anyone else was up.

Her decision felt devilish, yet independent. She filled her favorite mug with hot, black coffee, found an ashtray in the cupboard, and moved to the dining room table.

As morning light greyed in through the windows, she looked out through the sliding glass doors at the sea. She tasted the coffee, rich and hot. The fancy lighter operated with a delicate *click!*, and the first cloud of smoke issued like blue fairy fog rising from dewy moss. The morning's rough edges smoothed over.

She wondered if the hurricane was still on course—she would have to check the Weather Channel, later. She thought about the many storms the old house around her must have weathered.

She heard Mark on the stairs. Her hand reflexively darted to stab out the butt, but she stopped herself.

Mark hated cigarettes. He made rude, whining remarks to smokers in restaurants. But what did she care? If he didn't like it, maybe he'd have to leave, that's all.

At first he didn't see her there, in the next room. But he saw the coffee pot, and responded with a delighted sigh.

"*Ahh!*" He closed his eyes and inhaled deeply, cherishing the aroma. You'd think he never had coffee before.

She nearly called out, "Have fun last night?" in sarcasm, like a typical, wounded wifey. But he turned to her, and smiled. "The coffee woke me," he said. "The scent of it. I was so dead last night I nearly collapsed before reaching the bed. But now! My senses are so alive!"

What was with him?!

He crossed from behind the counter, with his coffee mug in one hand, and in the other a large, polished stone, the color of citrine, which glistened as he twirled it lightly in his fingertips.

She glared at him. Then she studied the cigarette pack and she fingered the lighter, debating.

"I made a decision last night," he said, seriously. "From this point on, there's only you."

"Oh, please. I'm not interested."

"I'm sorry if I've hurt you, Anne," he said.

This was not what she wanted today. Not to suddenly begin with truth telling and heart to heart dialogue, not with him. Maybe five years ago, before saving lives in the O.R. gave him such a sense of worth that he lost the necessity to try hard in other areas. Back then they were still hoping to build something.

She clicked the lighter.

"I brought these home." He took another stone from the pocket of his robe. This one was marbleized white and blue, the colors of a full moon in a daytime summer sky.

"Well, that's wonderful, dear," she said, detached. She stood up and took her cup to the kitchen. "You didn't happen to get my locket, did you? In the excitement of your travels?"

He said nothing, but poured over his gems.

Had he finally lost it? Had all the stress of a high-profile, anal-retentive surgeon's life finally snapped his upper branches?

"Don't worry," she filled in, embarrassed by his strange behavior. "I'm sure that guy in town will keep his word."

"Everything's different," he said. He stood up and faced her, with a smile. "You'll see."

As she rinsed her cup, he came to her, and stood close behind. Then he placed his hands on her upper arms, and her spine tensed. He kissed her neck.

She spun around, appalled. "What are you doing?!"

"Anne, I adore you," he said, softly, pleadingly. There was an unusual smell about him, not unpleasant but earthy and bitter. The look in his eye was baffling. Unfamiliar.

"Mark—" She side-stepped her way out of the corner, and brushed past him.

He followed her back into the dining room. She sat down and picked up the cigarette pack and the lighter. "Look—" She held her palm up, a signal to back off. "Right now—"

He picked up his rocks and replaced them in his robe pocket. "Just wait here," he said, excitedly. "Just give me a minute. Wait for me. And I'll be back down."

He disappeared up the stairs.

Anne picked up the cigarette pack, then tossed it back on the table. This was asinine. She didn't have time for this. Whatever he thought was going to happen—he was wrong.

She wasn't going to start smoking again, either.

She was going to put a few touches on the painting she worked on last night. She was going to walk her daughter to school, like a normal mom. And she was going to contact a lawyer.

CHAPTER 22

Van Rensselaer took a small, leather sack of polished crystals from the bureau, where he'd left it before losing consciousness the previous night. He poured them onto the bed and they splashed across the white bedspread like candy-colored rain.

They brought luster back to the room, which had grown drab in his absence. When this room was his, it had more character—like the bed chamber of a prince, a holy man.

In the master bathroom, he removed his robe and tossed it onto the clothes hamper. The lights around the mirror highlighted his defined biceps and pectorals—muscles like those he admired as a boy staring at the covers of war novels. Mark Clausin had spent countless, self-absorbed hours perfecting his physique in the gymnasium. To Van Rensselaer the notion of labor with the sole intended outcome of defined physique was sheer vanity. A waste of time and energy. When Man built machines to do work, who suspected the impending invention of machines to simulate work?

Nevertheless he had to admit, his new muscle tone was quite olympian. Clausin would never have guessed that the true purpose of his monotonous strain was to build a god-like form for the New Creator.

Van Rensselaer felt strong.

He ran the bathwater, and tested its temperature. When the stream was tepid, he stopped up the tub and let it fill. He passed back into the bedroom, and fingered the stones on the bed.

They were from Nepal, Egypt, Borneo, Mazatlan, Haiti, Bali, Mexico, and the United States. He had shipped five large crates of them to this address in 1937. Those scattered before him now were the only ones he could currently access. Among them intermingled bits of rotted wood and rotted bone and other assorted debris. But with these gems he would gather the rest of his collection. He would get back so many things. All he had to do was open the window between worlds.

He turned a few stones over, and made his selections. He arranged some on the floor along the bedroom's perimeter, dropped a handful of crystalline between the headboard and the wall, and lined the upper ledge of the bedroom mirror with others in solid colors—they were almost hidden by the frame.

He switched on lamps, and the tv and radio, and he turned the volume down low. He plugged in Clausin's electric shaver.

He flushed the toilet, removed the ceramic lid from the tank, plunked a blue agate down, and arranged the stopper so the water would continuously flow.

Into the full tub he dropped a stone of blood-red.

Then he knelt on one knee beside the tub, and with his fingertips he stroked the surface of the clear water. The hum of electricity was all around him.

The Mind was like water, and the world was a ripple on its surface. He swirled his hand above the carnelian-like stone in the tub. It looked like a tiny, pulsating heart in the center of concentric circles which lifted, and rolled out toward ceramic shores.

A clear bubble appeared below the surface of the water. It was tiny at first, but it ballooned and wiggled with fluid cellular orbishness as it grew. He beheld, within its sheer walls, his old bedroom. The room to which he was currently adjacent appeared as it was long ago.

There stood the massive, four-poster bed which had been shipped from Denmark more than a hundred years earlier. His wife, before her death, slept beside him night after night in that bed, and the sight of it brought to mind her shiny, puffy-white cheeks.

That anemic and compliant simp. She'd been more helpful to him than she knew.

Beyond the bed, in the miniature, snow globe-like world, stood his armoire. The skeleton key protruded from the lock.

With a process akin to visualization, he turned the key. Garments parted, and he saw, at the rear of the cupboard, a glittering, gilded box.

He was in his room, then. The room as he had known it—with its own scent. He sat on the edge of the bed and opened the box on his lap. The amber colored stones were revealed. So was the magnet invention. Magnets the color of emeralds encrusted in silver. The device was shaped like a tiny dagger, but it worked like a key.

He returned to the world of white, in the 21st century bathroom, where he knelt by the tub. The objects he retrieved lay dripping on the tub ledge. With them in his possession, he was again in control.

CHAPTER 23

Anne went back up to her studio, gathered the blankets from the couch and folded them. She was about to go upstairs to check on her daughter when Julia appeared in the third-floor stairwell looking sleepy-eyed and pretty in her nightgown.

"Morning, bright eyes!"

"Hi mom."

"Hungry?"

Julia nodded, and Anne led her down to the kitchen. They made french toast and ate it with butter and sugar.

"I still don't know how they get butter," Julia said. "They just keep stirring it, then 'poof!'?"

"Butter."

"But why?"

"We should try it. We should get a churn."

"Really?!"

"Why not?"

"It must be like cooking," Julia said, contemplatively. "*That* changes things. Like eggs get white and meat gets brown."

"Stirring something does add some heat," Anne said. "But I think it has more to do with the motion."

"Can you look for one today?"

"Maybe."

Later, as Anne rinsed the dishes, Julia suddenly giggled, jumped up from her seat, and ran to the coat hooks by the porch doorway. She threw her red coat on over her nightgown, and pulled rubber boots onto bare feet.

"Whatchya doing?"

"Be right back, mommy!" She had that secretive air, like she was planning a gift.

She dashed to the sliding door and stepped out onto the deck, then ran down the stairs and across the yard.

Anne watched from the kitchen window. Had Julia seen something? Did she have the sudden idea to collect a seashell or a periwinkle?

Julia climbed onto the big rocks.

Be careful honey! Remember—don't pass the water line, not without an adult.

But as if her independence was the only consideration, Julia stepped boldly from one rock to the next, out toward the middle of the break-water.

Julia!

Anne leaned forward over the kitchen sink. Julia knew better than that!

Oh, stop being overprotective! Let her explore, like a normal kid.

Nonsense! She was being disobedient, and it was dangerous. She had those loose boots on—

Anne moved to the sliding door, and opened it. Julia was like a red speck, now, out at the very end of the jetty. Jesus!

Then, as Anne took a breath—about to yell to her daughter—Julia faced home, as if seeking her mother's attention. In her quick, turning motion, Julia's foot slipped. She wheeled her arms for a split second. Then she toppled. Backward. A wave broke on the spot where she vanished.

Running across a yard, her yard, but not comprehending the reason. In a moment she would have Julia in her arms. *Julia, that was so bad! You knew you weren't supposed to*—But no, no this was unthinkable.

Her climb was so furious it could have injured the rocks. She topped the highest one. Her daughter floated in the water, already some distance out. Julia's bottom was above the surface, her face down below. The rhythm of Julia's movement was not her own, but the ocean's. Pulling her away.

Oh God oh God...

An injured elbow, as Anne's dive scraped corners of submerged rock. Then, wet cold dark brine. Masses of seaweed brushed her body. Have to get her, rescue her baby.

The drifting away child. Strenuous breast-strokes, desperate pursuit. Fighting the ocean.

Then—clutching at a slippery rubber coat. Turn her over, for God's sake, so she'll breathe!

...lifeguard class, junior-high school, grab her hair, hold her chin. Swim.

She drags Julia over the smaller rocks, then across pebbles. Bloody pebbles, bloody hands. Someone does CPR on someone. Someone inside Anne's head counts, and presses on her little daughter's chest. She kisses her daughter goodnight- no she pushes breath into the little mouth, lungs that won't breathe. No. This isn't. Oh God please.

She's not a doll. She's a *baby!*

God—She's my daughter! Don't do this!

CHAPTER 24

Alice made her rounds in B-wing of the treatment facility, and was tending to a forty-year-old manic-depressive woman with bandaged wrists, when the A-wing tone sounded. She scrawled the remainder of her notes on the chart, handed it to the nurse and hurried along the corridor and up the winding stairs.

The pain in her ankles didn't slow her. Near the top of the stairs her heart palpitated and she made another mental note to cut down on caffeine.

"Nash attacked Ronnie!" the nurse exclaimed. "He almost killed her!"

"Oh, Jesus." Nash was a long-time patient, a paranoid schizophrenic with a true violent side he usually kept reserved for small animals. "Is he secure?"

The nurse nodded. Alice crossed into the nurse's station. Ronnie sat behind the semi-circular desk and massaged the bridge of her nose. She was visibly shaken—her eyes were red, her breath was labored, and her throat was marked with red blotches.

"What happened?"

"I'm... so sorry!" The young girl hiccupped.

Alice sat beside her, patted her hand, and tried to soothe Ronnie.

"He took me totally by surprise. If you'd heard his breathing, you'd have sworn he was asleep. But when I opened the curtains—he was right behind me!"

Alice handed her a fresh tissue from the box on the desk.

"I put him down with a knee, doctor. I can't believe I—"

"You had to defend yourself."

A patient materialized at the nurses desk. "I didn't do something though," John Wilson said in his nasal monotone, his brows knitted in worry. "I didn't goddamn do something anyhow, ya know, ya know."

"No dear, I know," Alice said.

"Yeah, okay," he said. "But what's a matter her—she thought I did something ya know?"

"It's not about you, John," Alice said firmly. "But would you like to help out, and go get your shower done?"

"Okay beautiful."

"Okay pookie," Alice said.

"Yeahh—" John turned and left.

"How's your throat?"

Ronette rubbed the red marks. "Sore. But okay."

"And the rest of you?"

"He had me good—" She took a deep breath, and wiped her eyes.

"Go on downstairs. I'll meet you in the caf."

Ronnie nodded, and went. Alice met the other nurse at the door to Mr. Nash's room. "Who locked this door?" she demanded.

"I thought under the circumstances—"

Alice held her tongue. "We'll talk about it later," she said authoritatively and peered in through the glass rectangle. Nash was curled on the floor in his pajamas, motionless. The sounds of other patients, who sensed turmoil in the air, echoed from both ends of the ward.

"He hasn't moved," the nurse said.

"Fine. Go check on Mrs. Michaels," Alice said, turning the door handle.

The room was designed to be a comfort, to look as un-sterile and un-institutional as possible. But the fabrics which covered seat cushions, pillows and the bed were all in solid colors, to avoid patterns which some patients could find dizzying. The safety features weren't obvious—like the cordless lamp built into a polished oak table, which was bolted to the floor, and the clear, shatter-proof glass in the windows and picture frames. Alice sat by the door. "Howard?—"

He didn't move.

"It smells bad in here. You're going to have to use the bathroom."

He pretended to be dead, and he was so still he might have half believed it.

"Do you realize what happened? Do you know you attacked a nurse, whose only reason for being here is to help you?"

"That wasn't a nurse."

"Who do you think she was?"

"She was an usher."

This was a strange fantasy of his, where figures like theater ushers would come to guide him to a place like hell.

"Howard, look at me."

The head tilted slowly, and from within the protective cavern, which the body carved, peered the red-rimmed eyes of agony.

"Do you still trust my frame of reference?"

He blinked in affirmation.

"And you remember the things we've discussed about your ailment?"

Another blink, and a subtle nod.

"The nurse you attacked is Ronette Baker. She works here full-time, and she's also a full-time student. She's studying to become a doctor like me, because she wants to spend her life helping people who suffer from conditions like yours. You injured her, and you scared her half to death. We need to file a police report. Do you understand?"

His gaze reverted to the inner sanctum. "She was an usher, an usher—"

"No! She's a nurse and a student!"

"Why, then, did she want to lead me down there, down the dark aisle—"

"She wasn't. You thought she was, but you were mistaken. She came in here with your medication. She wanted it to be bright for you, so she went to open the curtains."

Nash curled deeper, then rocked into a kneeling position and lifted his face toward the windows. "I smell like shit."

"A knee to the testicles can have that effect," Alice said. "Do you understand why it happened?"

"I know why she decked me. She was within her rights there, no question. She should have gouged my eyes…"

"She should have been left alone."

"She should have been left alone," he repeated. "But I thought she saw my ticket. I would have killed her. Cuz, you know… Once they see your ticket…"

"Did she see your ticket?"

"No. Like you said… You see how things are, on the outside…" Outside his head, he meant.

"Go get cleaned up, okay?"

"Yep." He stood in one motion, and walked with exaggerated control to the bathroom, then closed the door behind him.

Alice sat with Ronette and described her conversation with Nash. She felt no need to remind the nurse of body-positioning issues, like not turning one's back on violence-prone, schizophrenic patients. Ronette would never repeat that mistake. Alice was inclined, though, to give Ronnie the choice of taking the rest of the day off. "…if you need it," she said.

"Think I should?"

"I think you should focus on being around Howard Nash for the rest of your shift. I'm sure that's not what you want to hear, though."

Ronnie said she thought she'd like to go, if it was okay.

"It's fine," Alice said. "But I'm afraid you'll spend every minute wor-rying about seeing him again. You might wonder if all this is worth it, when you're a registered nurse to begin with, and why change careers anyway? You're gifted in this field, Ronnie. You're very caring."

Ronnie sighed a breath of ultra-sobriety. "Fine," she said, rising. "I'll stay. But right now I'm going to visit Steve down in the kitchen. He's gonna roll me a big, fat dube, and the second my wheels roll off the lot today…"

Inside, Alice grinned. "Well, I appreciate your honesty."

A few moments later, while she sat alone drinking coffee, Alice suffered first an olfactory, and then a visual hallucination.

It started with the smell. The familiar smell. She stiffened, and looked all around for anything she might have confused for it, something with an odor that disguised itself. But there was nothing. She held her napkin over her mouth and fought the gag reflex, trying not to draw attention to herself.

Then she saw, along all the window ledges in the dining area, clumps of writhing meal worms, clumps that quivered and curled and fell to the floor in chunks that shattered like plaster.

Good Christ!

Her cup and saucer clanked and coffee slurped over the side as she stood from the table.

"Doctor?" a voice came behind her.

She spun to face it. An aide wheeling a bus cart had frozen, and stared at her, startled. "Are you all right?"

Alice shot another glance at the windows. The ledges were white with new paint, and clean from last night's dusting. The morning sun warmed them.

"I'm fine, thanks. There was a hornet—"

"Eeew!" The girl covered her mouth. "I hate those things—they get in here all the time. But he scared you bad, huh? A little hornet…"

"You want to get him?" Alice menacingly challenged.

"Not me!" Denise wheeled down the aisle, smiling in the glow of having seen the psych director rattled by a little winged creature.

But Alice knew what really disturbed her, and it was no bug. It was a monster.

All at once, the State Hospital was in her memory: painted cinder block walls stained from corner to corner with blood and shit and semen, human beings reduced to grizzly lumps like unshaped clay, with muscle gnarled by horror, hair frizzed by dementia and bones angled in positions of extreme defense. The six inch windows were ten feet apart and twenty feet off the ground; her eyes used to train on them for hours. A sliver of sky in hell's ceiling.

Those tiny windows. They were often the first thing she saw when her hallucinations ended.

But all that was a lifetime ago. By the time she received her doctorate, she thought she'd come full-circle.

But maybe not. Maybe coming full-circle meant that as a daft old woman she would begin a slow descending return into the mental chaos from which she'd come. And only when all contact with her current sense of reality was lost, would the circle be completed.

Stop it! she told herself, as she made her way back to B-wing. It was only a mild hallucination. It could have been triggered by any number of things. It was surprising that she'd gone this long with no relapse of any kind. Maybe it was just a scar.

She'd talk to Carl later. She'd have him do a full work-up on her. Whatever the problem was, they'd identify it in a hurry—and deal with it.

But that smell.

There was a time, long ago, when that smell was a kind of death to her. But now the past was dead. The beast was dead. Only its corpse reeked. And a corpse couldn't hurt you.

Not if you were sane.

CHAPTER 25

Anne's sister Mary was a housewife in Virginia. She spent a night at Anne's house and got dressed up for the funeral. Mary's husband was in the Navy. He and their two boys joked around and helped themselves to what was in the refrigerator.

Anne's brothers were at the funeral. Tom wore a plaid shirt under his suit jacket and tie. He and Mike were considerably older than Anne. They ran a construction business together. They didn't know what to say.

"Look at you," her brother Tom said. "You've done all right for yourself, Annie."

Not *I'm sorry for your trouble...* None of that. They weren't good at those things. Even hugging was awkward.

Anne hadn't seen any of these people in five years, and her brother Jimmy, the one she would have most liked to see, was not in attendance. The last she knew, his drug addiction had led him to California. But that was seven years ago.

Her sister tried to comfort her, talking about when they were kids. But Anne didn't want comfort. She didn't want to sit and chat and be nostalgic. She wanted to be alone with her pain. She wanted these people to go away so she could sit in the dark and torment herself with memories of Julia. She wanted to be so alone that she could shriek like a dismembered cat and no one would hear.

Ironically, Mark was the only person she could tolerate. Julia was his daughter, too. And his loss was in his eyes like a hundred years of prison. She knew he was the only one who could come close to understanding.

At one point during the wake she watched as he sat alone, hunched forward. He pushed tears aside as if he thought he'd be rid of them. Right cheek, left cheek, right cheek. There seemed a certain surprise, a kind of bafflement, when the tears kept coming, when they dropped from his cheeks like rain from leaves. It was an unfamiliar experience for him. She supposed he had never really mourned before.

Anne found herself wondering if his girlfriend would turn up. Of course that was nonsense. Lucy would stay far away out of respect for the grieving mother, the wife she'd injured. But Anne wanted to tell her it was okay, she could come if she wanted. Mark needed someone who could comfort him.

His parents said the customary things. They were the direct opposite of Anne's family. At one point, returning from the ladies room, she heard her father-in-law discussing stock quotes with a stranger.

She hid deep inside herself until the relatives cleared off.

During the next month, Mark took a leave of absence from his job. He cooked for Anne, who was too heartbroken to do much of anything. Mark got the laundry done and kept the house clean.

After that month, with Anne still not painting, still not eating much, still mostly just sitting where Julia used to watch tv in the deck room, and staring out at the ocean, Mark suggested she see a therapist to help her get through this phase of her grief. Then he returned to his job and Anne was left with long hours in the empty house.

Mark worked at the hospital for as many as forty-eight straight hours, grabbing cat naps on a gurney when he could. That's what he said, and she believed him. He didn't see Lucy anymore. He wanted to lose himself in work, he said.

Sometimes when he came home he'd say they ought to hire a cleaning service. "It's not like we can't afford it. The way this place gets, it's no wonder you still feel depressed all the time."

Anne agreed, but she knew she would never allow strangers to go through the rooms of this house, which now were a kind of shrine to her daughter's memory. Julia's sweet voice reverberated in the silence of the still walls and the wind-rattled windows of every room.

She saw the therapist Mark recommended, but she canceled more appointments than she kept, and said little when she did go. I miss my daughter.

Of course. But you have to live your life.

I am living it.

What are you doing to get back in the swing of things?

I don't want to.

I can only imagine it seems impossible?

But I don't want it. Not to be happy. Not really. Not ever.

She was given a prescription for anti-depressants. But it wasn't until she found a small black bag of Mark's, with samples of medication furnished by various pharmaceutical companies, that she finally found something to help with the pain.

They are pain killers, she thought. So why the hell not?

They gave her distance. Sometimes they let her feel that nothing had changed. Nothing had ever changed, since the dawn of time. She was connected with Julia, still connected…

One night Mark had people over. The idea, she was sure, was to help her, to bring her around once again to the world of people. But that was never her world. She excused herself from the dinner table, went up to the master bathroom and swallowed three Percosets. Then she returned to her guests, and her wine. She gave a fine performance that evening. When she started to clear the table, Mark stepped in to help. She let him take over, and she went back upstairs. Two more pills.

At the top of the stairs, she hesitated. Why should she go back down, if she dreaded it? Surely they would understand if she retired unannounced.

She took the flight up, instead, with uncertain panic at her heels. She went into the playroom. It was dark in there, and the ocean whispered. Let's make up a story. In her mind, she pleaded with Julia.

She switched on the light.

Something was wrong.

The room was arid and dusty. Nothing on the shelves but cobweb. Julia's toys, and her miniature furniture, were all gone. The murals, which Anne completed years ago, suddenly had the appearance of being unfinished. An iguana and a sloth on the south wall were missing half their bodies, and the jungle ended in jagged green lines where the blank, yellowed wall took over. The forest on the north wall was a charcoal sketch.

Her scream caused a clatter on the stairway—but she did not want them up here. She hurried down to the second floor. Her husband was at the top of the stairs, with concerned guests behind him. Sweetheart, sweetheart.

"No! You can't take all of her! Not like that," Anne said, crying. "She can't leave me completely…"

Mark guided her to their bedroom.

Later, he explained. They needed to remove sources of painful memory. He was going to redo the upstairs, make it a kind of doctor's office and examination room. He was thinking about semi-retirement from the hospital, and could practice general medicine at home. He could be home half the week, to help her. What she saw upstairs was white-wash, where it had been applied to the walls.

No, that's Julia's mural. Please. I painted it, I know how it looked when I was painting it. I saw my own line drawings. My sketches. No, we can't undo it. It's all that's left of her.

"Anne, I swear to God, I'm doing this for you. Please trust me, this once."

CHAPTER 26

There is a house on Bow Lee Point which is believed, by all the neighborhood children, and many of the adults, to be haunted. It is a house grown ugly with disrepair and neglect; shingles are missing from its gabled roof, and nearly a decade worth of accumulated autumn leaves have killed the grass and filled the corners of the yard with muck.

The kids do the customary things. They make up stories about the house, and they make wild claims about having visited it and what the crazy woman there tried to do to them. They throw rocks, apples, cans. They dare each other up to the door on Halloween, but flee before reaching the midpoint of the front walk.

Parents chastise the children when they hear stories about who dared whom to look in the window, or what horrible thing was left in the mailbox.

"Leave that poor woman alone, do you understand!"

To most locals, the house represents something different. It's an eyesore, and a depressing place. It seems more cursed than haunted, and they wish it would be sold and renovated. Or better yet, razed to the ground and transformed into a picnic area.

On subtle levels, some of them accept at face value the rumors that the child's death, years ago, was no accident. That the woman, suffering from mental illness and depression, pushed her little girl, and nothing could ever be proved. Others see the place as a reminder that anyone could fall to the depths of despair, and remain there, if tragedy strikes and is not surmounted.

In any case, the house is something to be put out of mind, like an evil hideaway in a buried dream. Those who walk past it often stare straight ahead, pretending something or someone up the road commands attention—because they feel eyes peering out from an upper window. They search the wildlife sanctuary as a distraction from the sudden gloom, which emanates from the house and seems to penetrate their skin.

This feeling is like unwelcome time travel—as if the house was stuck in a moment from the past, and that moment would draw objects into itself like a black hole.

The once-fine, ocean-front dwelling was built in the early 1800's, and it has seen many occupants. Fine furniture of different periods has made its way in and out through the front door. In long ago times, floors were polished, walls painted, renovations undertaken and completed. The living room mantle has, through the years, supported hundreds of vases of fresh cut flowers.

But at a certain point during the current occupancy, the upkeep fell away. Paint chipped and crumbled. Dust accumulated. Small rectangular sections of carpets faded from too-long stationary exposure to window light. The rooms took on the smell of the past. The air itself became a relic.

The air circulated within those rooms, and seemed never to commingle with the outdoors, so there was a staleness to Anne's every breath, day in and day out, as she stared into the fog of mental paralysis which pervaded each moment.

Nights had become nightmarish, and days bore no significant difference, one to the next. Sometimes she sat in her studio, a room fallen into as much decay as any inner-city flop house, and if she felt like it, she slapped black oil paint lethargically onto canvases: cold blacks cross-hatched over warmer ones in angry, unsalable pieces with no discernable form. Her chief concern in these endeavors was that upon completion of each she was closer to another dose of medication, and another long sleep. Each brought her closer to the grave.

Other times she sat in the reading room, on the second floor, and she paid attention to the way words on a page faded into uniform grey lines when her eyes unfocused.

Mark tolerated her living like this. He even eased the gloom by regularly procuring prescription pain-killers for her. She assured him they were effective in ways that her anti-depressants were not. Vicodin. Percoset. Darvocet. Demerol. Dilaudid.

One sunny afternoon she went outside and sat on the deck chair, reclining, as a spectacle of fantasy drifted through her mind.

Julia. At age four, tearing the Christmas wrapping off of a new baby doll. "Oh, Marianne!" she exclaimed.

Marianne? Where did the name come from? It was like she recognized the doll.

Another memory. Julia nestled close to Anne in the reading room. After a story about Babar the Elephant, Julia spontaneously invented a sequel of publishable merit. She was about five.

Julia, rail-thin in her nightgown, helping with the makeshift bed, the blankets. Auburn hair, fanned on the pillow, when Anne tucked her in. "I'll be all right, mamma."

Anne opened her eyes.

Don't start again. You'll only cause yourself more pain. Accept the truth. She's dead.

"How could she be?!"

You remember. You were there.

A June bug skittered up her thigh, and she screamed. She swept at it with her hands, but it didn't move—as if her hand passed right through it. She tried to clutch it with her fingernails. But it skittered up her arm. Its sharp pincers dug into her neck.

She leapt to her feet, and the aluminum lawn chair clattered against the deck. She screamed, and clawed at her neck. A sailboat cruised slowly by in the distance. Someone could be watching, and would know she was insane, on drugs.

She felt the bug on her arm, and looked. Nothing there but itchy skin.

The outdoor world spun like a malfunctioning carousel as she fumbled with the handle on the sliding door, and staggered inside.

*   *   *   *   *   *   *   *   *   *

Each day she dreamt the vivid dreams of the narcotics user.

In one dream, Anne went out to her screened-in porch, and sat. She was wearing one of Mark's old shirts. Rain pounded outside: a million leaves slapped by angry water. She rubbed her eyes, and the lively wind cleansed the world behind them. The weather breezed through her. It was dangerous, and made the skin tingle. What could be better than a screened-in porch during a storm?

Her cigarettes waited for her beside a brassy ashtray, on the old travel trunk used for an end table. She lit one up, and drew deeply.

She heard coughing. Out in back, in the rain. Must be Mark, she thought. *Was it Friday?*

The man appeared on the flagstone path that led from the ocean to the back door. He seemed oblivious to the rain, though his long, black coat was heavy with it. From a distance, his eyes were trained on her.

It occurred to her that if he meant her harm, he could achieve it. The doors and windows were all unlocked. He could kill her. No one would hear her screams in this storm.

And so what? She would bow to the Angel of Death.

As he walked steadily up the flagstones, she calmly finished her cigarette. He paused by the porch steps, a tall man. He stood there, silently, watching her.

She watched the rain drip from his flattened hair. Even his skin, as water rolled down it, looked strong. Strong skin. She thought: how much more attractive he is than my husband. How weak my husband is, compared to him.

She glanced at the wet hook-and-eye on the flimsy screen-door frame. The "eye" was an empty hole, a pupil-less socket. The hook, a limp, dangling, backwards "el".

His swift tug dispensed with the resistance of swelled wood, and the door frame shuddered. He stepped inside, and let the door slam behind him. Anne's cigarette butt smoldered in the ashtray on the trunk.

How amazing, the warmth that flooded her belly, the lightness filling her from her own dicey breath as this stranger came near to her.

Alone with her. He would do things.

He reached behind himself, and one end of his dangling coat belt receded with a hiss. It landed like a dead snake at her feet.

"What do I do with it?" she said.

"Pick it up."

It was damp, black wool, its fibers coarse.

"Bring it inside."

He followed her through the kitchen. She led him to the stairs, and hurried up to the master bedroom. The filtered light of a charcoal sky filled the windows, and reflected in the dresser mirror. A canopy bed, like an unlit pyre, stood ready to inflame the center of the room. She draped the belt over the lustrous baseboard. Then, facing the window, with eyes fixed on the grey light, she quickly unbuttoned her pants and pulled them off. She removed her shirt. Her bra and panties. Naked, she touched the belt, and carefully took it in her hands. She faced him and smiled.

"Kneel down," he said, "and offer it to me."

She understood how he wanted her to do it: in a ceremonial way. The oriental carpet fibers were soft to her knees.

She tilted her head back, watching him, and held the belt up with both hands.

From an inner coat pocket he pulled out a double-edged knife, and with an angry, upward slash, he sliced through the belt. Then he tossed the knife onto the bed.

With the short end of the belt he tied her hands to the baseboard. The longer one was for punishment. For letting her own child die.

"Yess!" she cried. "Owww... Goddd!" She was sobbing. "Yess plee-hee-hease..."

CHAPTER 27

Anne sat in the reading room with a blend of pain killers and scotch greying out the too-rigid lines of mid-day. A chemically born quiver of excited peace warmed her and carried a wave of euphoria from her stomach to her forehead. Each exhalation of cigarette smoke was a heavenly cloud, and she was born up on the recognition that only time kept her from death, a state where all things combined and where she and Julia would surely be reunited.

She heard her daughter's voice. "Mommy?"

It made her sit up, and take full notice of the empty room around her. The voice was so close. "Mommy?"

"Julia?" Anne rose, and turned a complete, slow circle. "Sweetheart?!"

For the rest of the day, she tried to make contact. But she didn't know enough about ghosts. She was up against silence, and was forced to settle for this new understanding—Julia was hiding behind a metaphysical curtain.

Although she didn't know it then, subsequent connections were imminent.

Julia's visitations always occurred unexpectedly, and never when Anne tried to initiate them. Her mind would drift off into some bubble of neutralized thought, and she'd hear her child's voice beside her. She'd look for Julia. And then… nothing.

There seemed a correlation between the likelihood of these audial encounters and the amount of opiates in her bloodstream. Painkillers assisted in opening the window of consciousness through which the ghostly presence passed.

She increased her drug intake, and the moments of contact grew frequent. They expanded in duration, as well. At times, Anne could close her eyes and listen to Julia's ramblings for hours.

She couldn't catch the meaning of Julia's words, though. It was as if the part of the brain which allowed Anne to hear Julia, filtered out linguistic interpretation. But it didn't matter. The sound of Julia's voice, her enthusiastic intonation, musically relating details that mattered to her, was so satisfying. Tears streamed from Anne's closed eyes as she pictured the face to accompany the voice.

Once, she caught a brief glimpse of Julia in peripheral vision. Anne was building a fire in the living room—lulled by the sight of paper blackening at the edges and crumpling in flame—when her little girl appeared at the dining room doorway, complaining of hunger. Anne raced to the vacant passage, arms outstretched.

Anguished, she cried out so strenuously she thought her vocal chords would be damaged. She hunted the empty space into which Julia vanished. And the space beyond that. But she could not regain the salve she'd enjoyed when permanent connectedness with her daughter was taken for granted. She could not hold Julia, or touch her warmth or smell her sweet skin.

The poor child was trapped in a ghostly world—in some mirror image of this stale, lonely house.

Anne swallowed three more pills with a tumbler of scotch—to blur the lines between the worlds, blur them. She knew the risks. But she was not afraid to plummet. She wrapped herself in an afghan and stared into the fire, hoping for something more than the haze which crept over her. She hoped the haze would prove a medium for contact.

But instead of another encounter, she fell into vivid dreams, opiate dreams, which are more clear than life.

The short slope behind her house was a vast field of daisies, and the ocean rose in the distance behind it. There were many children among the flowers. They must have been her own, although some of them, at ages of nine or eleven, were new to her. There was a dark haired girl in a green dress standing at a picnic table, who cut an apple, first into quarters, then eighths, then sixteenths.

Julia was out on the rocks, facing the horizon, arms held out to her sides for balance as she stepped onto the next stone, and the next, navigating toward the end of the breakwater.

*   *   *   *   *   *   *   *   *   *

When Anne woke, the fireplace was cold. Her joints ached. A peculiar, nervous flutter filled her and she had to pee terribly. Her head throbbed with white menace.

She went to the kitchen, and grabbed the vial he'd left on the counter. It had a nice heaviness in her hand: the promise of a newly filled prescription. Was this the reason she stayed with him? Most couples separated after the death of a child.

Was it love?

Or simple dependency. She hadn't the will or the energy to rely on anything but his capacity to procure pain killers, and his ability to earn a living.

And—there was the secret wish. A new baby with Mark would be Julia's full brother or sister.

*   *   *   *   *   *   *   *   *   *

The house was dark. None of the overhead lights were on, and the few lamps seemed to swallow their own glow; the house was filled with a weird, middle-of-the day darkness, like a house charred by fire, where the embers were cold and rain clouds had moved in. A damp draft coursed through it.

She walked as if underwater, and the rooms tilted this way and that. Something was happening.

She made her way upstairs to lie down, and rest. Dreams were a world which were sometimes sweet, and sometimes bitter. She liked they way they always dissolved in the end.

She stepped into the bedroom, and stood still. A moment stood still. In the confusion, her mind suffered. Questions fired rapidly, but clipped themselves off in mid-formation because they made no sense.

The bedroom… *wasn't* the bedroom. Not *her* bedroom.

She backed into the hall and spun around. Across from her was the deck room. The linen closet. At the other end of the hall was the door to Julia's old room. Anne's studio came after the stairway entrances. All was familiar.

She stepped back into the bedroom, but it was a room she'd never seen. A room in a stranger's house. It was so dark, she crossed to red velvet drapes that covered the windows and she drew them open. Instead of vanishing in the light of day, the strange, opulent room only brightened.

Oriental rugs covered polished, hard wood. Where had her carpet gone?

Whose canopy bed? Where the hell did that armoire—and that dresser—come from?

Were those gaslight fixtures?!

The wall paper was elaborate, expensive. A well-crafted tapestry next to the bed depicted something like a sacrificial rite, with Meso-American swastikas in its borders. And across from that hung a mounted, military sword.

"This is fucked up!"

She spun, again, to the window—to verify that the view outside was the same as the one she'd always known. In the wildlife sanctuary across the street, some of the leaves had started changing. Birds hopped and fluttered in the brush.

She spun back to the horror show of elegance that threatened her mind with collapse. When had he done this? Could a room be totally redecorated overnight? It was too much, like a museum that showed the lavish decor of a dead millionaire or president.

No… there hadn't been time for this. To re-paper the walls? Move in a bed? Tear up the wall-to-wall carpet and buff the floorboards?

What happened?

How long had she slept?

She touched the ornate post at the foot of the bed, and something returned to her—a vague but disturbing *deja vu*, maybe some erotic dream she'd once had.

She squelched the thought of it, and rounded the bed to the dresser, situated where her own had been. She yanked open the top drawer. Her own familiar undergarments were there. Silk and cotton and lace. Someone's filthy hands had transferred them from her dresser.

She clutched a handful of these belongings. She clung to them like they were her lost, fragmented past, and she sat on the bed and cried.

But the feather mattress beneath her was the softest thing in the world. Along with her weight, it seemed a thousand sorrows sank into it. Suddenly drowsy, she lay back and curled to her side. She drew her satin slip to her cheek, like a baby blanket, and she wiped tears, and nuzzled it.

*   *   *   *   *   *   *   *   *   *

"Mark!" she yelled, when she awakened and heard footsteps down below. He came upstairs, and in the bedroom doorway, he grinned.

"What is all this?" she said.

"Like it?"

"What in the world…?" She sat up in what should have been her bedroom. "Why did you—? How on earth—?"

He crossed to the other side of the bed and parted the veil. Then he smoothed the bedspread on the feather mattress. "Bet you thought you never slept in a real bed."

She fell back into the bed, which was pure luxury, with four pillows the size of children's sleeping bags. It held her like a magnet, and she sighed.

Mark smiled. "Not bad, eh?"

She turned her head and looked at him, and the way he smiled brought her back to when they were younger. "I don't see how you could have done all this—"

"Easier that you might think," he said.

There was something strange about him. So sure of himself.

"What got into you?"

He lay down facing her, and propped his head above his bent elbow. "You could say I have a new outlook on life. That I've experienced a rebirth."

She rolled onto her back and looked up at the canopy. Was she prepared for this? After all this time? He was a stranger.

He put his hand on her belly, and it felt nice.

"How long has it been?" he said.

She considered the question. The answer was amusing, in a distorted way. The time could be measured in years or lives.

He slid closer, and snaked his arm up along her side. "I want another chance, you know. To try to start over, with a fresh commitment."

Something in his voice made heat prickle along her skin. He spoke with a strange inflection. Was he trying to sound sophisticated? Create himself anew? She worried for him. Surely he was injured by their loss, and had issues to deal with. And she was no help. As supportive as he tried to be, she had given him nothing of any worth for a long, long time.

His smell met her again, like a mixture of sweat, rained on leaves, tilled earth and cinnamon. Something inside her relaxed. And when he kissed her neck, she didn't stop him. She felt her eyelids droop.

He unbuttoned her blouse, and slid his hand inside. His palm felt rough as a stone, but he touched her so gently.

He licked her ear, and she gasped. Her breath quickened, and she suppressed a moan of pleasure.

"I can't get pregnant—" she said. As much as her secret wish compelled her—the time wasn't right. Not with the poisons in her. Deep inside, she understood what it would take to extract those poisons. Her body, in such a state, was no place to begin a life.

"I'll get your diaphragm," he said, rising. "I'll help you with it."

He crossed toward the bathroom, then stopped and turned. "Give me a moment. And while you're waiting, Anne, listen to the sea," he said. He closed his eyes. "Listen to the way the waves lift and fall."

Then he sighed deeply. "Yes. They begin in silence. Then, a sound like drawn air, as it meets the back of the throat, in a deep inhalation. There is a shape to the sound, like a 'c.'"

His voice was soothing, and she envisioned the waves with a clarity normally reserved for the cinema.

"'C' for 'crest,'" he said, "for the shape of the wave. It roars as it breaks, then quiets again for an instant, before the crash of foam on the sand, the hiss that scatters water molecules in all directions. An atom of hydrogen, two of oxygen, all so simple. The wave recedes."

He must have gone into the bathroom then. All she could be sure of was that she was floating.

"Mommy?"

Julia. Was here. Her ghost.

Somewhere in this house. Her old bedroom maybe!

Anne wanted to check. But that would mean upsetting this serenity and causing the lovely view to vanish. The view of the ocean in her mind's eye.

But… Julia wanted her mama. Anne rolled to her side.

Her eyes refused to open—the surging sea refused to evaporate, but kept pounding the shore before her like an angry goddess.

Anne panicked, and shook her head. The scene remained before her. With amplified effort, she pounded her fists against her forehead. The vision ripped apart and her eyelids sprung open.

She sat up in the strange room. There was a gnawing in her gut. Why were things so different?

She stood, and crossed toward the door, thinking she would quickly check Julia's room, and if she found nothing, she would return.

When she reached the door, his voice stopped her.

"What are you doing?" The sound was hurt, embittered.

She faced him from the doorway. "I'll be right back."

An incredulous look crossed his face. He shook his head. "Darling, don't…"

She glanced around the room again, and again it struck her—it made no sense. How could anyone have moved furniture up the stairs without waking her? Not to mention the work required on the flooring.

"Come, now," he said, his tone patronizing as he crossed back to the elegant bed. "Do as I say."

Suddenly he made her skin crawl. The way he talked!

"Mark…" She gestured to the new decor. "How did you do all this? Really?"

He sat down and removed his slippers. Then, with a sardonic tone, he said, "…you slept so *soundly*."

"What's that supposed to mean?!"

How long was she unconscious?

"Darling, come here this instant." Mark peeled back the covers. "Or do I have to tie a rope around your ankles?"

Anne marched into the hall. The fucking jerk. It was all a sick game. Son of a bitch.

She raced down the hall, and threw on the light in Julia's room.

It looked like a small guest bedroom. With a single bed, plainly covered, and a lady's writing desk in the corner, the room lambasted her with its neutrality, its sterility. Its *otherness*.

Behind her, he leaned in the doorway, hands in his pockets.

"What is this?!" she shouted.

"What do you mean?"

"How did you change all this?"

"Anne—"

"This was her room! Don't you understand?! How can I find her if you—" She spun around, facing the room again. "But how?! This doesn't fucking make sense, Mark!"

"God dammit, Anne!" he exploded, "The room was redone last year! You agreed it was best, and you helped. Julia's dead, okay?! You think I don't miss her? Do you think I don't want her back? I'd do anything. But she's not coming back. She's dead! I'm not!" He pummeled his chest. "But for all you care, I might as well be!"

*   *   *   *   *   *   *   *   *   *

She spent the night in her studio. Early in the morning, before the sun was up, she went downstairs and made coffee. Her body hungered for her pain killers, now, they way it used to hunger for cigarettes. She knew where the nearest vial of her medication was. She always knew exactly where to reach for it. She knew there was a full bottle in the kitchen drawer.

For now, though, she told herself, she would sit and have coffee, only, like a normal person. The pills weren't going anywhere.

She sat at the dining room table with her cup of coffee. She closed her eyes and took a long, hot sip.

When she opened her eyes, she saw the pack of cigarettes, and the silver-encased lighter.

Have one, she thought.

The lighter felt heavy. There was an image engraved on the side, and she studied it closely. It looked like a drawing room scene from an Elizabethan novel: some fop with a handkerchief delighting the seated ladies with his wit.

It wasn't her lighter. That woman left it.

With sunrise burning in through the windows, Anne raced up and down stairs.

She searched the first floor, shouting for Julia at every turn. She bolted down to the cellar and scanned for spaces where a child could be hidden. The utility room. The garage. She stalked the outdoors in their yard, down by the surf, and in the wildlife sanctuary, calling and calling, visualizing Julia at play in her favorite places; frantic when that image refused to materialize.

She steadied herself against the kitchen counter. She had to stop this. Stop panicking. She had to stay in control.

"Don't you think you should calm down?"

Mark stood by the glass doors in the dining room. The morning had grown bright, and he stared out at the sea, dressed and clean shaven, blue daylight adorning him.

"Where is she?" Anne asked.

He sighed. "Anne—"

"God damn it!" she screamed. "What are you doing? Have you lost your mind?"

"Get hold of yourself," he snapped.

"Tell me—"

"Why don't you sit down?" he said. He turned again and looked out over the deck. "Why don't you go outside? You could at least have a seat out in the fresh air and let the surroundings calm you."

"Stop it!" Anne grabbed a mason jar filled with tea bags and slammed it on the counter. "Why are you pretending? Mark, *please!* I don't like this! You're so—"

"You're being irrational," he said, turning again toward the horizon.

"Mark, if this is because— Jesus! She needs her mother!"

He moved toward her, nonchalantly. He came around the divider. She fumed, motionless and loathing, as he put his hands on her shoulders. Then he leaned in to kiss her forehead, and she shoved him back.

"Temper," he said.

"Stay away from me! If you hurt her—I swear to God—"

She grabbed the phone, ready to block him if he tried to snatch it, and she hit 9-1-1.

It didn't make sense, not any of it.

The voice on the phone prompted her.

"…the *police*…" she said. "…*yes*……my *daughter!*……she's *missing*…" Her voice rose to a squeal. "…yes, please hurry!"

She took another look at his smug expression. Then she ran out through the back door.

Her mind and her heart shrieked as she hurried down to the shore, toward the rocks where she and Julia once talked about snails. Where was her baby?!

She looked back at the house. Its outline was familiar, every plane and curve. But the windows had become like two-way mirrors, and they concealed something from her. The house had secrets.

Part of her shut down and grew detached from the confusion. She had to stabilize—to be poised—for anything that would help find Julia. Up the road, the police siren blared.

✳   ✳   ✳   ✳   ✳   ✳   ✳   ✳   ✳   ✳

The cruiser pulled up to the lawn, and two uniformed officers got out and sauntered toward the house. Anne rushed over to intercept them. "Please help… I don't know where she is, I haven't seen her…"

"Your daughter?"

"She's only eight," Anne said.

They followed her to the house. One of their radios blared static, and the taller, dark skinned officer quickly silenced it.

When they entered, Mark came down the stairs and spoke to the shorter man.

"Steve…"

"Dr. Clausin."

"Come on in." Mark led them into the study at the right of the stairs. "How's Marie?"

"Fine, sir."

"For God's sake!" Anne broke in. "Anything could be happening to her—"

"It's all right Anne," Mark said, gently. "Take it easy, sweetheart."

"Don't you—!" she yelled. Then she spoke to the officers in a controlled manner. "He may be responsible—"

"Anne—"

"Let's start at the beginning," Steve said.

She understood—they needed facts before they could search. She hoped they would listen to her. Then they'd do a quick sweep of the house and the property. There would be a radio call. Then the place would be swarming with police. They would collect evidence, clues. Whatever Mark had done, they would know. They would bring dogs. They'd put out an all points bulletin, and alert the community. Somebody would find her.

"Whatever you need, please, just get it quickly," she said.

"Would you men like to sit down?" Mark asked. "Anne, come in and sit down for a minute."

"NO!" she shouted. "She's my DAUGHTER!"

"We're here to help," the other officer said, stepping nearer to her.

Mark spoke quietly to the cop he knew. "You know what this is about…"

Steve seemed uncomfortable, embarrassed. "Yeah. I guess I'm afraid I do, doctor."

Anne watched from the doorway. Mark took a seat behind his desk. His eyes darted at the standing officer, then he sat back and gazed at the cop named Steve, his brow wrinkled with vexation. "Maybe you should fill your partner in," he said.

Steve glanced uneasily at Anne. He seemed to want to ask Mark something, but he hesitated.

Mark's voice dropped. "She's got to confront this."

What the hell were they saying? "Don't listen to him!" she exclaimed.

"Take it easy, ma'am," the officer beside her said.

Steve calmly informed his partner. "It's been years," he said. "But the Clausin's daughter…" He cautiously regarded Anne. "Well…"

"It's okay," Mark said.

"Well… she was killed, some time ago."

To Anne it felt like the temperature dropped to twenty, like a rancid storm cloud filled the house.

"*What?!*" Anne heard herself say. But she was the only one listening.

"It was terrible," the officer continued, "and I'm sorry, Mrs. Clausin. But I remember when it was on the news. I remember the day of the funeral. She fell down the cellar stairs in this house, and took a fatal blow to the head… Dr. Clausin was at work, or he might have…"

Mark leaned forward on his desk and crossed his hands.

"You monster!" she shouted.

The officer beside her stepped closer, and put his hand on her arm. "Let's step out, Ma'am… "

"…these episodes before," Mark said, a long way off, "but this is the worst yet…" He continued as the policeman pulled Anne to the living room. "…consultations with colleagues… I wonder if you could… show her." She heard his desk drawer slide open.

Had she responded to the raging signals in her nerves, she might have torn through the cop to get to that liar in the next room…

She kept control. For Julia's sake. But something was terribly wrong. And these men could not be trusted. They wouldn't believe her. Should she tell them that rooms in this house changed overnight? They'd think she was crazy.

She sat in the living room. It was a sunny day. But the room was cold. The fireplace was empty. There was no cinnamon-haired little girl to warm her with humor.

Suddenly Julia's face appeared before her eyes. It was a color photograph, of Julia at age two, on the front page of the newspaper that Steve handed to her. The headline blackened the universe.

She gasped, and covered her mouth. Then she dropped the paper, and hurried toward the stairs.

She reached the hallway above, and rushed into the next stairwell. Half way up the flight to the third floor, her legs crumpled beneath her. She rubbed her forehead against the railing, as the memories forced themselves.

She remembered cooking, and Julia was playing on the kitchen floor, banging a toy xylophone with a wooden spoon. But the random musical tones stopped as the spoon sailed through the air.

There's a clatter. The spoon tumbles down stairs.

"Hey!" Julia says, amused. And she's on her feet.

Damn it, why is the cellar door open? There's raised, bent aluminum molding at the base of the doorway, and the stairs are unguarded, railless.

"Wait a minute, honey!" She turns down the gas on the stove and faces the cellar door.

But Julia trips. There's a thump, and a tumble, on the upper-most stairs.

Anne rushes over. She's frightened, Julia is on the upper stairs. Anne can scoop her up. Rescue her from the danger, real quick. She expects to spend the next several minutes comforting a crying little girl.

Julia is face down on the stairs, head toward the basement. In that stunned moment, she tries to pick herself up. But she is disoriented, and moves in the wrong direction. She drops from view.

A pair of quick, dull thuds sound below.

Anne races down the stairs, screaming.

The stack of newspapers, piled five feet high, appears to have tipped under Julia. Now the papers are scattered. The furnace is a blue, steel box, its sharp corner holds a wet clump of gore, with strands of hair protruding. Blood is smeared down the side. Newspapers are splattered red. And there's a dead child, with a gash in her temple.

On the upper stairway, with the distant murmurs of men's voices below, Anne pulled so hard on the railing it jerked. She thought it would tear free of the wall. But, as if all bone and muscle in her legs had vaporized—leaving nothing there but blood— she could not lift herself.

CHAPTER 28

Mark was already up and gone, and Anne had the entire morning to work in her studio. At noon was her Narcotics Anonymous meeting, then her appointment with Dr. Leister. After that, her yoga class. Busy, busy. Maybe she'd skip yoga today, though. She felt inspired to get some good work done.

She sat awhile and watched the sun come up—a morning ritual like nourishment to sustain her all day. When the sun peeked over the horizon, the prism dangling on the glass door broke the rays into dozens of scattered spectra, and she felt like a sightseer in a garden of light.

It seemed odd that she wasn't craving a cigarette. This was the kind of moment when smokers expected the biological urge to fill the veins. Moments like after panic, or after an adrenaline rush. After a meal, after sex. Or like now, sitting with a cup of coffee first thing in the morning.

Taking one out of the pack used to be an unconscious act. But now, for some reason, it seemed unfamiliar. Less than routine. Even her lighter seemed strange to her.

"Mommy?"

Anne gasped. The strangest image fired through her mind: a little girl, alone in a jungle, on a bed of sheets and couch cushions. Who was the little girl who called out for her mother? Did the image come from a dream?

It was an emotionally charged image—a portrait of vulnerability. Anne guessed it stemmed from her own longing, after years of trying to get pregnant, without success. Poor little kid, alone in the wilderness. Maybe it was her own, unborn child, unable to enter the world through this barren mother. Thinking about that faraway little girl made Anne feel weepy.

She decided to work with the image. It seemed important. It seemed to mean something. Beginning a painting with that image in mind would be a powerful exercise. A kind of inner-child embracing art-therapy.

She took a pen and some note paper from the kitchen counter and began to sketch. Animal faces surrounding the poor lost little girl. This one is sick, rabid. That deer heard a shot.

A deer in the jungle? No—several environments, in collage. Surrounding her.

When Anne stood up and looked at the sketch, she felt horrified. She felt like poison ink had spilled in her gut and was spreading into a complex Rorsharch blot. How strange.

She had to get to work, immediately. She had to work through this. She'd race up to her studio and grab one of the smaller canvasses, one of the six by twelves, and then she'd run up to—

Where?

What was upstairs from the studio?

The attic.

Was that right?

No. Upstairs from the studio was the third floor. Up there was Mark's… his other office, his doctor's office. The examination room.

But had she ever seen it?

No, because he locked the door.

But Christ, it was a room in her own house. She should at least see it! *What's upstairs from the studio?*

She started up the first-floor stairs, feeling strange, her insides fluttering. Between floors, she noticed, with some perplexity, that the stairway seemed to lengthen itself as she climbed. The thin, gate-leg table in the hallway above came no nearer, as her thighs pumped and her hand slid along the railing. She hurried up another five steps. Still she was in the middle of the stairway. Half a dozen more steps. The second floor kept its distance.

"Goddamn it!" she screamed to the upper hall. The silence of solitude, of old libraries and churches and basement record rooms in the middle of the night, answered her.

Why was she so alone?

With eyes accustomed to the strange darkness of her home, she retreated down to the kitchen and opened her refrigerator door. Cold air and harsh light fumed out with a gaseous hiss. It was blinding.

She squinted, turned her head, and grabbed a carton off a shelf.

She knew how many stairs there were on the first flight in her own home. And the egg carton was full: one complete dozen. One for each stair. Markers. Counters. The shells white, and unbroken. They glowed with promise.

CHAPTER 29

No—it couldn't have really happened like that. No way.

Willie sat in the Dunkin Donuts around the corner from a shitty neighborhood known as *the tracks,* called that for two reasons: the train tracks ran through it, and most of the rejects who lived there had needle marks in their arms. He'd just come from a score, and was enjoying the fine, floating feeling only a warm injection could give. Junk gave him the distance he needed from the thing that made his teeth hurt, and would not let him sleep.

It was the coke. That was all. He'd never had a hallucination on it before—but hey, he never fucked a ninety year old lady before either, that didn't mean it couldn't happen.

It was kind of funny, when you though about it. Why piss away eight bucks to see *Halloween 30* when your brain could screen its own horror flics, with such great special effects?

Yeah, junk made him feel delicious. Dunkin' Donuts never looked so good. And finally, he had it all figured out. It was the coke. He'd been tripping on it.

Still, somewhere deep inside, he felt queasy over the whole thing. Because a part of him wasn't sure.

Moments ago, while he was sweating, waiting in his low-life smack dealer's living room for the shithead to get the stuff cooked, he'd stared nervously at the tube. The chick who did the local news looked straight at him, and she talked like she needed a stiff one up her ass. But she didn't say nothing about that dead asshole in Bow Lee Point, whose neck had a second smile on it.

And there was nothing in the paper. So maybe the guy leaked and rotted through the night, and maybe he lived alone, and no one found him yet.

He was sure he knifed the guy. No doubt about that. There was still blood on the blade. And he was sure he poked the artery. The guy was dead. He was sure of that.

When he sat down to eat the guy's dessert, the rush of power-pleasure must have been like a long pull off the crack pipe. That's what it was. That's what triggered it.

Unless the guy stopped being dead, for real.

No no no. Willie pushed the thought down with a shudder. Because shit like that didn't happen. Because if it did, that would mean there was someone walking around out there who Willie killed. And that guy would be a freak. And what would the freak do? What would anyone do?

Seek revenge.

"Fuck off!" Willie shouted.

"Excuse me?" The spic faggot behind the counter held a pot of coffee like a fairy wand.

"You heard me, asshole," Willie said.

The kid walked away, shaking his head, and lisped, "Goddamn people in this place, I swear…"

Maybe, Willie thought, he should cruise by the house. Maybe they would have just found the guy, and Willie would get to see all the excitement he'd caused. Lingering cops, and yellow tape. The news van. He could watch the story on tv later, and he'd know he had nothing to worry about because the asshole stayed dead.

Don't be stupid, he told himself. Nothing like returning to the scene to get pinched.

Besides what difference did it make? In his pocket now was a forty dollar bag, enough to keep him off for days. Plus the eight-ball in his dresser drawer.

And seeing as how he'd defended his territory from that rich prick, he could still drift along his river under the pavement, and watch the ladies float by above.

But once he was in his car, the fine weather and his mellow buzz made him feel like taking a scenic drive. What better place to visit than Bow Lee Point? He would just happen to cruise by that house, no crime in that. Couldn't get busted for that.

The thing was, he had to know. Because just beyond the edges of the pastel world he painted with heroin, was a vague, shadowy figure waiting to take the shape of a demon. Willie had to know the man he killed was dead. Or the question alone would drive him nuts.

He caught himself crossing the double yellow line into on-coming traffic, and he swerved, and checked his rearview for cops, and proceeded on toward Bow Lee Point.

CHAPTER 30

Anne placed one egg on the bottom most stair and mentally counted off *one*. Likewise, she used the other eggs as counters to mark of each stair.

It was a mental battle, a contest of wills. But who was she competing against? Midway up the flight, she got a little confused. Her head got fuzzy, and she nearly forgot what she was doing—overcome with sleepy-dreaminess as she was, and with images of drifting boats and clouds and kites.

"…seven…" She willed the stairway back into focus.

When she finally placed the last egg from the carton onto the top stair, the egg started to quiver.

Hair-like cracks appeared in the shell, and a triangular flap popped outward giving birth to a kind of liquid darkness. Bugs skittered from the cracks onto the stairs.

"Jesus!" She leapt into the upper hall as bugs skattered in all directions, zig-zagging up the walls and running circles across the floorboards. She backed toward the bathroom, as they gathered and multiplied, filing like an upward flowing river from the stairwell until they had formed a massive heap the size of a coffin.

"Not real," she whispered. "…it's an hallucination."

Her heart thudded.

The mound of writhing black disappeared like a sandcastle in a hurricane.

When that happened, she heard two voices. A little girl screamed, and a strange, man's voice yelled, "God damn it!"

Anne slammed the bathroom door and locked herself in.

What the hell was going on? Had she lost her mind? Who was was out there?!

She rummaged through drawers, through cabinets under the sink and below built-in shelves, looking for anything she might use to fend off an attacker. Was a child in danger?!

Those eggs.

There was something wrong with them.

No! The problem was with her. Not the eggs! Eggs are a symbol of life, of motherhood. They're what you have when you…cook eggs—they change when you cook them, when you make egg-in-a-hole.

She found a trial-sized, cylindrical aerosol spray can, no larger than a canister of MACE. It was only hairspray, But still. It could sting the eyes if she aimed it well.

She also found a package of straight pins, and stuck a few into her sweater sleeve. She opened the next drawer. With simultaneous relief and apprehension, she beheld a small, hinged, leather case. She opened it, and withdrew an object which, without a doubt, could be used as a weapon. She never thought she'd be so grateful for Mark's yuppie sensibilities. And when she unfolded the pearl-handled, straight razor, its shiny steel glistened. She closed it against itself, and slipped it into her back pocket.

Then, on one panel of the bathroom mirror, she wrote with lipstick.

A) *I've lost my fucking mind.*

B) *My husband is psychotic, or evil.*

C) *Something else. Screwing up my head. Trying to hurt -*

D) *Trapped in a different world. The house is haunted.*

And on the other panel, she made a large, capital "J". She wasn't sure what it meant.

On the floor of the water heater closet were six short lengths of lead pipe and a handful of nuts and bolts—remnants of an inattentive plumber's work. She grabbed a cotton laundry bag, placed the heavy objects into it, and tied a knot above where they settled. The weapon dangled ready at her side.

She looked at the closed door. White, four panels. A cross in their center. Lord Jesus help me now.

CHAPTER 31

Alice made the call from her office. Her one-time mentor, and the previous director of the Lewiston home, answered after the second ring—easily reached in semi-retirement.

"Carl," she said. "Can I pull you away from Elmore Leonard for an afternoon?"

His reply was cheerful, but the increased frailness in his voice worried her. "I suppose I could pencil you in," he said. "Everything all right?"

She hesitated, unsure what to tell him. "I'm going to need some tests."

No. That wasn't right. She was going to be tested, yes, but not in a clinical way, as she previously thought.

"You sound frightened," he said. "What is it?"

She sighed. "Nothing much. Just the wee man in the toaster has been telling my fortune again."

He paused. "Ah. The past cries out. Have there been triggers recently?"

"I'm not sure what it is, hon," she said. "I'm working on it."

When she hung up, it was with a twinge of emotion. He was a great man, who had given her a father's love and guidance, and sometimes, something in her affection swelled like a sprained elbow.

She arrived at his house, went in without knocking, and found him in his chair, with the quilt his wife had made draped over his lap. He was motionless, and for an instant her anxiety rose. Then she saw the peaceful rise and fall of his skin-and-bone frame, and everything was okay.

She sat and waited, watching some ducks on the lake and taking in the pleasantness of his well-kept household. One thing she always found amusing was the juxtaposition of the Audubon loon painting over the mantle and the chinese mandala that hung behind him. He was an old-time swamp yankee on one hand, a student of Carl Jung on the other.

When he opened his eyes, he caught her staring. "How long you been here?" he asked grumpily.

"You've gone in and out of R.E.M. twice."

"Why didn't you wake me?"

"You said *keister*," she told him.

"Wha?"

"'*Keister.*' That's what you said in your sleep."

He grinned. "Probably about knocking someone on theirs."

"You go around saying *keister* in your sleep?" she harped.

"If it's called for. Didn't realize there was a *lady* present."

He lit his pipe and offered her tea, which she got up and made. And when they were comfortable with hot cups beside them, she talked about her recent troubling experiences. She described the meal-worm hallucination, and he took his pen and leather-bound notebook from the table beside him.

His note-taking technique, something she'd observed often and had imitated, was never a distraction, and usually amounted to a single written word at a time. Later, he would transcribe the notes into long prosaic passages, diverse in their exploration.

"I had a nightmare about Gorsham State," she continued. "How I love revisiting that place. In the dream, Charlie Arsenault, unshaven, bug-eyed, crawls over to me on his stumps. *Cribs here have plastic bars, and the doctors are like fathers,* he says."

"Explain that."

"To be honest, Carl… I think it goes to the old question. Plastic being a constructed reality."

"You've been compelled in that direction?!" he asked with some shock, some anger.

"It was never solved!"

"How can it be, ever?"

"It could be addressed."

He tapped his pipe on the ashtray. "I thought we'd addressed it quite a bit."

"You never gave me the space to look at it with validity."

"I've tried to be reasonable."

"I understand that. Obviously, I value your approach. But none of us know the big answers."

"That's right. Usually when we think we do—"

"I know that, damn it!"

She rose hastily, crossed to the windows and lit a cigarette. "There's more to it, Carl. Remember my warrior mask—"

"Of course."

Naturally, he knew what a powerful symbol the shamanistic mask was to her, and why the first time she saw it, it struck a chord of terror, prompting her to purchase it. An exotic shell of defense, black space where facial orifi were expected. A shadowy magician. A man-made object which she could face directly, every day.

In the seventies, she'd done a considerable amount of therapeutic work with the mask, and with masks in general. Carl had participated in some of those workshops. Admittedly, he found the work intense.

"When I woke from my dream, the mask was on my dresser, leaning against the mirror. It's been above the mantle for years, Carl. I certainly don't recollect taking it down. Of course, either of us could say I did it unconsciously, or that someone else did it. But at the time, I didn't even feel the need to step back and objectively evaluate. I just felt that I was witnessing, or participating in, a miracle.

"Okay, so I stepped up to the mirror. I didn't try to recall the emotional nature of the work I'd done twenty years ago with the mask. I stayed neutral. But when I put it on, and saw my reflection, it all came back. I was flooded with the vitality of that warrior-persona, just like the first time I wore it. But there was more. That figure had been maturing all the time. She had grown stronger. I felt the transformation from my toes to the top of my head: animalistic strength and warrior courage. With it came a kind of understanding I've never known.

"And now, quite simply, I believe there are truths I've hidden from. But I'm no longer afraid. I could enter that realm any time, Carl. Maybe it's taken me this long to prepare. But I'm not afraid."

Carl stared straight ahead. "I am, though."

He lay his pipe in the ashtray and folded his hands. "I remember—"

She stepped away from the window. "I know what you're going to say. How you once sat and watched a videotape of a skinny girl battling invisible demons. How I once believed suicide was growth oriented behavior... la la la." She returned to her seat and faced him directly. "Look, I need you more than ever. But try to remember what being open minded is like, okay?"

His sense of humor kicked in, and he shook his head. "Ha! You saying I'm narrow minded?"

They both laughed at the idea.

Then, "Let's go back," she said. "Way back..."

The past always lived. It lived and grew as people lived and grew. It was right there with them, and would not be denied.

The memories which throughout her early years were buried, now were like the daily paper. She was in her twenties when she first recovered fragments of her lost childhood, and she clung to them for dear life. In the ensuing years it all came back. And with Carl's help, she both regained and released the past. But it was never behind her. Now it was time to delve into it, once more, like a diver into the deep.

"I want to walk through all of it," she said.

He guided her into a relaxed state with his voice. Aloud, she recounted her earliest memories first, mostly sights and images. Then, "I was five years old, and I was strapped to a table. Because of that green crap, the taste still in my mouth, the room around me was flashing and swirling…"

Faces on the ceiling formed and popped like soap bubbles. Colors like dancing snakes, assumed personalities and lived lives before her little eyes, wide open. At times, watching this spectacle was soothing, like the whole universe had fallen in love with her.

But the euphoria was brief, and when it was ripped away, the only thing left was unspeakable terror.

Terror over the contorted demon faces that lunged at her with sharp teeth. Terror over the snakes that wriggled inside her gut, angry, and convulsing with electricity.

Then there was the voice. She didn't know what it said, although a part of her was listening. It seemed far away, but it was constant, and droning. It moved things around inside of her. Her father's voice.

"The bubble grew inside me. It did what father said. I felt sick. I was going to throw up—

"I tried to say something, to ask for help, because I didn't want to make a mess. Also, I was afraid I would choke to death. But I couldn't say anything. The bubble made my stomach too big. Then it forced its way up through my chest, into my throat. And I thought I would die."

She took a moment to adjust physically to the recalled trauma.

"It came out of my mouth. Like vomiting. But everything came out. All the things I needed. My dreams. They left me, they were torn out. My ideas, and my prayers. The speaking voice inside my head left me. It went with the bubble. -

"I was nothing but a shell, with eyes. And those eyes saw what happened next.

"The bubble floated above me, and grew. Everything was inside it. Colors, and music, and worlds. My imagination. My voice. -

"My father spoke to the bubble. He put his face near it, and directed it with his words.

"'*My own face!*' he said, in an excited voice. '*Show it to me!*' And the bubble obeyed. In it, appeared a reflection of the man.

"But the reflection didn't mimic his movements, the way reflections do. The face peered out at him, awed and in wonder. As if it had its own awareness of him looking in."

"'*Give me a doorway!*' my father commanded, '*To a city!*' And city lights coalesced inside the bubble. It filled and filled with bricks and movement. The entire population of a large metropolis.

"The bubble stretched tall, to accommodate the multitudes. The automobiles and the sky scrapers. But it could not maintain its integrity.

"…And it burst." With a gasp of pain, Alice bent forward and held herself. She breathed with determination.

"You're safe, Alice," Carl said, ever so gently. "He can't hurt you now. You know that don't you?"

She turned to look out at the lake and the evergreens. A flock of geese flew south, and their shadows made the scenery quiver.

She shook her head, and answered. "No. I don't know it, Carl. Not for sure. And honestly, neither do you."

CHAPTER 32

By the time the wood floors in Ed's living room and bedroom had been washed and waxed, giving the whole apartment a wonderful, lemony fragrance, and by the time all his laundry was washed and put away, and the dishes were done, and all the greasy kitchen surfaces had become smooth and shiny, by the time everything in the whole apartment that could be thrown away had made it out to the dumpster, and his new plants were greening up the rooms from hanging holders and from shelves, and the framed prints he'd bought, a Matisse and a Cassat, were sending rays of hope in colored bands from the walls, he had begun to think of Anne as a mysterious angel, who'd entered his life for the purpose of sparking a change, and had disappeared just as suddenly.

Now he was scrubbing the ceramic tiles by the base of his sliding doors. They had been covered with a black film, but with half of the grout whitened from his efforts with the scrub brush, the colors and designs of each were unique and brilliant. He daydreamed Anne sitting in the room, someone who shared his living space. "Come look at these things!" he'd say. "They're amazing!" And she'd join him—she'd crouch beside him, her hand on his back, and he'd caress her leg (she'd be wearing tan shorts.) They'd marvel over the craftsmanship of the long-ago artisan.

Had he seen her at all? He was beginning to wonder. Maybe she was just another part of that disturbing hallucination at his door.

Yet there was evidence of her visit tucked into the top drawer of his bedroom dresser. He'd put the locket there, ostensibly because it was a "safe place." But deep down he knew there was another reason. In his mind he played the scene of her ultimate arrival to retrieve the locket. With it stored safely in the next room, there was a reason to invite her into his immaculate, personal space.

His vision of what happened after that point varied. Sometimes she declined his offer of coffee, and when he gave her the locket she expressed her polite gratitude, and departed. He saw himself alone in his clean apartment, dejected, plunged into deafening silence.

In other versions of the imagined event, he told her of the change that had come over him since he met her. He was forthcoming with his feelings, and with his wish to spend some time together. She took a seat in his tidy living room, and somehow he managed to describe, in only a few words, what things had been like for him for so long.

It was a crush. And even though that was a silly thing to indulge in, which could only set him up for disappointment, still, it made him happy. It was refreshing to feel something pure. His only fantasies for years had been rude, dismal things. Now he was daydreaming like a kid again.

The feelings were his to keep, and if the captivating, autumn-haired lady, with a face like a 1940's movie star, picked up her jewelry and left forever, he would still be able to live a life of dreams and hope, in his clean apartment. It wasn't only the spark of meeting her. He was ready for the change.

He'd thought over and over about his bizarre hallucination. And he played with several possible meanings for it, aside from the obvious fact that he'd been corroding his brain with habitual drinking.

For ten years it seemed adulterous to even look at another woman. The thought of having a relationship, with the culturally embedded notion that Sandra and Maddy were somehow "looking down" on him, made him physically nauseous.

Who decided how these things worked?

So maybe Sandra's and Maddy's spirits were sending him a signal, telling him to get on with his life. It would be nice to think that was possible. And they would sure as hell have a point. But sensing the truth made it too sad, too thin a wish, to dwell on.

More likely, his fuzzy brain, roused from unconsciousness, had grasped the symbol of *Mother and Daughter* and immediately made the morbid connection. He wondered if all the interest he'd since invested was born of that momentary association.

It wasn't like he wanted replacements. No one in the world could finish what was started with his family.

Anne seemed a different creature entirely from his late wife. More modern, perhaps. More quirky. The presence of the daughter, a younger child than Maddy had grown into, didn't affect Anne's attractiveness one way or the other—but Ed had to admit, he liked that they would be a package deal. He wanted all the company he could get, and he missed being a daddy.

"Yeah, like we'll be marching down the aisle next week..." he said to himself.

Ultimately, the horrific imagery of his hallucination had been symbolic of stagnation. His memories of Sandra and Maddy had become demons, the vision said. His attachment to those memories had fostered decay. But he was in the world of the living, and other members of that tribe could radiate the beauty of life itself, right before his eyes.

A couple of hours earlier, as he was organizing his bedroom closet, he pulled out a box that was filled with some of Maddy's best loved possessions. They were mostly books, a couple of stuffed animals, a bracelet, two journals and a boxed pen and pencil set. He decided that, with the exception of Maddy's writing, clinging to these items was, in a way, morbid. He decided that it would be freeing, and a better expression of his love for his daughter, if some other child could have these things, and use them, and treasure them like she had. The box made it as far as the trunk of his car.

Now he looked up at the Mary Cassat picture of a woman holding her child. Each of them soft, with tenderness in their features. Each of them with something different on their minds—although they were, in a sense, unified. He knew when he bought the picture that it was an important symbol for him. He knew the mother and child could live inside of him, if he would only let them.

He was finally letting them.

With a wet rag from the bucket beside him, he wiped away the grey lather he'd worked up with his brush. Another white line of grout materialized before him.

Did he need treatment? Were his senses so deprived, that it was necessary for his mind to invent these connections, to give him something to think and feel?

He'd been relieved when Anne didn't show up for the locket that first morning, because he had more time to make his place presentable. Something must have come up, or she'd forgotten what her schedule allowed. But could getting the locket back have become unimportant? She'd seemed so distressed. The locket meant a lot to her.

So what was keeping her?

He dumped the bucket in the kitchen sink and returned with fresh water, which streamed down onto the colored tiles, rinsing them clean.

CHAPTER 33

Willie loved to drive when he was high. It was a helluva day, and his vehicle was smooth as a starship.

On the curving, coastal road he tried to remember where the house was. Everything looked different in the daylight. And he couldn't crane his neck or he'd look suspicious.

Nope, he was just a guy driving. Nothing suspicious about that.

Then he spotted a flagstone path which led to a sloping back yard— and the alarm clock in his head sounded.

There were no cops around as he'd expected, though. (...*back to life!*) Guess nobody's found the dude yet.

Okay—but someone had to be wondering why the motherfucker didn't show up for work, right? But hell—the guy was a rich prick. He could do whatever he wanted. Nobody was gonna say his shit smelled. Maybe by tomorrow someone would have the balls to call the cops and report him missing.

And who gave a shit? Not Willie. It was none of his concern.

After cruising past the house, he looked for a place to turn around, and he spotted a crescent of dirt on the embankment up ahead. It turned out to be a church parking lot.

Our father. Hallelujah.

He pulled in, and circled in front of the white building.

That's when he saw the guy. As he had done once before, Willie identified him from a distance.

The creep strolled along the far edge of the churchyard in back. The creep wasn't dead at all. Not like he was supposed to be. Cuz there he was. In hot daylight.

Willie remembered when the guy's face was so shocked, and how he choked on his own blood. He remembered the pleasure of watching the eyes bulge, and knowing the shithead was powerless to ever screw with Willie Prager again. And he remembered when the eyes blinked open...

"What the fuck?!!"

The smack in his veins wanted to assure him that nothing in the world could be against him and win. He switched his car off.

At first he pretended like he was headed inside the church for some quiet prayer time. In case anyone was watching. Then he sauntered alongside the building.

His blood was all over the floor, man! I remember that!

He peered from white-washed clap board down into the sloping cemetery. The freak disappeared behind a hill near the water. Willie hurried down into the yard. Near a statue that hovered over the final drop in the land, Willie caught sight of the freak again, and he ducked behind a granite angel.

The freak was at the entrance to a crypt, near the cemetery's border of hillside scrub and blue sea. The crypt sunk into the slope, above a sea wall. The freak glanced behind him, self-consciously, before stepping inside the stone archway.

Holy Fucking God!

This shit was too weird.

Willie ducked low, and scrambled back among the grey headstones, up the slope toward the church. From there, the crypt was invisible, tucked well below the hump of grass and stone.

Willie ran into the dirt parking lot in front of the church, hopped into his car, and kicked up a spray of dust as he swiveled back onto the road.

CHAPTER 34

So this was what haunted houses were like. They trapped you, over and over, in secret regions of themselves. Perhaps a time would come when she'd forget all of this. She'd know only that something terrifying occurred, but she'd lose the particulars...until next time.

She was tricked into believing things. Tricked. The bugs were a hallucinatory outcropping of belief. A product of her mind.

Anne stepped into the hallway. It was empty.

At the top of the stairs she looked down. On every level—a fresh egg.

Beside the stairwell, where she naturally expected to see the entrance to the next flight up, was, instead, a closed door. She opened it, and smelled mothballs. Winter coats hung there. Boots, still muddy, were carelessly jumbled on the floor. Up top, on a shelf, a few of her sweaters were neatly folded.

Her homemade blackjack dropped to the floor. She parted the hangers in the closet and pounded the back wall with her fist.

Then she staggered into the drab guest bedroom, which no guest ever attended in her memory. Her memory, or something like it, seemed to assert that the room had been redecorated, that the current decor was merely a way to fill space.

She closed the door behind her, sat on the un-cozy guest bed, and cried.

In the pounding of grief, a different look for the room began to materialize in her imagination. A child's bed, the frame painted white with vines climbing up the headboard and entwining, a patchwork quilt folded across the bottom of the mattress. On the pillows—a doll named Marianne, with a matching velvet jacket and dress, a bow at her collar, like a young lady from the pages of Victoria Magazine. The bookshelf, with its bright-spined, narrow volumes, and seashell clock. Faerie pictures along the wall. The dresser, with a ballerina music box, and toy jewelry.

All those things seemed, suddenly, like vivid memory. Were they visions of a child's room from a previous era? Did the girl's ghost haunt this space? How long since the room looked that way?

Anne longed for a child of her own with an ache like surgery.

But suddenly she felt angry. She marched across the hall and returned with three tubes of oil paint and a couple of brushes, and she removed a framed print from the wall—one that she could not have selected because it was junk that belonged in a hotel: a farm scene with a well pump. She tossed it face down to the floor, uncapped the tubes and squeezed thick globs of color onto the wall.

The work exploded out of her. Fast strokes, long and sweeping, delineated an abstract field of daisies. A slight, elegant form among them. Cool sea beyond.

She used her whole body in the act of painting, a vigorous and aerobic act. She smeared color with her hands. Thought vanished, the wall filled with form, and emotion surged from her feet, from her belly, into her face and fingertips. The brunt of it was grief. It flooded her until the world blossoming before her liquified.

"*Julia!*"

The memory eased itself into view, attention-starved and longing for a touch. While her heart leapt with joy for the face that came to mind, it also swelled with grief, and with horror over *the very implication!*...that Anne had, for a time, forgotten her daughter.

It was unforgivable. Had she repressed memories of Julia, and of her death, so grief might, for a time, be alleviated? Such sorrow flooded her now. Because Julia fell! Fell from -

Nausea churned with self loathing. She couldn't even be certain how her own daughter died.

Julia fell into the cellar.

No. Julia fell from the rocks, and drowned.

My poor sweet baby where are you?

Anne wiped her face, annoyed with her cloudy thoughts. She turned her back on the mural, and studied herself in the sterile, grey-framed, "guest bedroom" mirror. She breathed slowly, and kept still, and waited until she had a hold on herself.

Staring at her reflection reminded her of something.

When she was young, she and her siblings played a game they called "Mary Witches." They lit a candle in the bathroom, and turned out the lights, and stared into the mirror. Then they chanted, some specified number of times, "I don't believe in Mary Witches." After the last of the chants, the group voice intensified with the expectation that a host of strange faces would appear. They all chimed in, "I do believe in Mary Witches!!!" And they shared the thrill of fright as they observed dramatic shifts in the images they beheld.

She was the littlest, and it frightened her terribly. Years later, at about age seventeen or so, she did it again on her own. She challenged herself to face the terror.

The candle light, and the staring, were what did it. It was optical. And truly, the illusion presented some frightening versions of your reflection. But if you stared long enough, you realized that no murderous demon leapt out at you from the mirror and clutched at your soul. It was just you, a piece of glass, and your beliefs.

"I don't believe in Mary Witches," she said to the mirror.

She stared, and waited.

"I do believe in Mary Witches."

"I don't believe in Mary Witches."

I do believe in...

...a presence here, who has somehow taken my daughter...

"Son of a bitch!" she shouted. "I'll get her back! Do you hear me?!"

The face in the mirror changed.

Within seconds, it sped through a hundred years of aging. Her hair turned to ash. Her skin pleated with wrinkles thick as snakes. Her skin corroded as if with the disease of time. The eyelids evaporated, and round eyeballs rolled in the sockets. Leathery pieces of skin withered off the cheekbones. The eyeballs shriveled into dehydrated pulp like chewing gum. A human skull maniacally grinned.

The impulse to scream bloody murder, and to flee, was fierce. But she resisted. She felt her nostrils flare, and glared at the horrific image.

"I don't believe in Mary Witches," she said.

As the bones in the mirror began to crumble, the lower jaw dropped, and dangled. Then it fell away.

"I do believe in Mary Witches."

The mirror tilted. With the sound of a crash, a web-like fissure crackled through it, and triangular shards toppled out and splintered on the dresser below. Of the arrow-shaped, metallic wedges still clinging in the framed and fractured mosaic, one quivered on its hinge of mirror paint like a loose tooth tied to a wire, with tension increasing. Then it popped free, and discharged missile-like through the air toward her. She flinched, and cried out as it struck her in the face, and as it punctured soft skin below her eye.

Then the glass fell still. The commotion ended. In the grey frame was a fragmented jigsaw puzzle of her face.

She stared as if in a dream at the shocking, bright red streaks on her fingertips. Then she examined the wound in a piece of the broken mirror, to see if anything lodged in the skin.

"Just a scratch," she said brightly, with red tears dripping down. Then, in a voice like cold steel, she addressed her unknown assailant. "You broke it," she said, "for you, that's bad luck."

She heard a sound. It was familiar, a sound she had heard dozens of times from this very room, when she tucked her sweetie in at night. A high pitched squeal of metal against metal, followed by the rumblings of running water.

Someone, in the bath off the master bedroom, turned on the shower.

CHAPTER 35

She felt accustomed to the way he had their bedroom decorated. It was lavish, and on previous occasions, when opiates ran in her blood, the room transported her like cinema into historic regality.

At least that was how it seemed. The way she remembered it.

At the same time, she recalled the bewilderment of first seeing it this way. The sensation of displacement was still strong.

She sat in the claw-foot chair, sunk into its soft velvet, a small pillow clutched to her belly. She rested her feet on the ottoman, and waited for the shower to stop. With her sleeve she dabbed the cut below her eye until the blood ceased.

When the bathroom door finally opened, steam tumbled out in thick billows. He passed through it, into the cooler, bedroom air. Her husband.

A red silk robe clung to him, and he was clean shaven. Smells of soap and cologne floated to her on clouds of steam, which moistened her skin like perspiration. Beneath a fragrance of carnations was the earthier one, faintly dung-like, though not repellant.

Like everything else, he was familiar and strange.

"Where's Julia?" she asked, coldly.

He shot her a hostile look, and sighed. "Oh for Christ's sake. Must we go through this again?"

Shaking his head, he crossed to the armoire.

The breeze of his movement reached her, and a sensation like euca-
lyptus spread over her skin, from her feet to her scalp. She concealed
her startled reaction, and studied him through the parted veil of the
canopy bed.

From the armoire he withdrew clothing, including two dress shirts
still in packages, and socks still banded together as if newly bought. He
placed them neatly on the bed.

"I'm going to find her," she said.

He smirked in an annoyed way. Then he studied his shirts, made a
selection and absently asked, "…that right?"

When he disrobed, she spied a mark on his neck. It stood out against
his peachy skin like a burned candle wick.

What in the world? she wondered, and she stood up. Casually, she
rounded the bed and homed in on the mirror to observe the reflected
blemish. It was thick, purple and black, and curled like a snake tatoo: a
scar across his throat.

Mark pulled his shirt on, closed it at the collar and buttoned it all the
way down.

"Slip up with your razor?" she asked.

Already, he'd concealed the fact of the wound. Now he ignored mention of its evidence.

He pulled wool trousers over his silk boxer shorts. Then he selected a
necktie, and studied the inside of the armoire door as he put it on.

"Mark—" she said, steadying herself on the bedpost and drawing her
hand to her breast. "Please. Help me. It's worse than ever. I have to be
committed… something! Electroshock, or—I don't know!"

He came nearer, then, and put an arm around her. She let him hold
her.

"It's all right," he said softly. He rubbed her back. "Don't worry."

"I've got it in my head, now, that you're a vampire or something. Ha.
That's how bad it is. I start imagining I'm under a dark spell. So psychotic!
I'm one those lunatics who rave about conspiracies. Mind-control drugs

in the water. Jesus Christ issuing detailed instructions to murder." Anger and manic intensity filled her voice. "But it seems real. It's compelling, it makes sense. That's the trouble with delusions, when you're lost in them!"

"Anne. Don't worry. Calm down—" He seemed uncertain how to react, but there was a note of alarm in his voice.

"I can't! I'm afraid of what will happen. When I find myself on trial for your murder, how will I explain it, huh? I had to stop you—because you're Satan?! A demon or a body snatcher, something like that? All those stories of vampires and aliens… I realize they must be based in truth, you know. And you're as close as they come, you fucking monster!"

He was about to respond harshly, but she nestled against him and changed her tone. "Oh Mark. I'm sorry for I've put you through all this. We lost Julia,…but then your wife turns into this basket case on top of everything. You go to work, earn a living, carry on. You try to comfort me…"

Embracing her, he sighed, his breath tremulous. "I don't know what to say, Anne. When I saw you as an equal, perhaps I should have— You're very strong. And it's not as if you could understand…"

He turned toward the bed. "Come on," he said, gently guiding her. "Lie down awhile. For now, there's nothing you have to worry about. Please. Just let everything slip away…"

"Yes, alright," she said obediently. She did as he told her, and the bed was soft.

He drew the veil on all sides. White gossamer enveloped her like a castle in the clouds, and she listened to the steady beat of his words. Willfully, she followed them down into the hypnotic abyss.

Because somehow, deep inside, she was ready for the worst he could bring on.

* * * * * * * * * *

She awoke to a golden morning with a warm breeze sensuously fluttering the white veil. It was like summer, and the sheets smelled fresh.

She sat up, and parted the veil. Across a wide and airy room, open casements in whitewashed walls revealed a breathtaking sight, and she crossed through sweet-smelling breezes to the windows. A village below stretched between plum colored mountains and white sands. From a nearby crag gushed a pure white waterfall, and endless beaches reclined against lush hillsides, by a brilliant blue ocean.

It was Italy. Or Greece. Or some less-frequented, more serene paradise.

The fragrance of a powerful brew enticed her. Mark sat on the veranda, his shirt open in the sun, his hair softly blown. He drank from an espresso cup. A separate table setting awaited her.

She walked out into the sun, into air so clean it was intoxicating.

"Feeling better today?" he asked, and smiled.

"All this—" She stood at the railing, awestruck, and she tilted her face toward the sun's warmth.

"I thought we could use a little vacation. It's amazing, when you think about it," he said, buttering a muffin and placing it on her plate, "how little it takes to make people happy. Food. Pleasant surroundings. Pleasant company. Some security that these things won't vanish, or be stolen."

He lifted a shiny cover from a food tray. A puff of steam rose from a cushion of scrambled eggs.

Her head hurt, suddenly. She remembered eggs. The stairs. She remembered lipstick in the bathroom, and "Mary Witches."

She sat down, fighting for control of herself.

Then she asked him, forcefully, "What *are* you?"

He sighed to himself. "…a guy," he said. "Your husband. A surgeon…"

There was a moment's quiet. Then -

"No," she said. "You're a liar."

He leaned back and glared at her, hostile and incredulous. He raised his voice. "A *liar?!*"

"You're not my husband," she said numbly.

"Oh really?!" His brows arched. "That's funny. I've got your husband's face! I sign your husband's name with your husband's handwriting!"

He thumped the table, and rose, and approached her with an arm swiftly curled as if to strike, backhanded. Anne flinched. "Isn't this your husband's wedding ring?" he asked. His hand shook by her face. "*My* wedding ring?"

He crossed to the balcony, and increased the volume of his speech to accommodate the open air. "I operate on your husband's patients. The nurses address me as *Doctor Clausin*. 'Good morning Doctor Clausin.'"

Then he spun back to face her, and his voice dropped low. The look in his eyes demonstrated that if she were insane, she wasn't the only one. "…and you call me a *LIAR?!!!*"

Nor was she the only one who could be manipulated, she realized. "None of that makes a difference."

"Yes! It does!" He smiled, now. "Of course it does. What makes anything anything? I have a medical degree, right? A piece of paper with my name on it. So I'm a doctor! It's official!"

"No…" She spoke with an even tone. She had to be cautious. She'd pressed a button, and it was a pressure she wasn't about to release. "The only thing official," she said, "is that you're a *fucking liar!*"

His anger flared. His face, and the tips of his ears reddened as he forced restraint.

"You're wrong there!" he chided. "I have your husband's memories. I live your husband's *life! I—am—your husband!*" Then his voice turned raspy, a fierce whisper, and he spat the words— "…you ought to begin acting like it."

He turned again toward the view, and she waited. When he faced her again, his demeanor had changed. He softened, smiled at her, sat down and poured himself some juice. "Actually, the truth is I'm less of a liar now than I was before. Before Me. You want to talk about liars?" He chuckled. "Before Me, I told you dozens of lies, big lies, all the time. You wanted them, you needed them. Depended on them. Oh all right—so there's been a shift. You're much too perceptive to miss something like that. But still. When I say I'm your husband, it's no lie. Really! I have his mind, his experience! I am him, I'm what he is now. So don't call me a liar," he added coldly, "when you don't know what the truth is!"

"You sound like a goddamned lunatic," she said.

He laughed.

With forced calm, she asked, "Where is my daughter?!"

He stiffened, then affected a casual air. Sardonically, he chatted. "It's fortunate I'm not sentimental. Otherwise I might be offended. You're frantic for her, but your poor husband, myself—Me—, I garner barely any fuss at all with my passing."

"I assume you murdered him."

"I TOLD YOU!" Again the china and cutlery rattled with a display of his anger. "I—didn't—kill—him! I'm alive!"

She returned the table thumping and vocal intensity. "Where's my *daughter?!*"

He seemed to back down. Laughing, he said, "You're so damn persistent."

He downed the remainder of his juice, wiped his mouth on a linen napkin, and said, with no emotion, "She's dead."

Fright and panic threatened to explode in her heart, as he spoke with a tenderness more startling than his anger. "I'm sorry Anne," he said, "but it's true. You remember it, and so do I. You were there when it happened. She was too young to die. But sometimes that's how it goes."

All his forceful claims of honesty—they were persuasive, in their way. He, at least, believed them. But now their implications threatened her in a way she could not handle.

He was a liar.

He had to be.

She sincerely hoped he was the dirtiest of goddamned liars.

"I remember her," she gushed. "I'd forgotten, for a while. But I remember her now. How could I have forgotten her? Please," she begged, unable to stop tears and snot dripping. "It isn't like that, is it? She'll be frightened without me. Please. What do you want?"

He shook his head, and felt around in his shirt pocket.

She pounded her fists in rage, and screamed. "WHAT DO YOU WANT?!"

"It's what you want that matters. Give me your trust. That's all. These things are complicated. I know this is difficult... "

He wanted something, all right. He was reluctant to say what. But she had to reject the confusion he inspired. It was his weapon, like puppet strings with which he meant to entangle her. "You know what I want," she said.

"You can have so much! *We* can."

"I want my baby."

"We shall have one."

Her furious look drove a falter into his tone, and for a moment his eye could not meet her. "Anne, you're a fountain of desires, like everyone else. Look around you. Look at all this. There's no limit to what you can have, now. No limit at all."

"Super. Is this the part where I try to guess your name? Or what? Let's see. Rumpelstiltskin? No? Mephistopheles? Count Fucking Dracula? Are we near the end of the Faust Cliffnotes, yet?"

He glared, frustrated and indignant. Then his anger melted.

His mood swings were thorough. His softer side could seem genuine and charismatic. Of his rage, she felt she'd seen a snowflake atop an iceberg.

"So you've read your cautionary tales," he said. "I swear they weren't designed to enlighten you. You simply have no idea, Anne— " He became quiet for a moment. He stood, came abreast of her, and placed a hand on her shoulder. "I want you to trust me," he said. "Please. It will be magnificent."

He began to gently caress her shoulders. "Take a good look at the beauty around you. Who wouldn't be happy here? Most people want nothing more than an environment as lovely, and the freedom to relax and enjoy it. Paradise. Right? Eden. A harmonious existence. Simple pleasures. Why is it that every god ever known has denied us? Everybody hopes and prays for a better life. Maybe in the next world, huh? Heaven. Where everyone enjoys beauty, and serenity. And love. Where suffering is extinct. Where every desire is satisfied the moment it's born. Anyone who's ever fallen asleep and beheld the world of dreams has known better worlds were possible." He paused. "Perhaps it really is intended that we all find paradise. But the plan and the method differ from expectation. What if we're meant to find it in this life? And what if the time is now?" He leaned down and whispered in her ear. "Anne—I'm here to usher it in. It's going to be wonderful! And Anne, in the next world, your daughter Julia will hold the place of a revered and mighty goddess!"

She spun in her seat, and faced him. How dare he think of her daughter as— How dare he include her in this! And *what?!* What was he saying?! What had he done with her?!

She wanted to choke the truth out of him, once and for all.

"Where is she?!"

"You remember her death—"

"Who knows what I remember! My head's been rearranged! I see her falling off rocks, I remember her dying in the basement! But that doesn't add up! So I believe that those terrible things were put in my head—" She lurched out of her seat and stood face to face. Two fisted, she hauled off and pounded his chest. "You put them there, you SON OF A BITCH!"

He caught her by the wrists. "Ow! Watch it!" he growled.

She pulled away, and marched to the railing.

He shouted after her. "Your memories hardly contradict one another. You think reality is so constant? That events are carved in stone, that time flows in some fixed, linear track? I thought you'd have known better! You obviously have a gift. Which proves that you're up for this. That you're equipped to be my—"

She glared at him.

"Look," he said, "You recall your daughter's tragic end because it happened. But in this world I'm showing you—isn't anything possible? What if we could make it so the bad thing never occurred? So the terrible accident never was?"

"Do it," she commanded. "Do it now."

"I will. For you. But will you trust me? Will you help me open the gates of paradise?"

Suddenly, she felt very still inside. "Anything."

He closed his eyes, and in all directions the far reaches seemed filled by a violent whoosh of air and metal.

It was as if worlds of weakness and disease, endless grief, endless torture, were ripped from her gut, and from her mind, and a stream of warmth and affection replaced them.

She covered her mouth, but she couldn't stop the laughter that bubbled out.

The whole, horrible turmoil—of losing Julia twice over— seemed less, now, than a remembered, bad dream. It seemed no more than an unpleasant thought which once crossed her mind and was immediately dismissed.

"Where is she?" she asked, excitedly. "Where's my baby?"

"She's safe. Don't worry. She's hiding, now, because she's frightened."

The playroom!

Anne turned, and ran inside, and as she did, the master bedroom, as he'd done it—with its masculine decor and the wall-sized tapestry, dropped back into view.

"Wait!" he shouted, behind her. Anne rushed into the hallway.

But before she'd taken two steps into the hall, she realized the futility of her earnestness. In front of her was the open coat closet, where the stairs to the third floor had once been.

She returned to the bedroom.

"I know you're anxious," he said, one hand absently caressing the post at the foot of the bed. "Things are complex right now. Please understand. I must be certain that you trust me. That we are united in this cause."

It's going to be all right, she told herself. And she could believe it now, knowing Julia was alive. She learned more about this devil every minute.

He had human qualities, insecurities. Weakness. Chinks in his armor. Despite his God complex, he was far from almighty.

She knew what he wanted. Servitude. Adoration. She could imagine how he'd see it best expressed. And she'd do what she had to.

None of it mattered much. She held on to the one, pure thought that sooner or later she would be with Julia again, somewhere safe.

She pressed against him, her hands and cheek against his muscular chest, and he stiffened. She looked up into his face and saw a kind of fright. Then she parted his shirt front, and pushed it back over his shoulders. He trembled as she kissed the skin on his chest, as she pretended to be enraptured by his pungent fragrance.

She missed the real Mark, and grieved; she longed for the familiar touch of her vanished, doctorly husband.

Something shifted in the man. This was what he hungered for. It was something he could not satisfy alone with his clever magic. He needed to believe she acted of her own will, out of her own desire.

He tried to enclose her in an embrace, and she grabbed his wrists and placed his hands on the baseboard. He needn't move, she said. She'd do everything.

She left his shirt loosely binding his wrists behind him. She lowered his trousers, and left them securing his ankles. Then she teased him with the soft silk of his own undergarment, his boxers, first lifting the fabric away from his tense prick, then lightly brushing it. She lowered the boxers. He groaned throatily, and his red cock danced.

When she was naked, she knelt before him, and felt his pleasure magnify. She ignored the strong odor, made an oval of her lips, and took him into her mouth, touching him with breath only. She tortured him with breath, and his penis bounced upward against the roof of her mouth. A slimy drop oozed onto the back of her tongue, unique from Mark's in its acridness.

Feeling his whole body rigid, and that he might in an instant become infuriated, grab her by the hair and mercilessly end it, she saturated him with movement, pressure, and wet tongue.

He screamed as if he'd been stabbed—and she stood, and grabbed his penis with both hands, and squeezed, hard.

"OW!" he yelled, and he shot her an angry, wounded look.

But his orgasm was staved off. And she smiled to let him know she was all sweetness, and still in charge.

She nudged him backward onto the bed and his legs dangled over the ornate baseboard. Then she mounted him.

It took her by surprise when she immediately started to climax. There was no build-up to it. Instead, it was like a switch had been thrown. There was a hollowness, a perceived absence of love that was painful. This was no different from his other manipulations. Yet primal screams hollowed out her lungs, making it the worst imaginable rape. Hot waves swept her, and when she thought they could grow no more intense, she was blinded by explosions of blue and red blood behind her eyes. She thought it would kill her.

At a point near loss-of-consciousness, she heard his monstrous screams, and felt scalding liquid pump into her.

It was afterwards, lying in a state of numb wonder beside the sleeping devil, that the horribleness threatened to swallow her.

She was his whore. This demon, or whatever the hell he was. A murderer, who killed her husband. Who killed Julia, and brought her back from the dead.

The fact that pleasure had been involved, hollow as it was, like narcotics, made her hate herself. How did this stranger manage to rape her mind, her metabolism, her memories?

He breathed in slumber rhythm beside her while she wept in silence.

It was willful deception, then, the attitude of warmth she put on as she woke him. He was reluctant to stir, but soon responded to her mouey entreaties.

"I miss Julia," she said. "I want to see her!"

"That may take time."

"What do you mean?! You—"

"Perhaps you can speak with her. Would that make you happy, for now?"

"Hurry," she said.

While he dressed, she put on a pair of tennis shoes from beneath the dresser, and she arranged the straight razor in her pocket for easy access.

He led her up the stairs, which had inexplicably regained their rightful location. He spoke of Julia in clinical terms that stirred frenzied, murderous rage. She listened carefully to him, and at the top of the stairs she nodded and smiled.

"But together we may convince her," he said, selecting a skeleton key and unlocking a massive door which had materialized up top, blocking the entrance to the upper hall. "Any child can be willful and disobedient at times. If you hear her voice, you must encourage her cooperation." Then, more to himself than to her, he added, "...if she's to remain more than a memory."

With his hand on the doorknob, he smiled shyly, then reached out and lovingly touched Anne's hair. "I've worked alone up here endlessly. It's very... comforting to..."

Timorous, he left the sentence unfinished, and opened the door.

In yet another sad transformation, the third floor had become a single, open space which held nothing of Julia's. The spirited collaboration of the mural was erased. This man had stolen it. He'd put it in a dark place, and replaced it with a dark room.

Like a chapel lit by candles, the room flickered and rocked. The windows were all darkened with black paint, closed shutters and heavy drapes, and darkness, mossy, pressed into corners, and disjointed the walls and ceiling. The white-washed walls tilted, as if on alternating planes, and they held a faint, grayish glow, upon which the yellow of the candles dissolved. A circular chandelier, like something from a gothic dungeon, dripped wax in the center of the room.

"I never use electric light up here. Lightbulbs are an unsuitable use of the electric force. Anyway, the old methods are better, don't you think? For ambience?"

The room was like an opium addict's hovel, or a religious freak's sanctuary. Some tables were piled with junk—odds and ends, books, pieces of machinery. He closed the door after her, then crossed to a desk against the left wall, and busied himself. A glass-globed oil lamp and a candelabra stood among scattered papers and books on the desk. Other disordered literature behind him protruded from a stocked bookshelf, one of many that lined the room.

Against the wall to the right, with ensconced candles burning above at each end, was a ceiling-high stack of wooden cubbies built into the wall. In those were numerous scrolls bunched together, and jars with smudged, hand-written labels. Anne stepped nearer to it. Many of the jars held dried plants, others—liquids of red, blue and black. In some jars, though, the cloudy, submerged shapes were recognizably of animal origin. The fingered-segment of a reptilian corpse clawed for escape. A bloated and grayed eyeball stared morosely at the floor of its glass casing. She'd touched nothing, but she wiped her hands on her sweater just the same.

On a nearby, massive table, among dung-heaps of black wax and by an old clock, were a pair of pendula, each subtly in motion, dangling from separate, artfully crafted supports. Black velvet swathed raw stones alongside cutting and polishing tools and piles of crystal dust. A fat journal lay open, apparently to the most recent entry of illegible scrawl.

Anne moved toward the center of the room. In the far corner, half a dozen import-stamped, wooden crates gave the appearance of a hastily abandoned loading dock. A crow bar rested on one box ledge. The top most crates were pried open, and nails and packing straw jutted out.

There was something bizarre by the far wall, the east wall, where the ocean view used to be. Heavy curtains parted in a tent shape over a darkened, stage-like area. A web of brassy wires, with set gemstones and metal disks embedded mobile-like through it, extended from the top of the blackened window to a chair in the center of a platform. It was intricate, and regal. The chair, with red cushions, exhibited restraints for the feet and arms. It was the size of those used in classrooms, by first graders.

Anne whirled around. The man with her husband's face hunched over his desk and made marks down the length of a piece of paper, as if checking items on a list.

Murder him, she thought. Before he can do another evil thing.

He finished his task and glanced up at her with raised eyebrows, as if he'd forgotten of her presence. Then, with a pleased sort of recognition he said, "Ah, yes." He rounded his desk, and walked past her. "You may be able to hear her. Do you know what's up there?"

He pointed to the ceiling, where the trap door to the widow's watch should have been. He dug into his pocket and withdrew some keys—iron keys, a medieval jailer's keys. He inserted one into a slot in the wall. When he turned it, a hum filled the room. A large platform up above slowly began to lower toward them. He turned the key again, and the lift came to an abrupt halt. But there came another sound from up above, in the darkness. It was similar to the roar of surf, with a papery static blended into it.

The lift had dropped just low enough that Anne could see the bottom edge of a rectangular object. The sounds seemed to come from far above. Something glinted dully in the darkness, way up there—a petal shaped piece of brass. Anne recognized the handle of Julia's toy chest.

"Call up to her."

"*What?!*"

"Easy now. It's not what you think."

But she imagined Julia up there, a prisoner in a darkened cell, suffocating in that cramped box. Anne backed toward the crates in the corner, peering upward.

"Go ahead," he insisted.

She called with a hollow voice into the space above, which seemed to encompass a starless universe.

"Julia? Honey?"

She suspected a trick.

She called louder. "Julia! It's mommy, sweetheart. Can you hear me?"

The sound above intensified. To the distant, oceanic roar, with its electrical quality, was added the violent snap of heavy current. It grew louder, and from deep within its crackling came another sound, a very faint, human voice. A little girl's voice.

"*Mommy...?*"

Anne gasped. The voice was so distant, so disconnected. Her arms ached for her daughter.

Julia spoke again, but the words were lost in static.

"...Mommy! I..."

Anne craned her neck, straining to see into the darkness. "Julia! I'm coming up!"

"...Mom you...No!...Go away!"

Anne shoved one of the crates to the floor, unconcerned for its scattered contents, and she began to drag another, which offered heavy resistance. "I'm getting her out."

"No, I don't think so."

She stepped onto the box, and the man grabbed her, with an arm around her waist. Anne stumbled to the floor. "She's up there! You get her down now!"

"Either she'll talk with you, or she won't."

He held her back as she screamed toward the ceiling. "Julia!"

When he turned the key, and the platform began to rise, Anne struggled to free herself. "Let me go! Please! Let her down!"

"Forget it!" he said, authoritively, as he dragged her away from the lift. Her hand dipped into her pocket.

As if to paint a furious horizon across a barn wall with one mad stroke, she swung at him.

The razor slashed his face. A red line appeared from his cheekbone to his bottom lip.

He was stunned a moment. Then his scream registered shock and pain. In the moment it took him to see the blood coating his hand, his disbelief turned to fury.

"BITCH!!!"

Anne dashed toward the mechanism, where the key still protruded. The lift continued to rise. As she reached for the key, she was grabbed from behind. Her arm twisted, and the razor clattered onto the floor. The sound from the portal above filled her ears as the lift neared the ceiling. Just as the space above was sealed closed, she was enveloped in a bear-like grip. She kicked at him, and he shoved her, and she fell onto splintery boxes. Then he grabbed her leg, below the knee, with a fierce grip, and he tugged brutally. She slid downward, scraping her arms against jagged wood and nails.

She saw the razor as she hit the floor, and she reached for it. As her fingers brushed the handle, he kicked her in the crook of her underarm, and she went down. She heard the razor spinning somewhere on the floor, and coming to rest.

He dragged her violently by both arms. As she thrashed free, he threw her to the floor. She rolled, and faced him, crab-like, and tried to back away, kicking, until he grabbed her foot and twisted. She was forced to roll to her stomach.

The razor was a few feet away. When his grip on her foot loosened, she lurched forward, and grabbed the pearl-handle. Then she twisted her back to the wall, ready to slash in lightning fast arcs.

The hard toe of his shoe rammed into the soft skin under her chin, and her whole head jerked backward and went numb. Her neck hurt terribly, and she heard a distant, delicate rattle of steel against the floor.

Then he delivered a thunderous punch to her lower jaw. Her teeth scraped against themselves. A visual disturbance like white noise danced through her head. She tasted blood.

"I gave you a chance." He drew back and delivered a forceful, merciless kick to her ribs and breast. It was followed by another and another. "You!—Should have!—Listened!"

As she curled, breathless, he casually stooped down for the razor.

Then he stood over her, and turned the razor in his hand. Its blade glinted with the reflection of candles. Calmly, he walked across the room, removed the lift key, turned, and walked past her again.

Glass clinked. Watching him through a blur, in a state of paralysis, she was vaguely aware of him reaching into the cubbies along the far wall. He mixed ingredients. Anne fought to regain her composure, and to re-learn movement in the presence of such pain. Waves of dizziness, black at the edges, washed over her.

Then she was on her knees with something close to normal breathing in her good lung. He sat across the room, behind the desk, with a white compress pressed against his cheek. His angry face glowed orange by the candelabra, and he snapped through pages in a wide book. "So. You failed. Miserable failure. So what? You won't die in vain."

She teetered, a hand on the floor for support. She rose to her feet, but remained hunched over to ease the pain in her side. Gradually straightening up, she limped across the room and approached his desk. Candles reflected yellow on his fingernails.

"Why are you doing this?" It hurt to speak, and the words sounded thick.

He didn't even look up. "This is my house," he said. "You were guests, and you've been rude." He picked up the razor and gestured, flicking it to wave her back. Adhered to his cheek wound, the white compress looked like a torn halloween mask. "Would you? Remove yourself? Let's have a moments peace."

"Let me get her, and we'll leave. You can—"

He rose, suddenly, rounded the desk, and grabbed her hair. He shouted, "Should I cut your face off now?" His voice turned hoarse as he pressed the razor blade against her cheek. "I don't want to make a mistake! Don't make me! Just sit down, and shut up, and let me figure this out."

If she flinched, the skin on her cheek would divide. If she freed herself, and rushed the door, he would cut her off and end her life. He held her with a look so severe she thought it wise to obey him.

"Are you LISTENING?" he yelled.

She nodded, carefully.

"Good!" He released her, and returned to his chair. "Now back off."

But her hands, concealed behind her, had been busy. And with a smooth motion, she drew them up and sprayed hairspray into the candle flames.

Blue mist exploded in the air, and a cloud of flame burst forth. He raised his hands in defense, but she sprayed past them and coated his face and shoulders with liquid fire. He turned away as strands of hair and eyebrow crackled and curled like melted plastic.

The salve in his compress must have held high isomer content, for the cloth combusted. He did not seem to notice. He reached forward to grab the spray from her, his face flaming, and she gave more fire to his hands and wrists. Then he screamed, and jumped back, covering his face with both arms. He began smashing his own forearm into his face.

"IT FUCKING BURNS!!!"

He dove for the desk, grabbing at one of the drawers, and as he did, an oil lamp spilled, liquid splattered and combusted. Fluid soaked the base of a stack of notes, and seeped along the edges of papers and books. Page edges ignited, and flame danced along the desk top.

He dove for his papers.

Where was the key? He would soon have the fire out.

Anne bolted to the door, slammed it behind her, and hurried as fast as she could down the stairs.

In moments, the flames would be quelched, and he would use his strange powers to change walls and corridors, and to trap her.

She raced down the second flight. The eggs which lined it began to quiver, to crackle, sizzle, foam and smoke.

She reached the foyer, flung open the front door, and stumbled out into sunlight.

The memory loomed up.

And it was true.

All this was part of the delusion, part of her psychotic reaction to unbearable trauma, to the nightmarish truth that her little girl, her sweet, defenseless Julia fell from the rocks to her death.

Anne wailed, limping out into the road.

CHAPTER 36

At first he didn't realize anything was wrong.

Ed had gone outside to sweep off the front stairs, and when the last stair was done, he swept the walk. Then, because it was so wonderful outside, with the sun beginning to sink low at the end of a colorful day, and because he was enjoying the smell of fresh air, and the criss-cross pattern of the bricks, he continued down along the walk until he was mid-way up the block.

It was getting difficult to remember her face clearly. He'd seen a couple of women that day who he'd taken for her, for an instant. Each time, he'd instinctively known it wasn't really her, but he'd maintained a certain openness of expression, with a friendly half-smile, ready to say hello, just in case.

Now his stomach did a little flip, like a sixth grader's. There was no mistaking her.

What timing! That he should be out here now. After a casual chat in the autumn air he'd smoothly invite her in for the locket. Maybe he'd kid her, at first, and pretend the locket was nowhere to be found.

She staggered, slightly. An expression of numbness and bewilderment darkened her bruised face.

"Well, hi!" he said. "I wondered when you'd be back. I was starting to think I dreamed you."

She stopped, and stared at him blankly.

Although he'd been impressed with his own ease in speaking to her, now he faltered. "I live here. I mean there." He pointed. "I manage the building. Remember?"

She searched his face. Her arms were strangely crossed—was she clutching her side? She hunched forward a bit.

"Your necklace…" he said.

Her expression changed so suddenly it startled him. "Oh God!" she erupted, wide-eyed. She grabbed his arm. "The locket! Please! Do you have it?!"

Her grip was tight, insistent.

"I have it," he assured her. "It's inside—"

"Please, give it to me, please!"

He rested the broom against the iron fence—but when he moved, she twitched and grimaced. Then she clung to his arm more desperately, as if supporting herself.

Maybe she'd been in an accident. More likely, she'd been assaulted.

"Let's go in," he said.

He turned, to guide her to the stoop. Her face distorted in a savage effort to suppress crying.

He wrapped his arm around her. "Hey…"

Her frown was like a crumpled photograph, and she leaned into him. Her lashes filtered the streams. And he held her.

Inside, he led her to a seat on the couch. "I'll make you some tea."

While the water heated, he brought out the locket and placed it safely in her eager hands. She draped it against her palm with tenderness, then clicked it open. She gazed at it like it dazzled her with a million dreams.

"Do you remember my daughter?" Her voice trembled; her gaze was riveted on the necklace. She looked up, and her dewy eyes pleaded with him.

"The other day," he said.

She pressed the locket to her heart, closed her eyes, and her face smoothed into something prayerful. "She's okay… She has to be…"

A year or two ago, he would have closed down at this point, sensing unknown danger. He would have written her off as a flake, someone who'd managed to get herself into more trouble than she could handle, and certainly more than he cared to be involved with. He'd have done the proper thing—if it was spousal abuse, he'd have found the number of a shelter. Drugs, and he'd have gotten her the 800 line for Narcotics Anonymous. Pass her off to a concerned party, and exit, stage left.

Instead, he felt concerned, and he was encouraged by that. Their earlier meeting seemed more purposeful now, more real. And he wanted to know what was wrong. He wanted to be intimate with her troubles, to share her burden. He wanted to make everything okay.

She drank some tea, and he stood there silently, embarrassed to be watching, feeling she needed privacy.

"What is it?" he said. "I'm not sure what… If I can help I -"

"Tell me about her," she said. "About when you saw her."

Anxiety gripped him. Not knowing the situation was hell. Like when the troopers came to his door to tell of his wife and daughter, with clenched jaws and a world of timidity in their eyes. They blurted nothing out, but asked to come inside. They gave him preliminary details first. But the horrible knowing was in him. They built up gradually to the facts uttered already by the death-grip in his gut.

"She's a cute little kid," he said. "A little sprinkle of freckles across her nose and cheeks."

Anne smiled.

"What happened?" he asked. He sat down beside her. "Where is she?"

She bit her lip, and clenched the locket. She didn't trust him completely. That made sense. But he feared her reluctance. Maybe she had reason to be secretive.

"I haven't been right," she sputtered. "My thoughts. I've been confused. Because of *him*."

She's hurt the child, was all he could think. He spoke gently. "Where's your little girl?"

"I don't know! She was in her playroom. I—can't explain…!"

"Is it a police matter?"

She looked terrified. "Don't call them, please!"

"But something's wrong."

"I don't know what happened. I don't know where she is. These strange things—!"

"What things?"

"Maybe I've lost my mind… I thought she was dead—my God!"

"I think I ought to call—"

"No! Please. Give me a minute."

With heavy breath, he placed his nervousness out in front of him. "All right."

He sat across from her and watched her jaw and her lips play around several false starts. Before long, once more regarding the locket meditatively, she undid her creased mouth in what seemed like determination to open up.

"The day we dropped this," she began, "seems like ages ago."

He listened, and listened.

Was she insane?

That would be the easiest explanation. But he'd encountered the highly delusional. They believed their truths with fierce conviction, and often made no bones about peddling their views. Anne was astonished. She seemed apart from it all, outside of it. She too thoroughly examined her own mind-set, and allowed for flaws in her thinking.

No, it was a scam. He was the mark. They turned up at his door, two damsels in distress. Make sure he sees the little girl, that's important somehow. Draw him in, we need a patsy.

He thought again of the frightful hallucination. Sandra and Maddy at his door. Was it a warning?

The bruise on Anne's cheek certainly looked real, and the way she seemed to suffer made him ache. Which was just how they wanted it. Pick a lonely guy, someone vulnerable and weak.

Now he was the paranoid, delusional one. Yet there was no good reason at all to believe her.

But he wanted to.

Maybe he was even willing to get himself used and abused. What the hell? Even that seemed better than the way things used to be.

But if this was a confidence game, why make up such an outlandish tale?

He thought of all those far-out, science fiction and horror movies where the heros pleaded with strangers to believe something that was nuts. You sit there mentally yelling at the ignorant character, 'Come on, it's the truth!' and you share the frustration of the other actor, who's stuck that kind of bad film to begin with.

Who could say?

Maybe her story was true. He could at least allow it as a working supposition. He could play along, until he understood better. The vision of his wife and daughter remained a compelling question mark.

"We'll get her back," he said. "Safely. Maybe she's not in danger."

"I told you, he—"

"You said he wanted your help with her. Maybe up in that widow's watch, she's out of his reach."

The way her face brightened was enough for him.

CHAPTER 37

Two days earlier, before sunset, Ed used two screwdrivers, a hammer, an acetylene torch and half a can of WD-40 and he finally unhitched the lock mechanism on the grate. After he retrieved the locket, he closed the grate, walked to the hardware store, and bought a pair of sturdy bicycle locks. They fit snugly around the bars in the grate, and dangled below the upper surface, one at each end. He left it safe and secure. And with the keys added to his ring, he was prepared for any eventual, similar need to get down there.

His trip to the hardware store had taken no more than twenty minutes. But he realized now it was possible, during that time, for someone to open the grate and crawl in. And he might have been like a jailer, locking the prison doors.

Since the grate was her husband's last known destination before all the weird shit started, he felt sure they should investigate. And, as she put it, "maybe that's where he came by those stones."

So, with the sun well below the chimneys of the town's many-leveled rooftops, and with antennas against the orange sky like sprung cages long escaped by ancient behemoths, he undid the locks, switched on his flashlight, and shined it down into the hole. "God knows where this leads," he said. "I started to explore it the other day, but it seems to go on forever. I didn't like it."

She held the light for him as he climbed in, and she tossed it down when he was ready. Then she started down after him. "Can I have some light?"

"Aren't you staying up there?"

"What for?" She proceeded down, carefully.

"Someone might fall in," he said.

"We'll close it."

"But you're hurt."

"I'm all right." She dropped to her feet beside him, with a wince. Then she confronted the discomfort with a pout, and stroked her side.

"You ought to be recuperating," he said. He wanted to tuck her in and kiss her cheek. He helped to steady her, a hand at her elbow. "You okay?"

She nodded, and took a shaky breath. He stepped up on a pipe, reached, and closed the grate over them.

They chose a direction, at random. Except for the suction of their feet, they walked in silence. The flashlight beam drowned in the tunnel like a yellow marble plunked down in a can of black paint.

After what would have been about two city blocks above, a wide gap in the tunnel wall offered a right turn.

"Which way?" Ed asked.

Anne debated a moment. "We could split up."

"We only have the one light."

They proceeded straight ahead for another hundred yards or so, when they reached yet another division in the path. "You never think about all this, under your feet," she said.

"All these old channels no one uses anymore…"

"Maybe we should have gone the other way."

"You want to look back in that direction?" he asked.

"We could cover areas nearer to the grate."

"Right," he said.

They started back the other way, and passed below the grate. Then, after a short distance, a voice resounded.

Ed paused. Anne heard it too, but she quickened, and followed it, ahead of him.

"Wait a sec," he whispered.

She turned.

He stood still. He wasn't sure. "Nothing," he said, and caught up with her.

The voice led them to a hole in the wall, three feet high, blocked with a piece of plywood that glowed orange in the flashlight beam. They stooped down, and Ed killed the light. The voice beyond the covered opening was loud, now. An angry voice.

"I'm telling you," the man inside shouted. "You better listen if you want my services… The guy was fucking dead!…Okay? I cut a ribbon in his neck the size of your ass crack, dude. I watched him die! Then he's up walking around? You find that strange?"

Ed's blood felt thick as glue.

"The hell you think?" the voice continued. "What you're best at. Isn't that what you people do?…I already iced the fucking creep once… Yeah, I know how it sounds! You think I'm stupid?… Yeah, yeah.…*Ghostbusters*, right, fuck you!"

The phone slammed down, and the voice yelled, "PIECE OF SHIT!"

Anne whispered. "Who the hell is that?"

Ed put a finger to his lips. He led her away from the voice, and when he felt a recess in the wall he ducked into it with her. Then he whispered, close to her ear, "Wait here. I'll be right back."

He passed the switched-off flashlight into her hands.

*   *   *   *   *   *   *   *   *   *

Ed disappeared into the darkness, and Anne stayed behind.

Had he abandoned her? She didn't think so. But maybe it was too much insanity for one day.

Now she was afraid, like a child left behind at the supermarket, and no nice lady to comfort her. She wanted to call out to him, but it was too late. The man down the hall would hear.

From down along the channel, the muffled voice muttered. Anne heard a noise which, for some reason, made her picture someone opening and closing an old fashioned, aluminum breadbox over and over. Someone obsessed, opening it and slamming it closed.

She decided to hurry back toward the grate, and wait for Ed there. The streetlights would give some illumination, and she'd be able to see her hands in front of her. She started in that direction. Then a thought froze her—actually locked her legs in place. The man back there killed Mark. That had to be what he was saying—he killed someone who came alive. But that meant the creature in her house had not done it. Just as he claimed. He was telling the truth! Not a liar!

Oh God! She shook her head to fight the confusion.

Something scraped, in the distance behind her. Wood against concrete. Then… footsteps in the muck of the tunnel floor.

She rushed along the wall as the steps came nearer, and she ducked back into the small alcove. But how could he not have heard all her rustling? His footsteps seemed to get slower, more cautious.

As the killer approached, she held her breath, and held her arms close to her body. Let him pass, let him not find me here.

Then he was close enough, in the narrow passage, to hear if she blinked. That's where he stopped. She held perfectly still, not breathing.

He must have smelled her.

A hand grabbed the flashlight, another found her wrist. The light went on and shined upwards. A gaunt, crazy-eyed face grimaced at her. Before she could cry out, his hand covered her mouth, and he rammed her head back into the alcove wall, muffling her shout of pain.

Then he dropped the flashlight, and spun her around. An arm curved under her chin and locked into place; he held her mouth and nose. "Thanks for dropping in!"

He hauled her backwards, out of the alcove and down the channel. She thrashed about, but she couldn't breathe or make a sound as her heels dragged through muck. In a moment, he kicked the plywood from its place, and forced Anne's knees to bend. Then he ducked, and pulled her. The grip around her throat loosened, and she sucked air. But she couldn't get his arm away. It was like steel, latched around her. Her forehead smacked the upper ridge of concrete as he pulled her in. Her calves scraped roughly against the jagged bottom of the hole.

He threw her to the floor and she struck a metal bed frame with a *clang!* She coughed, and gagged, and dizziness surrounded her.

He shifted the plywood back in place, and Anne clutched her throat. Barred light from a ground-level window above spilled over the floor and stretched across the rumpled bed beside her.

The man loomed above her. "Ever done movies, bitch?"

A car passed by on the street above, and in the arc of its headlights, Anne saw another figure in the room. This other person raised an object, and pointed it.

With a tense, metallic click, the pistol cocked. "Don't move—" Ed said, evenly.

The killer spun around. Ed smashed him across the face with the gun, and the man dropped to his knees.

Then the light went on. Ed's hand was on the switch.

There was a red gash across the killer's forehead—he groaned and nearly toppled from his three-legged stance. Anne scrambled away from him, and lifted herself by the foot of the bed.

"Aw, fuck!" the man growled. He looked up, holding his wound and shielding the light. "How'd you get in here, man?!"

Ed frowned, and held up a small, shiny object which dangled in place. "Master key," he said.

CHAPTER 38

Char-edged papers scattered across his desk soaked with paraffin oil. The stupid bitch. It was in her to see the importance of his work, yet she tried to destroy it. There was ignorance there, still. And blind attachment to her little brat. It was sickening, how Anne resisted his abilities.

But the Great Laws put Anne McGilvary in his path, and he was far from finished with her. Obviously she was meant to challenge him. To keep him on his toes.

The question remained why his control over her had faltered. Perhaps this was the ultimate question. Once solved, the rest of his work would fall into place.

The key to Anne McGilvary, clearly, was entwined with her daughter's fate. The girl was suspended up there, in the place Van Rensselaer intended for her since the day she first responded to his nocturnal whispers. She was the battery in a living, four-storied machine, and she accounted for much of his increased creative vigor. He hadn't even needed to indoctrinate her with customary methods. Such was his post-mortem potency. He'd expected that once his laboratory was newly intact, he would perform the procedure on the girl. He'd feed her body, and feed her mind, and alter her.

He transformed the third floor with a bubble. And when he re-entered the lab which he so long ago departed, she was already in the appropriate place. Perhaps the Great Laws had anticipated his whim.

Yet how could he know for certain that her will was leveled?

Van Rensselaer found an oil-splattered document which he thought could be useful. It was something he collected in Egypt, years ago, where it was conveyed to him orally, by a black-skinned woman whom he at first took for an old man. The spell was inscribed with ink on the piece of paper he now held. It was preserved from the ancients, who, supposedly, had used it to effect the return of runaway slaves.

Van Rensselaer didn't take much stock in such things, although their study had often guided him. Sorcerers and shamen through the ages consistently failed in locating the gate to true power.

And Julia Clausin was not a runaway. Still. He suspected that with some modifications, elements of the spell would remedy any lapses in the control he wielded over Julia's mindwaves. His authority in this household had to be absolute, before his work could progress. The spell was worth a try. He possessed the required materials.

He tidied up the pathetic mess on the desk before him. Then he unwrapped a white handkerchief and withdrew a cloud-shaped mass of human hair, which he'd extracted from a brush in one of the bathrooms below. The brush, a child's very own, was hand-painted with a scene from A.A. Milne's *Winnie the Pooh*. The hair had a gentle, reddish-brown tint, and a certain delicateness. How sweet.

The spell also called for an object beloved by the subject—a common element, to be sure. Every culture with traditions that embraced sorcery had a spell like this one. He smirked, picturing jailers who stared blankly at the numerous wares their escaped slaves were forced to leave behind. A natural and juvenile instinct: the hope of influencing persons through their pots. Form, too frequently, catered to convenience, alas.

Beloved by the child, surely though, was the piteous bundle of porcelain and rags now lying face down among the cut gems on his work table. Her Marianne. He'd tossed it there disgustedly after one look at the pouty smile on its lips.

He went to it now, and placed the ball of hair beside the doll.

All in all, it was good to be back. If his work had been easily completed upon his return, well… suffice to say he'd be immersed in pleasure, luxury and beauty this moment. But he'd always loved the challenge. And now it was like the old days—working long hours in his lab, puzzling over minor setbacks and dilemmas, holding his goal mentally up before him, knowing it was the worthiest goal any man ever sought. He loved the hunger, loved knowing that the Great Laws championed him. Today his goal was more within reach than ever. And as always, he knew it was a matter of time before he attained it. He would savor this final phase of the journey.

After searching the cubby holes for what he needed next, he turned the doll over on its back. She was still pouting. Perhaps she was beginning to comprehend the implications of her predicament.

From beneath a pile of quartz which he dumped onto the wood of the table, he extracted a swatch of black velvet, and wrapped it snugly around the thing's head. Then he opened one of the jars and poured a bright blue stream from it, staining the front of the doll's dress.

The second liquid he poured onto the beloved doll was clear in color, when the jar held it. When it soaked into the blue stain the whole smattering turned a bloody red. The doll began to corrode. He grinned, enjoying the imagery, careful not to breathe the smoke that spewed from the doll's abdomen.

Every problem had a solution. He'd learned that simple rule long ago. And he lived by it. It wasn't just the small problems which could be solved with the appropriate application of will, such as he now demonstrated. But the bigger ones too. The imperfection of the universe, for instance.

And that damned woman? He'd solve her as well. She'd see her errors.

When I am Lord, she will adore me. She will pray to kiss my feet. She'll give herself to me if it takes the fire of hell to convince her.

CHAPTER 39

She was in a beautiful field of daisies. Beth waved to her, far away. Eli was there, too, picking flowers. It was sunny, and warm. Julia's mother sat on the porch of an old house, and called out. "Julia—!"

"What mom? I'm right here."

"Julia, honey…" her mother said. "I'm coming up!"

"We'll just play in the field. Love you Mom! Are you all right? I have to hurry, before they go away!"

And she joined her playmates and they played for hours.

Later, at the playground with her mother, the air was filled with children's voices from everywhere. She climbed monkey bars: blue and yellow and red and orange. And she kept going up. Higher, higher.

Too high. The ground was too far, and up here the wind pulled on her.

"Mommm!"

She clung to the bars.

Way down below her, the jumping frogs and the see-saw were gone. The swing set was gone. Down there, it wasn't the playground anymore. Just a flat field of dirt, stretching.

Far away, at the edge of this wide, flat dirt, her mother was on a bench, near the town. The bench was on a sidewalk in front of a cluster of tall, brick buildings.

"Mother!" she yelled.

Her mother didn't look up, but sat very still and looked down at her knees.

"Mom-eeeey!" Julia screamed.

Then there was strange music, like chimes made out of tin. It meant someone was coming, from behind the brick buildings, from the maze of narrow streets behind them.

He appeared as a shadow that loomed in the alleyway near her mother. "Mommy!"

The music got louder.

Her mother sat still.

When the tall man emerged from the alleyway, her mother was gone.

He came to the monkey bars, and climbed to the first rung. The whole structure swayed with his weight, and the loose connections rattled—thin metal against rusted bolts.

She couldn't make a sound. The scream wouldn't come out. She had no voice. There was no air…

She woke up gasping. Afraid.

But she heard a sound then, like a loud seashell. Her breath copied it. One long breath that didn't stop.

It was so dark, she couldn't even be sure her eyes were open. This didn't feel like her bed, she couldn't move.

The coffin!

They were at my funeral. They were sad, because I was a little girl when I died.

Someone called her.

…Julia…!

Beth?

Do you want to come play now?

I can't. I'm stuck!

It's okay, Julia. Do what we tell you.

She listened to their voices. That feeling like foam started down at her toes, and moved up through the coffin. It moved up her legs, and her bottom, and her back, into her shoulders, into her neck, and her head. It covered her, her face, and her tummy, until the whole coffin felt like it was full of foam.

She could see. It was as if her eyelids opened, but not her regular eyelids, a different kind, that made you see in the dark. She could see inside the coffin, but it wasn't red, it was sort of bluish. There was no light in there, but she could see the hard pillows all around her. She could move, too. Like rolling over and over in warm water, but staying in one place. She could float.

She floated up to the coffin lid, rolled over in place, and saw herself lying there with closed eyes, not moving.

...Julia! Are you coming?

She rolled over again, and her face was close to the lining in the lid. Then she floated up some more, and she passed right through it.

It was freezing, and dark, and she wished she'd put clothes on instead of her nightgown.

The first thing she saw was the coffin, small enough for a child. There was another one behind it, a bigger one. She got all shaky again, and she had to pee.

The coffins were underneath a light. For a minute, she couldn't see anything but the coffins, and the light. Just brown, shiny wood. Then she saw some other colors, around the coffins. Flowers.

All kinds of flowers filled the room. Whoever's in those coffins must have been special. Everyone must have loved them, to send all those flowers. The whole room smelled like flowers.

"But it's me! I'm in the small one...!"

When she looked behind her, she saw chairs in rows on a red carpet. She stood at the top of an aisle, which ran down the middle of the room, and against every wall were huge bunches of flowers. At the far end of the aisle was a closed door.

"Beth?" she called.

But no one was there. The room was quiet. Completely still. The flowers were all still.

There were doors behind the coffins, one on each side of the room. She wondered if Eli or Beth were in the rooms back there. She called to them.

She wanted to go look through those doors, but the coffins stopped her.

She knew what you were supposed to do when you came up to the coffins, in one of these places. You were supposed to kneel down in front of the coffins and say a prayer. But she was afraid. What if Liza was lying in that big one, ready to play a joke? That would be too scary, if Liza jumped out. Or worse— if it was Bazil.

But you were supposed to kneel down and say a prayer.

If she didn't kneel down and say a prayer, some dead person might be mad.

She approached the coffins, but instead of looking at the shiny wood, she studied the flowers on the kneeler railing. It was easier to walk up to flowers. And when she knelt down, it was just like stooping down to smell flowers.

Then she folded her hands.

Dear God… Please help whoever's in there. Maybe they were good… Help them go to heaven…

Something distracted her.

Her name, whispered, made her look over her shoulder. She stood up. The voice spoke again, louder. It came from behind the door at the end of the aisle, in the back of the room. She stood up, and went to the top of the aisle, and she heard it again.

A man's voice. He shouted, like he was hurt, or very mad. Then he yelled swear words.

She recognized his voice.

She heard him come closer, his footsteps and his breath were loud. It sounded like he walked on microphones. Then his shadow filled the space under the door at the end of the aisle. It was the same shadow as in her dream. The tall man's shadow.

But that's daddy's voice…

She thought of running into one of the other rooms to hide. But a weird flash of light stopped her. It came from beneath the door at the end of the aisle, like lightning. Then it got dimmer, like a broken fluorescent bulb.

The door burst open, and the tall man stood there. Everything behind him was dark. Her father's face was the color of baby powder spilled in the yard at night. In his hand, he held her Marianne doll.

"Julia, come here for a moment, won't you?"

"You're not daddy!"

"Come get your doll, love."

For some reason, she knew she had to finish her prayer. So she turned her back to him and hurried back to the kneeler, as the man walked up the aisle. She watched the flowers again, as she knelt and bowed her head, and folded her hands.

Please God… Help whoever's in there get to heaven… If that's me in there, please help me get to heaven too. It's scary here. I don't like it.

The man walked up to her. As she opened her eyes, he arranged Marianne on the kneeler railing, amidst the flowers. Then he stood behind her, and placed his hands on her shoulders.

Julia closed her eyes again, so tightly they hurt.

I miss my mother. So please help. Help my mommy. And let me go to heaven, please…

Crraackkk!

She opened her new eyelids again. She was back in the coffin, and it was dark.

But at least now, Marianne was with her.

CHAPTER 40

It was dark, in the coffin, and she couldn't move. She was a statue. She felt the way a statue felt. Cold, but not uncomfortable. She thought about blinking. She remembered what blinking was. She knew how to blink. She had blinked in the dark before, and knew that you could feel it. But right now her eyes couldn't move like that.

She couldn't feel anything. She should have felt afraid. She should have felt lonely and sad, and she should have missed her mother. But all she felt was still, and all she heard was her own breath, one long breath that seemed like it would never stop.

She listened to that breath.

She knew it was a very long time going by—too long for a little girl to be alone in a box.

But the sound of her one long breath made the time seem like it had already gone by to begin with. In a way. Even all the time that had yet to go by—and that was a very long time—seemed to have already gone by to begin with. In a way.

She didn't have to go to the bathroom, and she wasn't hungry. She wasn't tired, and she wasn't antsy.

She was a statue.

Like the one in the park. The one of the soldier from a long time ago on his horse. She used to wonder how he felt. Now she knew. Like almost nothing at all.

This was how rocks at the ocean felt.

Or a doll, on a shelf for a long time.

Time kept passing.

She pictured a toy maker—an old man, like Gepetto—and he sat down at his organ and played. She listened to the organ music that played outside her coffin.

Then the box she was in shifted, tilted and rose. It moved along, unsteadily, with her in it. Someone was crying. This was how a statue felt when it was being carried to the park, where they had a spot all ready for it, surrounded by flowers. Or this was how a Christmas doll felt, in its package on its way to some boy or girl's house. Except nobody cried about that.

Moving through the dark.

Her box slid into a place. A car started, and drove with her in it.

Then she was lifted up again, and marched along like a balloon bouncing on waves of grass. And when she was set back down, and the box slid, head first, the sounds of wood against stone echoed all around her with a certain finality, like all the time that would come, now, which in her long breath seemed to have gone by to begin with.

Voices grew distant then stopped altogether. The silence stayed with her under the sound of her breath. Somewhere between one long, quiet time and another, she thought about her playmates, and the foam feeling they had helped her use. Some time after that, she decided to try to use it on her own.

She felt her feet. Her toes. Maybe the foam would help her feel like she could wiggle her toes.

Something started to happen. But it wasn't the foam feeling.

It was different. And it really hurt.

CHAPTER 41

"It's up to you, how you want to do this," Ed said, as Anne stood back. "Frankly, from what I know about you, I could live with it if my gun made you dead."

"Bite me." The man was still on the floor, holding his bleeding head.

"That cut looks bad," Ed said. "I wonder if the cops will get you the right attention." He rifled through some of the possessions on top of a dresser. "Nice hypodermic needles. You diabetic?"

"Keep your hands off my shit!"

"What are you gonna do, Willie? Bleed on me? You know—I should've guessed you were a junkie the day you walked in here."

Ed pulled a binder from among a row of video tapes.

"Don't touch that!"

He flipped through the folder, and his face registered disgust. From behind him, Anne caught glimpses of skin in the photographs, and young faces.

"You got a record, Willie? You strike me as the type who would. In fact—" He slammed the binder down. Tapes toppled off the dresser. "I'd say you're one shitty fucker."

"Yeah, well what's it to you?"

"We heard you on the phone. You start talking about dead people walking around, that's a curious thing, you know? Maybe computers listen to your conversations. Ever think about that? Maybe they pick up key words, then your neighborhood shows up in a big grid on a computer screen, and the computer zeros in on the exact shit-hole where you live. Maybe building managers are agents, of a sort."

Anne watched Willie's face. Ed's obvious tactics weren't wasted; he knew what he was doing, and how primed junkies were for paranoid mind-trips—never mind the ones who'd seen corpses rise. Willie scrunched and opened his eyes, as if trying to make a dream disappear. Then something like panic rose in his voice. "...Man?! This shit's fucked up, all right?"

"Come on, Willie. Tell us what you were talking about."

"I don't know nothing!" Willie thrashed his head violently back and forth. He banged the night table cabinet beside him, and squealed.

"Murder and child porn. You'll go up for life, Willie. But for now—" Ed grabbed a half-empty bottle of Jack Daniels from the dresser, tossed it to the floor in front of Willie, and whispered, angrily, "...all we care about is the crazy shit you said on the phone!"

Willie grabbed the bottle frantically, leaned back against the bed and took a long drink. Then he wiped his mouth, and his tone turned confidential. "Look. I went into that house -" he said, shaky. "I didn't think anyone was home. I needed money. I've got a drinking problem. He came at me with a knife. I had to protect myself. He got cut—by accident. That's the way it was....But the guy was dead."

All because of him, Anne thought. Mark dead. Julia missing. All because of this filthy creep. And to think of what might have happened, with him in her house. To think of the children in his book, who were lost, like Julia.

She spotted a hammer, next to a chisel on a small, cheap table near what passed for the kitchen, and she grabbed it.

"Then what?" Ed said.

"I saw him after that. Up the road from his house. In a graveyard. He went into one of the... whatayacallit? One of those tombs."

"A mausoleum?"

"Yeah."

"Good. You show us where."

"I ain't going back there," Willie said. "Nothing in hell…"

"Fine, Willie. Where's the phone?" Ed turned, picked some clothes off the dresser and found the black phone. "Good—What's the number for 911—?"

With Ed's back to him, Willie turned and reached into the night table drawer behind him, and grabbed a pistol.

In one motion, Anne hurled the hammer at Willie. It smashed him in the face, and knocked his head back. He grunted. His eyes rolled, and blood spurted from his nose.

Anne scrambled for the hammer, which bounced on the bed, as Willie, with half-shut eyes and a nose like a squashed beet, clawed like a dying animal for the gun in the drawer, his mind all-but insensible of what his spasming hand did.

She grabbed the hammer, raised it, and came down hard. The drawer splintered, spilling its contents. Willie screamed, rolled to his knees, and curled his whole body around his bent-wrong, bleeding hand.

Ed was beside the bed, then. Gun-in-fist, he backhanded Willie, who landed seated in the corner. Anne grabbed Willie's gun from the pile of debris and threw it. It struck the bathroom door and landed with a crash of metal against ceramic.

She pounced on Willie, and hooked the claw end of the hammer against his cheek. With violent pressure, she forced him down to the floor.

"SON OF A BITCH!" she screamed. "THIS IS YOUR FAULT, YOU FUCKING JERK!" Straddling him from above, with her fists choked by the hammer-head, she raised the weapon and delivered a ferocious vertical blow to his collar bone.

He grunted deep. "Ughh!"

Then he moaned, low and strangulated.

Her next blow was aimed for his skull. As she swung, Ed grabbed her from behind, and she toppled.

"You'll kill him!"

As Ed dragged her back, Anne delivered a fierce kick to Willie's groin. It finished him. He cried out in a high voice, and he curled up. On his side, he wretched on the cheap, thin carpet. Then he lay motionless.

A few minutes later, after Anne retrieved the flashlight from the tunnel, they revived Willie with a splash of cold water, and he talked in streams of gibberish nonsense.

"...all for a goddamn—fucking hell, she, oh for christ, no they can't—"

"Willie—Shut up, for Christ's sake!" Ed shouted. "Get up. You're taking us to the graveyard, remember?"

He looked at them through watery slits, and shook his head. Then his face crumpled, like a crying child's. "No—please—I don't want to—I didn't ask for this!"

CHAPTER 42

Anne felt she would be forever grateful to Ed Jones for returning her locket, and for the help he gave her. Fighting this alone was too dangerous. Having two minds to evaluate the illusions that passed, and maybe any to come, evened the playing field somewhat. She felt stronger now. And he seemed to share her determination.

He joined her, it seemed, with the simple reason that he cared. It was a rare thing finding a stranger who, despite horrifying opposition, would help when you needed it. She counted it a blessing. And she accepted it, gratefully.

He was afraid, though. She saw it in his face, through the rear-view mirror, as he guarded the deranged junkie in the back seat. Ed maintained a degree of exterior calm, which was comforting. But he was sweating, and he clutched the gun anxiously, near his chest.

Her own anxiety was like a cancer in her stomach. She kept thinking about what the *presence* in her house had told her. That he didn't lie, that reality could change. And although she recalled the morning when Julia dropped the locket, a memory which, with the help of Ed's supportive affirmations, she trusted, still, she was in possession of multiple, distinct sets of memories, and most of them were unbearable.

What if reality *had* been restructured? What if Julia…

No. She wouldn't accept that.

Anne pulled into the unlit church parking lot, and the three of them stepped uncertainly out of the car. Then she and Ed followed the other man to the hilly grounds where granite crosses and marble angels burned cold in the moonlight. They followed him through the thick of rolling darkness, dense with cut stone, and at the top of the highest mound, he froze, and spun around. "That's it. No further."

"Where is it?" Anne said.

Willie turned and pointed. "There. That last one."

It was a massive mausoleum, built into the far slope, above the sea wall.

"You sure?" Ed asked.

Willie laughed nervously. "Believe me, dude," he said. "I can't forget. I tried. Now if you don't mind—"

Something must have made a sound behind Willie. Maybe it was the wind scraping a fallen leaf against a nearby grave, but he whirled around and screamed "Wha?!"

When he faced them again, his eyes looked like shiny quarters. "IT'S COMING—!" he said.

He tossed another alarmed glance over his shoulder. Then, like a rabbit hearing a gunshot, he bolted. He brushed past Anne and sprinted up the path.

"Hey—!" Ed shouted, and charged after Willie. When he caught up, he grabbed Willie's sleeve, and Willie spun with a holler. With a violent swing, Willie smashed his arm against the underside of Ed's jaw.

Ed stumbled backward down the slope, a couple of steps, until a thin slate marker chopped into his calf. The gravestone cracked in two, and Ed crashed backward with it.

Willie kept running. His feet pounded the dirt as fast as rain, and like a ghost in flight, he disappeared past the church.

Anne shouted, and ran to Ed. He lay sprawled on the ground, with his head between two barely-separated cherubs, and his body twisted.

He wasn't moving. She crouched near him and saw wet mud splattered above his ear. No—it was blood.

"Hey—Oh Jesus—" She called his name, but his eyes remained closed. She felt his neck for a pulse and her hand warmed with a coating of sticky liquid. She snatched it away. The blood was black as oil in the night.

"Oh, Christ!"

She felt his neck again. With relief, she detected the delicate, rhythmic expansion of the vessel beneath her fingertips. She put her ear to his mouth, and heard a hoarse intake. She called his name again, and gently patted the side of his face.

Then his eyelids fluttered, and he looked up at her. For a moment he was serene, like a patient emerging from surgery, who floats on a stream of anesthetic. But when the pain awakened, a twinge overtook him from head to toe, a grimace distorted his features, and he groaned.

"Oww! Man!" He rolled to his side, and she helped him pull free of the cherubs.

"Are you all right?"

His hand reached for the wound at the side of his head. Then he struggled into a kneeling position, with his arm across the back of a headstone. "Eee, that smarts!"

Anne felt ashamed of her own urgency, realizing that her chief concern was not so much his personal safety, but the help which she so desperately needed. "You need a doctor," she said.

He felt around his skull for a moment, and checked his hand. "Ugh. No brains spilling out." His hand returned to the sore spot. "Big lump, though. I'll be okay."

"Are you sure?"

"Please help me up—"

She slid her hand across his shoulder blades, under his jacket, and struggled with him, as he stood. There was a clean smell about him, mixed with sweat, and earth, and blood.

"I'm sorry," she said. "I'm really sorry."

He walked to a taller stone, a sturdy cross, leaned against it and breathed in deeply through his nose a few times, with his eyes closed.

"Does the ground tilt over here?" he asked.

"Yes."

"Good."

In a moment, he pushed away from the gravestone, trudged up the slope and looked to the distance. She joined him there. At the edge of the moonlit field, near where the ocean lapped the sea wall, at the rim of the graveyard, the mausoleum squatted in dirt, malevolent.

"Who hasn't felt this before," Ed said. "I mean, you're in a graveyard, at night… It always seems like there's a haunted thing. The usual association. Kids or adults, it doesn't matter. Fear of the dark. The unknown. Death and evil spirits."

"Of an encounter," she said, "with something bewildering, and powerful, that confuses you, and threatens your soul."

Then she was quiet.

"Ready?" he asked. He took her hand.

She nodded. "You?"

"…for what though?" He stared off at the crypt.

They walked down the slope. "…aah, we're just a couple of kids, you know?" he said, and smiled at her. "Strolling out for a picnic. A moonlight stroll."

She returned the squeeze of his hand.

CHAPTER 43

Willie ran blind down the winding night road past sporadic, set-back residences and ocean winds. Flight drained all his energy, and occasionally he stopped, bent over, and sucked fast wheezing breaths into his pained lungs.

Now and again, a car passed him on the shore road. He challenged the glare of headlights and stuck out his thumb, shielding his injured hand under his jacket. Not one of the assholes had the decency to stop.

It seemed like forever since he'd had a fix. And goddamn it, he wanted one! Now! The pain in his hand raged.

As he made it into town, a twisting, low in his gut, made him as desperate to find a toilet as he was to poke a vein.

The world was under water. When he finally saw his block, his building seemed to recede like a safe haven in a nightmare. He dragged his legs through invisible mud, and finally made it across the street.

Everything was quiet. But his cover was blown, and the cops were coming. He didn't know when. But they were fucking coming, and he'd better take care of business, quick.

Inside his apartment, he crumpled onto the toilet—so scared and tired and sick. All he wanted was a good, shiny spike to knock him on his ass. Just to nod off, and be far away. But if he did, the cops would shake him from his delirium.

There was no time!

Fuck it! Who gave a shit? Who cared, as long as he could get off, this minute!

No, no. Got to clean up around here. Got to get the fuck out. Get somewhere safe, and shoot up!

He grabbed his gun from the bathroom floor, and he poured a pile of white powder onto a mirror, and snorted it fast. It was a mild rush, but enough to hold him.

Everything was fucked up now. Those two tonight had something to do with it. But it started when a fucking corpse came back to life.

He lined his gym bag with assorted baggies of illegal chemicals. Of his entire collection, he saved only two video tapes. He couldn't bring himself to part with those. The rest, he dumped into a garbage bag, along with the photographs, and as fast as he could, he brought them to a dumpster behind a printing company a block away and tossed them. Then he ran back to his apartment.

He added the gun and both his knives to the stuff in his gym bag. Then he filled a bucket with warm water, and crawled through the hole in the wall.

He used his video camera's light attachment as a flashlight, and he hurried along the tunnel until he reached the passage where he'd stashed the quick-drying mortar and the bricks. The entrance was small, like a cellar window, and beyond it stretched a corridor with no visible end. He shoved his gym bag through first, then climbed in, and began mixing the powdered mortar. Always be prepared.

He laughed when he finally finished the job. They were never gonna find him down here.

After he shot up, the underground highway called to him. It was a secret tunnel to another world. It led to escape—from the past, and from the hideous corpses which walked above ground.

He'd find a new life beyond the ancient tunnels.

CHAPTER 44

The crypt was a silent, dead thing. It infuriated Anne to think her search for Julia led to such a place. Ed shined the light on the imposing, stone structure, with its artfully engraved borders and iron door. Shadows leapt up on both sides.

He talked about breaking in, said his recent experience with lock picking was some preparation. But he didn't have his tools.

Together, they stared in horrific silence at the crypt. Ed shined the light on the engraving at the top. In block lettering was the name: *VAN RENSSELAER*.

"Think that's him?" he asked. "This guy in your house?"

Intuitively, she nodded.

"Van Rensselaer," he said. He tapped the iron door. "Maybe the stones were in here, buried with him."

They decided to traverse the coastal ridge, and to approach her house from the rear, quietly, no lights. They crept along the rim of the cemetery and crossed stony ground, skirting her neighbors' backyards. They trudged past tangled thicket, and scaled piles of rocks above black, reflective water. Finally, her house appeared in the distance.

"Looks haunted enough," Ed said.

It was an age old monstrosity, splintery shingled and silvery windowed, its dark gables oddly aimed at the night's creeping clouds.

"It never looked like that," she said. Then, "Let me have the gun—"

"Hang on."

"Please!"

"Wait a sec, okay?" Ed said.

She shivered then, in the ocean wind. He offered her his jacket, and she shook her head. He suggested they sit for a minute. Carved into the hillside scrub was a small cave of branches, and they sat below the wind.

He retrieved the gun from behind him. "I don't even want this thing around—"

She turned away, and pinched the bridge of her nose with enough pressure to swell the ache there. Then she massaged her ocular ridge.

"Julia used to make up holidays. We used to decorate the beach with shells and seaweed. We had August Day, and Whale Day in November. Do you know she'd remember the exact date a year later? We had our rituals. She never wanted to bring seashells home, though, even though she adored them, and loved to find the pretty ones. She didn't want to have to choose some over others. She felt bad for the ones she'd have to leave out."

Ed said, "My daughter used to cellophane the toilet every April Fool's Day."

Her laughter felt cleansing. "I did that once or twice."

"She was a little prankster," he continued. "Or she'd put shaving cream in the ear of the phone and have the operator ring back."

"Ah, that's a good one. So did she become a gag writer, or what?"

His lips formed a tight grin, and he shook his head.

Anne guessed the answer, but inquired nonetheless. "Where is she now?"

He shrugged up to his eyebrows, and asked, "…in heaven with her mommy?"

She felt the tomb again. It's cold silence.

"Do you want to tell me?"

"It was a drunk driver," he said. "My wife's face was…"

Anne rubbed his shoulder, feeling the thin tweed. She threaded her arm through his and leaned her head against him.

"Madeline, my daughter, flew about fifty yards through the air. When I heard that, I remembered how when she was eleven she had this thing about flying. She'd had this dream—where she discovered she could fly, and it wasn't make-believe, it was real. Then once, I saw her from the window. She stood on the picnic table in our yard. Closed her eyes and held perfectly still for the longest time. Slowly lifted her arms. Just a little, out to the sides. I watched her imagine she was flying. Eventually she opened her eyes. And even though the dream wasn't true, she turned it into play—she jumped off the table with a shout of joy, and ran across the yard."

She glanced up and saw it in his eyes, in his face—the still wanting her back. She understood even more why he was here beside her.

"So when I heard it," he continued, "that she'd flown through the air like that, I had this feeling. You know how the mind does things to help you deal. I had this image of her, flying to her death. It was peaceful, it just melted over me, I don't know."

"It's something you've held onto."

"By a thread."

She wished she knew him better.

"And your wife?" she asked.

He sort of half-shrugged, and spoke apologetically. "I don't imagine this is helping much—"

"...please. If you don't mind, I'd like to hear."

"Well—for me, I know what being in love is. I always remember this one night, after one of our earliest dates. I drove home by myself—and I just thanked God for the snow and the road and the night. For letting me inside the beautiful picture, and making me feel at home for the first time. Because my desire came back like a reflection. Because two people said yes, and it meant the same thing. Throughout our marriage, I thought about that. And the feeling never changed. I always considered her the truest affirmation of everything good."

She didn't say so, for fear of sounding trite, but he was lucky to have had that in his life, even if it ended so sadly. For herself, she hadn't hoped for as much since she was a young girl.

She took his hand and said, "We're headed over there, maybe to confront the most... I'm just glad you're here, and maybe together... I'm glad you understand what's good in this world."

After a long silence, there was an unspoken cue. The two of them rose, dusted off, and walked down to the lip of Anne's back yard.

With the house watchful of every step, they crept up the slope of her yard and crossed to the back door.

Anne yanked the screen door and the wood quivered. The inner door, however, was closed and locked.

"Let's try the garage," she said.

They rounded the house, past white trellises and flower boxes to a smooth slope of concrete which slanted toward the basement level carport. They crept beneath the guttered overhang, and went down.

Between borders of intermittent sewer drains, the parked BMW was cold and quiet. The cheap door to the utility room was, as she knew it would be, unlocked.

"Even when it's locked, it's unlocked," she said.

They went in. She turned on the light: a bare bulb hanging in the center of the room. Behind a work table, a wall was paneled with brown pegboard supporting utility hooks. A power drill was held in place on the wall, but the rest of the hooks were idle, and tools were scattered on the table.

Makeshift shelves in that room held everything from old cookbooks and plastic laundry baskets filled with toys, to vacuum cleaner parts in paper bags. At the far corner was the door to the pantry—steel, painted beige, with double locks.

"Can you try the door?" she said.

She spotted a stuffed lamb, a favorite when Julia was two. Anne freed the threadbare "lamby" from its constraints. Fondling it, she recalled a time from what seemed like another life, in another century, when Julia could not sleep without the pet.

Ed tested the doorknob. "Nope."

Anne crossed to the drawers below the worktable. "We always kept a spare key, but last time I used it—"

The key was missing from its former location. Anne opened the next drawer, on the off chance—

…and she beheld the baby monitor. "Look!" she said, snatching it out, with the AC adaptor behind it. "In her playroom. The transmitter… I left it—"

She crossed to a wall outlet, and plugged the adaptor in.

Then she turned the dial. A sound came to them. It was like the oceanic white noise she'd heard from below the widow's watch. Then it transformed. Ed went to her side, and the two of them listened to a strange, spacey melody, a cross of humpback whales and electronic dirge, echoing, unrepetitive, at once soaring, then folding back upon itself and blooming fresh from its center. Images leapt to her mind— colorful abstractions with a cellular quality. They widened and dissolved, cyclic, pulling her with their outward-reaching movement. Anxiety began to melt. She began to feel light.

"Turn it off!" he yelled.

She found the dial on the side of the device, and spun it until it clicked.

"What the hell was that?" Ed said.

Anne found herself leaning into the work table, half collapsed. She was out of breath. "I saw something."

"Yeah. You ain't kidding."

They compared the effects of the noise; they'd seen corresponding images. It took them a moment to shake off the drugged feeling.

Ed manipulated the ladder free of its position, Anne hunted for a fresh 9 volt battery, for the baby monitor, and she came up empty. She stashed the monitor and the adaptor in a cloth lunch bag and slung the bag over her shoulder.

"When we get outside," Ed said, "let's not make a sound."

They hauled the ladder, one at each end, with combined stealth. When there was room, they elongated it, tense with every little clank. They planted the feet, and Ed walked the ladder into its angled position, lowering it ever-so slowly when it neared the gutter. The contact was no louder than branches in the wind.

She climbed ahead of him, slowly, looking down from time to time. She crossed onto the shingled roof and scaled it, like a spider, toward the dark widow's watch. Then she stooped low, in warm wonder.

One pane of the glass was luminous. Beyond it was an amazing sight.

It was a room from memory. Wearing her 101 Dalmatians pajamas, and tucked under the covers of her own bed, in her own bedroom, Julia played with her little lamby, making it dance and lending it a light, musical voice.

Ed stooped beside Anne. "…Thank God—" he whispered, also taken with the illusion. "Wait! That *is* her isn't it?"

Anne placed her hands on the glass, to try to touch the warmth beyond. The scene was as familiar as her own breath.

"She's changed so much since then," she said. "See? She's just a baby."

Really, she was about three. Her face was rounder, her hands tinier than when Anne last saw her. Her eyes were committed to the lamb, like the eyes of a mystic watching the aurora borealis. Julia's expression deepened in delight when another figure passed into the room.

Five years.

Had Anne changed so much?

The sight of her own self, standing inside that warm room, was the opposite of shocking. Her own, younger face was like an old friend, with whom she'd shared the deepest intimacy. She'd lost a pound or two since then. But five years ago, she was neater about her appearance.

Even then she tried to make herself look pretty around the house. And she was happy. Her role was clear. Julia depended more on her then.

"It's what I was thinking about," she whispered, "when I plugged in the monitor."

Ed's reply was like a breath drawn out of the tide. "Unbelievable!"

He knelt beside her, and moved closer to the window. They watched the mother and daughter inside, who smiled and laughed. The mother sat on the bed and nuzzled the daughter.

Then the scene dissolved, and for an instant the room was replaced by a swirl of bright colored lights so intense the two of them shielded their eyes—before it all turned black.

Anne stared at the black window. Where had they gone? They were right there, those two. Right in front of her. Mommy and baby.

Why was it dark, now, like the cold, lifeless heart of a tomb?

Ed shined his flashlight through the window. Small wires and gears of brass and silver were set into the panes like watch parts. Behind them, several arcs of water danced, like in a fountain. The streams fully spanned the space within, and were caught in mounted trays. The octagonal wall-bench below was vacant, and the floor of the widow's watch not visible. Instead, it looked like a well that dropped endlessly through the house.

Anne's awareness shifted with a pulse of green light.

"Anne?"

She spun, and looked past him. "The lighthouse," she said. "Watch when the beam passes this way."

He stared out to sea for a moment, observing its rhythm. Then he looked back to the window. "They're in sync," he said. "Interacting. As if one sends a message to the other."

Each time the beam hit the window, a pulse spread throughout the wires like a school of fish fanning out, some changing direction.

Ed said, "Let me see the baby monitor."

"But there's no battery."

"Shit."

At that moment Anne swooned, and the house tilted beneath her, and the slanted roof heaved. She fell to her side and slid, and she slapped the roof with an outstretched arm keep from rolling off.

Ed scrambled toward her and grabbed her elbow. "Are you all right?!"

"I'm dizzy."

It took a few minutes before she felt able to move. Then she climbed shakily after Ed, who stayed close to her on the ladder, helping to steady her weary descent.

They hid the ladder behind a line of shrubs. Trudging back toward the churchyard, with eyes frequently cast toward the seaward beacon, they spoke in disjointed sentences, puzzling over the matter, brainstorming for possible theories.

Radio transmissions. Crystals. Thoughts projected. Paradise, with Julia as its god. A small chair below a strange device.

In the car he said, "You don't look well."

"Maybe it was this." She put the monitor on the seat between them. "My head hurts. I could collapse."

*   *   *   *   *   *   *   *   *   *

Anne fell asleep in the car. Ed drove into town to pick up his blow torch and other tools at his apartment. He told himself, in the bathroom mirror, that he looked like shit, and he washed blood from his face and hair. He put on a clean shirt.

Then he bought a 9 volt battery at a convenience store. At the all night Dunkin Donuts drive-thru he got two large coffees, and he drove back to the church lot. He'd let her rest. God knew she needed it.

He pushed the seat back, and when she shifted away from the passenger door he let her nestle against him. He touched her hair. His hand rested on her shoulder.

"It'll be all right," he said. "We'll find her."

Then he leaned his head back and closed his eyes.

CHAPTER 45

She dreamt she and Julia were trapped in an elevator, while her dead husband reached through the jammed doors with a razor in his hand.

She dreamt that Julia was a toddler, playing in the cemetery. Anne kept shouting at her, don't go near the open grave. But every time Julia ran in another direction, the grave was ahead of her. Anne ran for her daughter, but Julia thought it was a game, and fled.

Then Anne had another dream in which Julia was older, around seventeen. She sat at a desk, with school books piled beside her, and she was busy writing. Anne watched from another room, at first. Then approached, and kissed Julia's cheek.

Her daughter's desk faced a wall with assorted post cards and photographs taped on it. One image caught Anne's eye, because it blazed with light. It was a religious icon, a Madonna, with dark skin. The golden light behind the figure radiated into the room, and cast a circle over Julia's papers.

On one of those papers, Julia had written a note. The words filled Anne with understanding. Relief washed over her.

""What's up, Ma? You okay?"

"I had a bad dream."

Julia smiled, and patted her mother's hand. She looked so pretty, and so grown up.

*　*　*　*　*　*　*　*　*　*

197

Anne awoke, curled on the car seat with her head in Ed's lap. She sat up and wiped saliva from her lip, alarmed by the unfamiliar setting, unsure, for a second, who she was with. But then she remembered Ed, with some relief. He was slumped in an uncomfortable-seeming position that was fairly comic—one shoe off, a heel wedged between the dashboard and the windshield, and an arm linked through the steering wheel. She lifted his legs into her lap, and removed his remaining shoe.

She stared through the fogged glass to the dark cemetery, and to the lighthouse beyond.

Anxiety banished the peaceful feeling of her dream.

CHAPTER 46

It was no illusion, the courage that heroin inspired. And the raw power that cocaine tapped was pure life energy. The drugs freed him to realize there was nothing to fear—a constant truth that was hidden from most people. Uncovering that truth in this new, underground world, where every few steps offered a new choice, a new direction, was a blessing straight from heaven. He was free from his pursuers, and it was amazing, to fly underground. Willie was soaring. He kept hitting on the perfect blend for his speedballs. The leaf of the coca, the juice of the poppy. His stash would never dwindle, because the drugs were on his side—mystical friends who would always reach out to him. He was on a special journey. The drugs told him which turns to take.

He was lord of the underworld. He knew, when he peered down a dead-end corridor and saw hundreds of rats scrambling up a wall into an open duct, that it was out of reverence to him—and fear of his power—that they fled.

And when, after a short climb down a rusty ladder into a warm, ankle-deep stream, the worms writhed on the walls with a special vibrancy, he paused, and studied them expectantly. Sure enough, there was pattern in their frenetic posturing. Letters emerged. A message, for him. G—O—L—S—R—U—T—H.

He understood.

After burrowing through vast quadrants of the ever-changing net-work of tunnels, he grew tired. The hum of the walls grew tinny. The drip of water. Metallic smell like blood. The rats grew braver, and poked their narrow snouts out of fissures in the concrete, and out of pipe ends. They sat atop stony ledges and watched him.

He remembered the undead. The face of the man he'd killed, who meant to stalk him, who meant to have revenge. The face of the man, the face of the man…

He plunked his bag down, in a corner of the dark, mysterious maze. He cooked his works, and shot up. Then he rose, like Jesus on the mountain, and he journeyed onward.

No more brave rats. No more face of the man. Just glowing walls, and the coolest shit, the glimmer, in this underground maze where he ruled.

He was special, he knew that. Drugs loved him as much as he loved them. They would never leave him. They'd always find a way to bless his veins. They were helping him move toward something—his destiny. Something big.

CHAPTER 47

Van Rensselaer stood on the railed platform on top of the lighthouse. The sea was turbulent, though the sky was clear with a three-quarter moon. The wind rushed toward him, as if it needed to be near him, to brush against a force greater than itself.

Beneath his feet the latest application of his ideas whirred in crystal opulence. He thought of all the things he would have, in the new universe. Music and cinema, ballrooms filled with dancers, palaces in settings of natural splendor. Space ships. Angel wings with which to soar over mountains. Everything would be possible in his private heaven.

His house was a vessel containing the sum of all creative forces condensed into a nugget and answering his every whim, a fetus in the womb of nature. The next phase would flow with little effort. A few adjustments in his instruments, some new equations which would all but solve themselves.

A new universe would be born and he would be its God. He determined its laws, made all decisions about life and evolution, about the human condition and the passage of time. It was the Next Universe—a natural outcropping of the previous. It would swallow its predecessor hungrily. It would devour every mind and every molecule. A world of unlimited possibilities, of magic and wishes granted. A world of bliss.

Very soon, it would expand by concentric circles. Like the beam of light circling beneath his feet, it would emit illuminating energy and sweep the surroundings in a rhythmic pulse. His world would encompass those beaches and docks, those houses, the neighboring houses, the woods, the town, the bridge, tons of ocean water and air, the North Eastern quadrant of the United States. Once set into perpetual motion, the rapidity of growth and absorption would increase exponentially.

Every mind would fuel the new existence, according to his will. And as the New God, he would show greater sympathy than the previous one—to all forms of life, providing them with not only the sustenance, but the comfort and pleasure they sought.

Why then.

Up here, alone, he asked himself.

He offered her everything. She was his wife. Yet she'd turned her back on him.

She was his wife. And he missed her. He held more than a decade's worth of memories of her, and she'd always been there for him, dependable. He knew her through another man's eyes. But it was with his own heart that he loved her.

"Stupid bitch."

There would be many versions of her to come. Perhaps he would court her repeatedly, using inside knowledge to magnify his charm. Some versions of her he might induct into slavery—as an appeasement of fantasy—and he would enact every form of sexual punishment he could devise.

The thought of it wounded him, as if it was his own self he would be punishing. And could there really be an imitation of her to compare to the original?

He'd been certain she was to assume a place beside him. A place to which his previous wife could never have aspired. Only Anne had the chance to be his equal, and to enter the next world by his side. To witness the passage together.

She was an artist. She should have understood.

He cursed the Great Laws which led him here, which offered him everything but one thing.

The razor she cut him with was in his breast pocket, a symbol of her rejection kept near his heart. He pulled it out, lifted the handle to his nose, and leisurely inhaled.

Then he willfully nicked a chunk of flesh off the back of his thumb.

"Goddamned bitch!"

He imagined doing the same to her. Cutting her up—drawing red lines down her back and thighs, and horizontal slashes across her belly as she pleaded with him.

No, how could he ever hurt her, his darling. He would make her beg, make her wish she'd never betrayed him. He would destroy the thing she loved best, once and for all, and be done with it. Isolate her from all things, show her more and more. Show her what hell is. Show her what love is. Goddamn it, was there a time when she would understand? Would she ever love him back?

Don't be stupid. There are bigger matters to attend to.

Forget her.

But what about the pain?

CHAPTER 48

The night turned bluish with the approach of morning, and the air held the metallic smell of ozone as in the calm before the storm.

Ed installed the battery in the back of the baby monitor. When he snapped the back on, Anne opened her eyes, looking tired, and pretty.

He handed her a coffee, cold by now, and she took it.

Then he got out and opened the trunk. Feeling conspicuous to shoulder a duffel bag full of lock-cracking tools, he glanced around at the visible neighboring houses in the distance. One swatch of window peaked above clustered autumn leaves, another faded behind a network of branches.

Did the church have a rectory?

Nah. Many Baptist ministers drove to work like everybody else.

They walked through the slowly brightening graveyard, through intensifying wind that flicked their faces and smelled of distant tropics. They shuffled down the slope toward the shore. Carved into the embankment, the work of stone masons walled the furrow before the Van Rensselaer crypt, and Ed dropped his bag with a clank at the end of the furrow. He unzipped the bag, spread the tools on the ground, and set to work.

"This might take a minute. If I spring it just right, it will stay closed afterwards."

For a while Anne stood nearby, watching him work. But she must have grown tired of anticipating the lock-spring which would take them inside, because her gaze wandered toward the ocean, and her step soon followed.

From time to time, as he fiddled with lubricated metal, he glanced her way. She meandered along the water's edge, her face toward the horizon, the wind tossing her hair sporadically.

After heating the metal sufficiently, and branding his fingers on the pressure of an allen wrench, he finally drew back the iron deadbolt with an aggravated jostle, and sprung the door. The hinges groaned like a dying cat.

He stood, and addressed her in a brief, private shout. "…Got it!"

As she turned from the distant horizon, something up the north shore seized her attention. She covered her mouth, and for an instant her profile was motionless. Then she broke the tableau, and dashed out of sight.

Ed hurried out of the furrow and up the embankment, and he saw her, at a distance, as she rushed toward the rocks of the breakwater. Out at the tip of that bridge-to-nowhere stood a small figure, tiny, like a seagull, in a nightgown that fluttered.

Ed raced across marshy grasses as Anne struggled onto the rocks. He ran at a distance behind her, along the jetty, blending urgency with caution in giant steps from rock to precarious rock.

As he rushed across the tumbled boulders, he saw past Anne. Julia stood small against the ever-silvering sky, wind whipping her nightgown. She stared out to sea.

He caught up as Anne crouched behind Julia on a flat rock where the jetty came to a point.

Julia resisted when Anne tried to turn her. She wriggled from her mother's grasp, her attention urgently fixed on the horizon.

Ed caught a glimpse of Julia's face, and it seemed peculiar, the expression there—in some way disturbing.

Anne was in a state. She threw her arms around the child. She made high-pitched sounds and kissed Julia desperately. Again and again she tried to compel the child's attention, but Julia kept turning away. Anne pleaded in an urgent, mournful voice, "What is it, sweetheart?! What happened?!"

She turned the child forcefully toward her, and Ed felt horrified.

Julia's skin lacked all color, her face looked like an image carved from a white candle.

Her eyes were solid black.

No pupils. No irises, no whites. No reflecting surface. Just black, like a window onto the night. Black space, far-reaching.

"Oh God!" Anne scooped the child up in her arms, and brushed past Ed.

He caught her arm when she nearly slipped, and he helped her climb from a high rock.

"I'm taking her to the car!" Anne said, rushing over sand.

He followed her part of the way, wondering what in the world...? Then he ran to the mausoleum, and he stuffed his tools back in the duffel bag, stashed them inside the crypt, and left the iron door, for all appearances, locked up tight.

Those black eyes. That look on Julia's face. A sort of grin? He'd never seen anything so disturbing.

On the way up the cemetery slope, he heard Anne's scream. It sounded like the gravestones had all toppled, leaving wide-mouthed pits, from the depths of which howled the ghosts of hell. She ran toward him, white as frost, the child no longer in her arms.

"Where is she?" she yelled. "Christ almighty—*where is she?!*"

She stumbled past a tilted cross, and he thought she would collapse among the granite markers.

Instinctively, he looked back toward the rocks. For an instant, he thought memory was tricking him, projecting the image. Out there, at the end of the jetty, was the same, slight figure he'd seen before.

Mutely, he pointed.

Anne lifted her face to the shore. Then she fell into a wild run.

And so it seemed that the child was with them in this place, and only in this place. Again they stood on rocks, in the midst of crashing waves. He wanted to say something. What could he do? The only truth, it seemed, was an utter lack of comprehension.

The child's attention was kept out to sea, and soon Anne stopped trying to change that.

"It's not *really* her, is it?" Ed asked. He only meant it might be another illusion, a trick of Van Rensselaer's.

But the question seemed to wound Anne, to frighten her. "I know my own daughter!"

Then it occurred to him. Perhaps there was another area of speculation on Anne's mind. And he wondered himself—*was this Julia's ghost?*

A gust of wind, with unusual vigor that spoke to his body weight, came like a sharp signal. Drastic weather changes were imminent.

"The storm's coming," he said. "It won't be safe here."

She shot him an incredulous look. "I can't leave her!"

"If it's a trick—"

"Never mind. Go ahead if you want—"

Their attention was diverted by Julia, who for an instant seemed to respond to Anne's voice. Though her black eyes remained fixed on the horizon, she tilted her chin toward her mother. Then, with that peculiar grin still on her lips, she spoke, softly. No words. Just garbled syllables, like the ancient, primordial language of a child speaking in sleep.

"What is it, sweetie?" Anne said.

No response.

Another wind broadcasted the approaching storm. The sailboats in the harbor bobbed like scared boys on their momma's knees.

Holding Julia close, then, Anne looked solemnly down at the foam-sprayed rocks and the tide pools. Her voice was quiet amidst the crashing waves. "It makes no difference," she said.

Ed glanced back toward the crypt. And what he saw was shelter.

Anne clutched her daughter, and they all darted into the furrow which led to the crypt. When Ed opened the door, darkness tumbled out, with smells of rust and mold. He took his flashlight out of his bag, led Anne and Julia inside, and closed the wind out.

They stood in a narrow, stone room. Facing them was a stone partition with a doorway in the center, and dark portals on each side screened with iron filigree. Beyond the doorway, a short set of steps led downward to where, no doubt, the coffins were interred.

Julia wriggled in Anne's arms, and when Anne set her down, the child moved to a corner. She sat on the floor, and seemed to play with some imaginary toy.

"I'm going to find out about Van Rensselaer," Ed said, "Who the hell was he? There must be records—Something that would help—"

Anne moved closer to Julia, and knelt down. She covered her own mouth and wept.

"I'll hurry back," Ed said.

Anne pulled her sweater close, and stroked hair away from Julia's eyes. "We'll be all right," she said. "I think she wants to tell me something. Maybe if we're alone—"

"I've got a blanket, in the car," Ed said. And he hurried out into the blustery wind.

At the car, he had to move aside the box of Maddy's things to get at the emergency blanket. Then, with the blanket under his arm and one hand about to slam the trunk closed, he thought twice about that box of once-loved possessions. When he returned to the mausoleum he carried the emergency blanket on top of the cardboard box. He told Anne that the things in the box could be Julia's, now.

Julia sat in the corner, completely still—frozen, staring at nothing. Ed carefully handed his gun, butt-end first, to Anne. "In case he comes back here."

As Ed glanced back from the crypt door, Anne draped the thermal blanket around Julia's shoulders. Julia's black eyes peered out. The peculiar grin was gone from her young, ghostly face. Her expression was blank.

CHAPTER 49

The wind grew stronger and tempted Ed's steering wheel as he hurried back to town. It crossed his mind, at the sight of outside furniture being hauled into a corner cafe, that the Athenaeum, where the town records were kept, would be closed for the weather. But he remembered, the room was attended as-needed by an elderly woman who resided in the building.

He rushed from his car into a narrow stairwell. At the top of the flight was a hand-written sign—*Please ring buzzer for service.*

She came down in a few minutes, and unlocked the records room. He told her what he needed, and she checked a computer file. When she pointed to the ledger, he stepped up on a rolling stool and pulled it off a high shelf. Within ten minutes he found the name Victor Van Rensselaer printed above Anne's address on Shore Road.

He'd lived from 1877 to 1944, and he bought the house twenty-six years before his death. He was of Dutch origin. A world traveler. A financier. A published writer. He'd outlived his wife and one daughter, and left a daughter behind.

Ed stared at the blank space where Alice Van Rensselaer's death was yet to be recorded. She'd be an older woman now, maybe with a different last name.

He sat at a metal desk by a window overlooking the town square, and he used the computer to access the Web. One search engine turned up an e-mail address for an Alice Van Rensselaer in the Portland area. Great, if it was her. But sending e-mail wasn't going to be much use.

He decided to conduct a key-word search in the on-line archives of the local paper. He typed her name, entered it, and hit pay dirt. A Sunday feature article, *Her Tragedy Became Her Calling*, described the life of a woman who had once been a compulsory patient in a local sanitorium during the 1940's and 50's. When the institution was shut down, about half of the residents were relocated to scattered group homes, run by a couple of local agencies. The rest of the patients were to be released on their own... although they were ill, and required care. Alice Van Rensselaer convinced the trustee of her estate to use her funds for a new treatment facility at the hospital in Portland. Eventually her own treatment was completed, and she moved on to study pre-med at Yale. Psychiatry dominated her university career. Twenty years later she was the director of the facility where she'd been the first patient.

Ed was given permission to use the phone, and he called the Portland hospital. Most likely, she was retired. But if he could convince a hospital representative of his urgency, perhaps he could get her number.

"I'm trying to reach Dr. Alice Van Rensselaer," he told the receptionist.

"One moment, I'll page her."

Panic stricken, he listened to the muzak of the hospital's phone system.

When the woman answered, in a pleasant-professional tone, he was dumb struck. What could he say?

"Hello?" she prompted again.

"Doctor?"

"Yes?"

"It's about your father—"

Heavy silence fell at the other end of the line.

"He's dead..." She spoke with an edge of uncertainty unusual for such a factual statement.

"I'm not so sure—" Ed responded.

She made a sound, then. Like a gasp caught in her throat. "…I hope you're not trying to be funny—"

"Please… help us."

Portland was too far. She gave him directions to a group home in Lewiston where she kept an office.

Then she made a hesitant request. "For God's sake… tell me it doesn't involve a child—"

He pretended not to hear. He hung up the phone and panicked all the way to his car.

CHAPTER 50

At least Julia was with her now. With her momma, where she needed to be.

...Oh please God save her!

Don't cry. This isn't the time for worry.

Anne slid the cardboard box over to the corner where Julia huddled in the blanket. "What have we here?" she said. "It's a present for you, lucky..."

She gazed into Julia's face: the little nose and chin as familiar as her own breath, and then those other-worldly eyes. Her daughter. Altered beyond normal human understanding. Was this the last time they'd be together? A time for saying goodbye?

Stop it.

She opened the box, in the dim, circular glow from the flashlight, and pulled out a stuffed, black kitten with a jeweled collar and a mischievous face.

"What's this fellah's name? Hmm?" She made the kitten hop up Julia's arm and kiss her, and Julia vaguely brushed the place where she'd been touched.

The box held half a dozen chapter books, and three picture books. "Hmm, I've never seen this one. Have you, hon? *Princess Wysteria?* Looks good, huh? Pretty illustrations. Remember that one you had about The Lady of the Bay? Ooh, look at this palace!" She held the book up, and shined the light on it.

No response.

"Anyway, I can see why this was one of her favorites."

Anne looked over the other books. "Oh look, Julia. *'Madeline!'* Remember when you were little?"

Julia uttered a string of syllables that Anne wished she could understand. Was she dreaming? What did her lightless eyes see?

"Oh sweetie…" Anne suppressed a rush of salty tears. "Honey, I love you so much! Sweetie pie? Please come back to me, honey…"

How could she have failed her own daughter to this extent? God didn't ask much of her. I place this child in your care. Help her grow. Take care of her. Protect her. Why hadn't she protected Julia? Why wasn't Julia kept safe?

Damage had been done. There would never be a way to protect her from whatever already happened.

Oh God. Sickly waves washed over her. How could she have failed her daughter like this?

"You know, the girl who owned this was named Madeline. I guess we know why it was one of her favorites. Remember how I used to sing that Beatles song with your name?"

She sang it now.

"*Ju-lia, ocean child, calls me—sleeping sand, silent cloud, touch me— So I sing a song of love, for Ju—lia—*"

There was deep silence, as the flashlight dimmed. Outside, the storm strengthened, but it seemed millions of miles away.

Then Julia softly spoke. "Your voice is pretty."

"Oh sweetheart," Anne said, hugging her daughter. "I love you so much!"

Anne squeezed Julia's hand, which felt as light as a dandelion seed, neither warm nor cold. When she looked down, she gasped, horrified.

She could see her own hand on the other side of Julia's. She could see the glint of the aluminum blanket through the overlay of Julia's knuckles.

CHAPTER 51

Ed was lost.

An old man at a bus stop under a plexiglas dome sat on a metal bench with a closed umbrella by his side. Ed asked for directions.

"Oh sure," the guy said, "that your car? Proud to be American... My brother had a truck. He always didn't throw rocks, but then, he had the service..."

Next he asked a young mother-to-be, who sat on her front porch waiting for the weather to bring excitement. "I think it's a kind of nursing home," he said.

She wasn't sure. She asked if he meant "that big house on Elm street?"

And if he knew that, he wouldn't be asking. "Yeah, that's the one," he said.

The place was elegant. On a road lined with oaks and elms, it was one of those enormous Victorian houses set back from the road, with iron gates and a long circular drive in front.

He talked to a speaker, said he was there to see Alice Van Rensselaer, and the gate opened electronically.

The reception area was vast. There was a circular desk near the front entrance, and the room beyond it had shiny marble floors and beige columns. Various corners were furnished with small dining tables, rectangular carpeting, lamps and easy chairs. To the left, some serious-minded folks sat around a television watching the weather channel. To the right, a carpeted stairway wound past the portrait of some unhappy rich guy. At the far end of the room, a caretaker wheeled a harried woman to some french doors, and left her to peer out across a patio.

The receptionist spoke to him, and her displaced southern accent reminded Ed of the military installment nearby.

"I'm here to see Alice Van Rensselaer."

"Are you Mr. Jones?"

He nodded.

"Great. I'll just make sure she's free." She spoke into the phone.

The second floor was pretty, with tall windows that overlooked wind-whipped grounds. There were potted plants on tables, and oil landscapes on the walls.

She sat behind a desk, peering at a computer through half-lenses, and typing away. "Sorry! Almost through, just one sec!" she said energetically, and continued clicking away. Then she finished, and a flash from her monitor changed the color of the light on her face.

"There!" She looked up at him. "I apologize! I was on-line with a colleague and we were just wrapping things up. With the storm, who knows how long before the lines go down." She leaned back in the leather chair, and regarded him momentarily over her reading glasses. Then she removed the glasses, and stood. "I'm Alice Van Rensselaer."

He shook her extended hand.

"So it's about my father?"

He nodded.

She stiffened, and tightened her mouth. "If he were here now I'd spit on his corpse."

"I'm sorry—"

"Don't be. He's dead, Mr. Jones."

Ed hesitated. "On the phone, I was under the impression…"

He sensed that she was a brave woman, but also that something like dread gnawed at her. She guided him over to a sitting area where the floor was checkered black and white. The smell of coffee came from a nearby kitchen.

"About his work," Ed started.

His words hung in the room.

"I'm sorry, just one moment." Alice rose and hurried into the kitchen as Ed stared at the spines of old *Parabola* and *Journal of Modern Psychiatry* magazines in a tall, glass fronted cabinet.

When Alice returned, she held a half crumpled cigarette pack and a crystal ash tray. She took a seat across from him, and set the ashtray down. "Is there, uh…" she sighed, shakily, "…a little kid involved?"

Ed shifted on the couch, and in a disjointed, inarticulate way, he talked about Anne and Julia.

When he finished, Alice massaged her hands. Then she took a long pull off the cigarette and smoke breezed from her lips into a cloud above them. "Maybe he's the devil himself," she said. "I never knew what to believe. I suppose I figured… after all these years, Christ! He's dead in his grave! Right?"

She calmed herself with another drag of tobacco.

"What did he do?" Ed asked.

She shook her head solemnly. "Child abuse doesn't say it. It was more thorough. A rape of mind, body and soul. He forced hallucinogens on me. Untested ones, which he secreted from religious sects in remote regions. He used hypnosis on me before I was three years old. And not for therapeutic reasons, I assure you. But there was more. Technological methods of probing my mind.

"So he knew things, then," Ed said. "His work was no joke."

She took a long, slow breath. "All this time, I was never sure. But if it's true—if it's true, then he made the unimaginable possible. His beliefs were simplistic, really—that we're like radio transmitters, that we harness the creative powers of the universe and project them into reality. He believed a child's mind tapped the purest and most potent of such forces. So he saw children as ideal instruments, like magic wands, to manipulate the powers. If he could control a child's mind through post-hypnotic suggestion, if he could use drugs and technology to boost those projective impulses, he could mirror the primordial creative act. He could custom design any 'reality' he chose. Govern a child's beliefs, and through the process, those beliefs become outward reality. That was his theory. What more could a sorcerer hope for?"

"You had a little sister."

"Yes, she died. And her life was nothing but a bloody sacrifice which secured my redemption. I was six when she was born. He'd done considerable experimenting on me by that point, but he hadn't perfected his techniques. I possessed at least some, small ration of the personality and cognitive development normal for a child that age. Not that I was 'normal' in any sense of the word. Not then. I was damaged goods. But I had a small sense of my own identity. And for him, that was a detriment.—

"But then he had a brand new baby girl! A tabula rasa, a blank canvas to draw on. My mother died in childbirth. One less distraction for him. I was set aside, and quickly forgotten. And he plunged into his work with complete obsessiveness.

"He hired a nanny for me. But my little sister lived on the third floor, where he kept his laboratory, and not I nor anyone else was ever allowed up there. His pretense was that his youngest child was 'special' and required 'special care.' He told the world she was a deaf mute, and claimed that his life's work was her education and the fulfillment of her needs. But I knew differently. I knew what she was to him, really. What could I do? He was a powerful man. I couldn't contradict his lies. So I prayed for my little sister, and I lived my solitary life.

"Then one day there was a commotion. Our housekeeper complained that he'd not emerged from upstairs for two weeks. Authorities were contacted. The third floor was accessed with a battering ram. And they were both found dead.

"I've always believed something went wrong with his experiments, and it killed them both.

"But the really sad thing, for me, was when one of the policemen, who was jotting notes, asked me for my little sister's name. My own sister, who I had prayed for so often. I couldn't remember! The only *name* I could think of was the one he had used. The only way he ever referred to her.—

"'...the quiet child.'"

CHAPTER 52

Inside the mausoleum it grew colder as the rain outside pummeled earth and rock. The flashlight was nearly dead. Julia was transparent, all-but invisible, in the corner where they sat, with its ever deepening shadow. Suddenly she gripped Anne's hand tighter, and whispered, urgently, "Tell me another story, mamma. Tell me the one about The Quiet Child."

Anne guarded her reaction. She wouldn't gush, she wouldn't over-power Julia with her emotion. "I'm not sure I know that one, sweetie," she said.

"Please?"

"Okay. How does it go?"

Julia's voice was clear and dramatic. "Once, there was a little girl—"

Anne repeated the line, and Julia said, "…whose daddy, made her be quiet."

Anne repeated, "…whose daddy, made her be quiet."

"Tell the rest, mommy."

"He told her to be quiet—" Anne said.

"No! He *made* her be quiet."

"He made her be quiet…" Anne said, "because he didn't like a lot of noise. He was always busy, and he had a lot of things on his mind."

Julia squeezed her hand again, and nodded, engrossed in the story.

"So he made her be quiet," Anne continued. "But it was hard for her to be quiet."

"That's right…" Julia whispered.

"She didn't like being quiet," Anne said. "So she came up with a plan. She went to the kitchen cupboards, and grabbed all the pots and pans she could carry—"

"No, mamma. That isn't how it goes."

"No. No, it isn't."

"He made her be quiet," Julia said, somberly, "so she had to be quiet. And she was quiet all the time."

"Yes," Anne said. "She never spoke to anyone. People thought there was something wrong with her. Some thought she was deaf, and some thought she was feeble minded."

Julia spoke with a sigh. "…right…!"

"But all the while," Anne said, "in her mind, she was singing in the most beautiful way. In her mind, she was singing about all her sorrows."

"That's right, mom! And sometimes at night—" Julia prompted, in a tone growing ominous.

"Sometimes at night," Anne said, "people would hear strange music."

"…yess!"

"They'd think some neighbor had gotten new windchimes, and didn't they make the loveliest sound? Or they'd think—could those be whales, passing by in the ocean deep? It isn't time for their migration!"

"And then one day…?" Julia said.

"Then one day," Anne continued, "someone heard the music…"

"Another little girl—?"

"Yes. Another little girl. She heard the music, and she wondered what it was, and she kept wondering until she just had to know."

"So she followed it," Julia said.

"Yes, she followed it down to the water."

"But that's not where it came from."

"No," Anne said. "She looked everywhere, up and down the beach, and she listened to seashells. She heard beautiful sounds: the sounds of the waves, and the roar in the shells, seagulls singing their songs, and even a distant fog horn. But none of these sounds was as beautiful as the strange music—"

"Because the strange music was so sad?" Julia asked, and Anne felt like weeping.

"Yes," Anne said. "Everyone who heard the strange music felt so sorrowful, and sometimes it made them cry. So, the other little girl, the one who just had to know where that music came from, walked into town. On the way she heard churchbells. Then, in the park, there was a concert. Violins, and a harpsichord. A cello, and a flute. The music was beautiful. And sometimes, it was very sad. But it wasn't as beautiful or as sad as the strange music she heard."

"…right!"

"So she went back home," Anne continued. "And she listened. She listened for the rest of that day, and after the sun went down, and the house grew dark, she kept listening. And finally she heard a sound. Way off in the distance. *The same sweet, strange music!* And it grew louder, and louder. Until…"

"Until she could hear…" Julia prompted.

"…until she could hear…"

Julia finished, "…the words the other little girl was singing!"

"Yes," Anne said. "And do you know what they were?"

Julia took a breath. Her darkened features seemed to stare far off, and she sang, with a voice high and sweet:

>…*mee-I—quiet child—me hello*
>*I-ah-me the—quiet child—mee-I hello*

Bewildered, Anne asked, "What did the girl do, when she heard this song?!"

"…sang," Julia answered.

"What did she sing, sweetheart?"

"...mee-I—Julia—hello, hello..."

Anne squeezed her daughter's hand. "What happened then?! What happened, Julia?!"

"She sang her own songs to the quiet little girl," Julia said. "She taught the quiet girl other songs, so she wouldn't have to be quiet anymore. And she told her stories. They made up stories together!"

"And then what happened?!"

Julia looked up at Anne with normal, clear, life-filled eyes. She suddenly appeared solid, complete and unharmed. But there was terrible anxiety in her face.

"She's not dead, mommy!" she said urgently. Then she began to fade from sight. "I had to help her. Don't you see? She's not dead!"

Then Julia was gone.

Anne's horrified scream filled the mausoleum. She ran from the tomb into the raging storm. Battling hurricane winds, she zig-zagged toward the water. Waves heaved ten feet up and crashed onto the sea wall, and the ocean brimmed along the cemetery ridge. She blocked her eyes from the horizontal rain, and peered, between gusts, toward the space where she'd twice found Julia.

Way out, at the tip of the jetty, a spray of foam shot twenty feet high—but... had she glimpsed Julia standing there first? Did that enormous wave steal her baby?!

Nothing was there now but water, lashing the rock where Julia once stood.

Anne splashed through a pool of brine, and screamed her daughter's name into the commotion. Nothing came of her cries but consuming emptiness. And when she lost the spirit to resist the wind's force, it knocked her down into the rising tide.

Her daughter was a vanished ghost.

CHAPTER 53

Ed fought with the steering wheel. The winds were ferocious now. By the time he reached the town square in Lewiston, no one was on the street. Downed branches tumbled across the road. A garbage can rolled in an arc, and ricocheted off a lamppost.

Maybe there was a way out of this after all. He suspected Alice had the answers.

They'd agreed to meet at the tomb. She would see the child; she was a psychiatrist, after all. He would go with her to the house, and together they'd handle the son of a bitch.

Maybe Julia would be saved.

He was amazed to see the time on the clock in the church tower. It was as if he'd been walking through a dream. He'd left Anne and Julia in that dark place by themselves too long, especially considering Julia's condition.

Which was what? *Mystically affected?*

And, if the weather was this bad inland... Shit.

He heard a sound like machine gun fire. A wall of rain, as grey as steel, marched toward him from the square and hit his car with tidal-wave might.

It would be murder driving in this.

All the same, once he got on the highway, he exceeded by a good fifteen miles an hour the speed that would get a trooper to stop him. He had to get back to Anne. The thought of her, in that place…

At least he had the highway mostly to himself.

In part, he let fate do the steering. He couldn't see Jack on the road, except occasional headlights on the westbound side, and the tail lights, when he was all but on top of them, of the slower moving cars which he passed.

There was no reason for him to see the tractor trailer, because it's tail lights faced the breakdown lane, and its headlights shined at a peculiar angle into oncoming traffic. Its long body, which intersected the eastbound highway, was the exact color of rain.

CHAPTER 54

Julia's arm was itchy, near the shoulder. It had been itchy for a long time, and it bothered her. But somehow it took her a while to realize, and to know what to do. When the word finally floated through her mind, *itch*, she reached over and scratched. That felt good, getting rid of that itch.

But then she was left with a bigger problem.

It was cramped inside the box. It was black, and the air was stale. She was sick of it.

She lifted her hands and pushed on the lid. But it was no use. She twisted to her side, and pushed with her shoulder. She pushed with all her muscles.

"Julia?" a voice whispered outside. He sounded weak.

"Eli! Let me out—"

"Don't think I can, Julia. I don't feel too good."

"Well get one of the others! Where's Beth? Hurry up and get Liza, tell her to let me out—!"

"We can't find Beth. She went away. Now Liza is hiding because Bazil scared her. They had a fight…" His voice trailed off. "Julia… we're gonna die…"

"But I need to get out!" Julia called. "Eli? Where did you go? Eli help! Please!" She banged on the lid. "Let me out!"

CHAPTER 55

Alice drove toward the place she was most reluctant to visit: the past.

After twenty miles east through treacherous rain, the highway was blocked with an accident. She was forced to take winding route 78 for the next several miles. Driving nearer and nearer to Bow Lee Point, she watched a thousand dreams in her watery windshield.

Her father's beliefs may have been insane. But now it seemed there was truth to them. Maybe all truth was found in paradoxes. It was true that he died long ago. Yet she was about to pay him a visit.

In her stomach, the recalled sensation of the torturous bubble grew metal cold. And beside her, on the seat, her tribal mask was propped up as if watching the leaf-littered sky they passed under.

She was glad Carl couldn't see her now. He'd think she was lost. He'd call her behavior erratic, and she'd be inclined to agree.

Maybe she was insane. She was convinced, after all, that she was justified in what she meant to do. She believed things that would seem pretty spaced-out to most rational people.

So maybe she was insane, and about to commit murder.

CHAPTER 56

There had been an accident, and somebody was hurt. The rescuers had taken a man's body from the wreck. Ed wasn't sure if there was anything he could do to help. He wanted to help. But what could he do? He stood behind the rescuers, feeling useless. They brushed past him and shouted instructions and administered CPR. One of the young men prepared the de-fibrillator machine.

Ed backed away. Give them some room, let them do their job. The whole scene was ugly—blood and glass all over the pavement. He wished he were miles away. Maybe he shouldn't have stopped. There was nothing he could do.

He'd been in a such a rush. Over-anxious to reach his destination. It was so important, yet—now he couldn't remember.

A hundred feet or so up the road from the accident, he sat on the guard rail. The sky was a strange color, and leaves were tossed upward from the woods into the open space above the highway. He wondered why he felt no chill from the rain.

Then he glanced over his shoulder. Down the slope behind him, in the little valley by the edge of the woods, were his wife and daughter.

They sat on a fallen log. In her long, blue dress, Sandra sat with her hands folded in her lap. She smiled radiantly at him.

Maddy straddled the log, dressed in shorts and a tee shirt. She was looking at Ed and laughing sweetly. She said something to Sandra that he couldn't hear.

The two of them seemed so happy, and the sight cheered him immensely.

Run to them now, he thought. *Embrace them, hold them close.*

"Sweetheart?" his wife called to him.

"Yep?"

"Go to the ambulance, honey," she said. "They need you."

He looked back at the accident scene, where they were putting the stretcher with the man's body into the back of the ambulance. He didn't see what good he'd be to the paramedics.

But it had been so long since he could to do what Sandra asked. He longed to make her happy.

"Okay," he called to her.

"I love you Daddy," Madeline called out.

"Love you too, sweetheart! Be right back!"

"I've got a pulse!" someone shouted.

Ed opened his eyes in the back of the ambulance.

"He's breathing!" The young paramedic leaned over him. "Welcome back, sir!"

CHAPTER 57

Van Rensselaer awoke with his head on the desk. The vigors of his labor were often draining, and late that morning exhaustion had claimed him like a four-year-old. Now his back ached. He wished he'd had the sense to sleep in bed, instead of in a chair. His head throbbed.

Soon, of course, soon. It would all be feathers and luxury and warm, bubbling water. Vitamins and wilderness hikes, endless sunshine.

The terrible banging from above distorted his reverie.

What!? What is that racket!?

He stared at the far corner, at the trap door above the stack of crates. A distant, pathetically weak voice cried, "Let me out!"

She banged so hard the whole ceiling shuddered—or was that the heightened stab of blood behind his eyes? All his excitement and anticipation combined with a swell of fury.

That little brat's stubbornness, her unwillingness to once-and-for-all submit, was enough to derange his senses.

Just like her mother. A pair of willful, blind, ungrateful and selfish cunts. He needed them like a thorn in the eye.

The straight razor had been inches from his face as he slept. He picked it up now, and slid it carefully into his pocket.

Then he rose, walked across the room, turned the key, and stood by the stack of crates in the corner as the lift slowly descended.

"Just like your mother…"

231

CHAPTER 58

Ed sat up inside the swaying ambulance. "What's going on?"

"Take it easy," the young paramedic said.

"I can't do this—I—"

"Lie back down and relax, sir."

"Stop it!" he said, pulling the i.v. needle out of his arm. "I gotta get out."

"Sir, we can't—"

"Stop the van!" he yelled. The paramedic tried to restrain him, but Ed sat up and pushed the young man away. As the EMT lost his balance, and faltered against the IV stand, the driver veered to the side of the road, stopped the ambulance, and spoke into the radio. Ed flung the doors open, and jumped onto the wet and windy road.

He stumbled into the ditch by the highway, and ran for the woods.

Sandra and Maddy, alive! He remembered them vividly. In a different world, but one that was real. They were waiting for him. They were with him!

With the buoyancy of new understanding, he raced through the wind-bent, rain-splattered woods which all other creatures had seemingly vanquished in favor of safe burrows and dens.

Soon he reached a clearing, and a steep slope fell to a one-lane highway. He wondered how long before the next car would pass. And how far would his thumb get him? He looked like shit. His shirt was bloody. He probably looked like a maniac. But country folks were known to help, when you really needed it. And if he didn't look like someone who needed it...

A black car pulled into view, a VW Jetta. As it drew nearer he waved for it to stop. The driver was wearing a tie, and talking into a cell phone, and he sped right past.

Poor Anne, alone with her little girl in that dark place.

The next vehicle that pulled into sight was a red pick-up. Ed knew it would stop even before it reached him.

When he saw the blood on Ed's shirt, the driver, an old plump man with thick glasses, asked what happened.

"Accident. Listen, I've got to get to Bow Lee Point in a hurry."

"You want to stay away from the coast, fellah."

"This is urgent."

"There's a Gulf station up the road. I could take you as far as there."

Ed said he appreciated it. But really, he wished the guy would go the extra mile. Or thirty.

At the station, he tried to imagine who to call. He'd grown so solitary in recent years, that the list was short. He had a sister-in-law in South Beach. But when he tried, the lines along the Seacoast were down.

Through the plate glass of the office windows, he saw a corner of the lot where used cars lined up in a row. Prices were soaped in their windows.

He hung up the phone, and turned to the guy in greasy coveralls behind counter. "You the owner?"

The man nodded.

"Which one of those works?" he asked, pointing.

He paid eight hundred dollars with a credit card, and waited an eternity for authorization. Then he pushed the engine of the unregistered, aged Ford hard, down the road. The passenger windshield wiper was broken, and a soapy zero on that side resisted the washing action of the rain. He hoped the weather would conceal the fact that the car had no plates.

CHAPTER 59

Julia heard a squeal of metal, and wood scraping against wood outside of the box. Was it Eli? She wanted to call to him, but she was afraid.

There was a louder thump, and something scraped against the lid of her box, and the hinges squeaked a little. The box shifted, and she knew the lid had been unlocked. She could open it now, if she wanted.

What she really wanted was to throw open the lid and run all the way downstairs to her mother's arms. But she was too afraid to move.

When the lid was thrown open, it wasn't Eli who did it. The tall man—with her father's face—towered over her, and his hands came down like claws. He grabbed beneath her underarms and lifted her out of the box.

Julia screamed and kicked her legs, as he carried her, roughly. When he let go of her, she fell onto a broken wooden box, and she started bawling.

He yelled, "Knock it off!" louder and meaner than her real father would have. He grabbed her arm and yanked her down to the floor, then he dragged her across the room. He shoved her into a chair and her head got knocked back. He pressed his hand into her face, pulled a strap across her chest, and tightened it.

"It hurts!" she yelled.

"Quiet!" He pushed something down onto her head, then bound her wrists to the arms of the chair.

CHAPTER 60

She even looked like her mother. Two priceless venuses cut from the same block. Anne would whimper like this, surely, if she was in the same position. The thought of it excited him.

At his work table, Van Rensselaer mixed ingredients in a bowl, readying the charged substance which would blow apart the confines of Julia's consciousness. Then he began to wonder. Why had he kept the girl for so long? All children were gold mines, and all would eventually succumb. He'd been convinced that Julia was a special tool, that she yielded to his power even before he awakened. Now that seemed foolish.

No—his quiet child was the center of his resourcefulness, not Julia. The quiet child was the heart of his invention—she *was* his invention— and he hadn't needed any other instrument to get him to this point. Julia Clausin was a possession he'd stumbled upon, which he'd been unwilling to relinquish. A valuable resource, yes, but did she add so much to his strength? Of course not! He'd grown in power as a matter of course. It had nothing to do with her. He could dispose of her now.

Yet he was delighted by her features. The Great Laws, after all, had a certain way of doing things. This child's mother had evoked deep emotion in him, for some reason, and now, here was the child. Like an untainted version of the mother. She'd been more difficult to manage than he expected. Like her mother. But all kids, after a certain age, were rebellious like that.

Perhaps it was Julia, not Anne, who was meant for him.

No—she was just another distraction. He had no time for this. She'd only get in his way.

But she was still a resource. Why not utilize her as he would any other?

He poured a vial of botanical tincture into the mixing bowl, and the concoction turned dark green.

When he brought the bowl to her, she was sobbing like an infant. Again he was given pause. He set the bowl in her little lap, took the razor out of his pocket, and unfolded it.

Why infuse her with this valuable substance when she'd shown herself to be so contrary? It would be wasteful! Why invite her deeper into his scheme at all, when it would be so quick to end it, to be done with her.

Her eyes rolled like a frenzied shark's when he waved the razor before her.

"Just watch the light on it, my dear. See how it shines? You know daddy wouldn't hurt you. The light knows, too. See? Ask it, it will tell you."

The child did her best to squirm against the restraints. She wasn't very strong, though. With his mixture in her, and a bit of surgery on her frontal lobe, surely his improved device, now aligned with the machinations of the distant lighthouse, would blow her will apart like a sand painting in a hurricane. Her resistance would collapse and dissolve. She would be like the quiet child, and her mind's animating vigor would run through him like a steady dose of potent nutrients.

There was risk, of course. Julia was not properly molded. Why bother with such hazards, at this stage? Especially since there was one sure way to get back at the mother.

He looked at the reflection of Julia's mouth, and her neck, in the razor blade. This was what the mother dreaded.

Well guess what, Anne?

"I'm going to cut her fucking head off!"

CHAPTER 61

The hurricane was pushing her away! Julia's ghost was caught in these atrocious winds and she'd be dragged to the middle of the ocean!

"Julia! Please," Anne cried out. "If you don't come back, there's nothing left."

Too late. Anne had failed in every way imaginable.

It was over. Julia was nowhere, now.

Hunched against the powerful wind, she staggered back to the shelter of the crypt, and closed herself in darkness. She felt her way toward the corner where she'd sat with Julia, and she collapsed there. Her hand brushed the flashlight, but she did not bother with it. Her only intention was to remain there forever, holding the memory of her daughter, and holding it close. She would sleep endlessly in this tomb.

A dreamy voice in her thoughts sang, *this tomb, your womb…* as a wave of exhaustion swept over her. But she shook her head, suddenly, and snapped herself free from the grip of that tiredness. It wasn't over, not yet. "I won't give up on you, honey! I won't let that monster get away with—"

She felt around for the gun, then stood up and secured it in her waistband. She'd get back in that house, and she'd shoot him in the heart.

Wait, wait. Oh please God. To walk into that world, to become trapped again... What if Julia came back to the rocks, needing her mother?

...Mee-I quiet child me hello...

What did it mean? What was Julia trying to tell her?

...Mee-I, Julia...
She's not dead, mommy!

Anne took the baby monitor out of the sandwich pouch.

This crypt was so far from his lab, and the power of a 9-volt battery was so feeble. But why should that matter? The last time she turned this monitor on, a memory had been brought to life. She sensed it had more to do with the power of the mind, than with the flow of current. Besides, the beam from lighthouse swept over this area. Could something else be given incarnation, the way her five-year-old memory had? What about hopes, or prayers? Prayer seemed like the only thing that could combat all this. What about the dream she'd had of Julia as a young woman? That was such a positive, strong image of Julia. Would a sharp evocation of that dream bring *that* Julia to life? What about made-up stories?

She needed to decide, quickly. Where to direct her thoughts, what to focus on, before turning the dial.

The choice was instinctive, and natural, and the calm focus she required draped over her, unforced, like a gift from heaven. With a prayerful, meditative disposition, she clicked the switch.

The sound began, as before, like someone stuffing crinkled foil into her ears, into her brain. Then the colors. The shapes. Bedazzling. Cellular. Within and without, representing a force which underlied the material realm. Form and chaos. Creativity.

In the dark tomb, there was nothing to obscure the images. Every color in the spectrum blossomed and seemlessly transmuted into its compliment. Every minuscule point on every image embodied the whole of the image as well.

She felt her body slip, and drain of energy. But with no one there to hold her back, to turn off the monitor, the connection became a journey. She crossed a threshold of light and sound, into a realm of formlessness.

...and darkness.

CHAPTER 62

When she reached the shore road in Bow Lee Point, a place last viewed receding from the rear window of a police cruiser in another life, the wind was kicking off the water, threatening to tip her car, and Alice felt she could any minute regress to the state of a terrified six year old. On the outside, though, she was all metal.

Most of the houses on the street were new, and with the oddness of taped "exes" in many of the windows, she imagined she was journeying into a stormy, three-dimensional game of tic-tac-toe—a game she remembered playing on fogged glass as a child, in the years after her release from torment.

She veered into the driveway, and she scurried through raging weather. It didn't take long to discover the unlocked entrance from the carport. This part of the house was an addition to her childhood home, a useful addition, too, where useful things were stored. Like the long-handled axe she found suspended on nails behind a forgotten exercise machine.

She stared at a wall of shelves in the utility room. Whatever was on the other side had once been the library, where her nanny read to her. It had been a good room for solitude, too, safer than her own room because it was on the first floor, and distant from the third. It was fitting point of entry.

She leaned her mask against the leg of a table, and she cleared the shelves quickly, dumping the contents to the floor. She removed the shelves from their metal braces and revealed a gritty wall, with faded areas in the paint.

She raised the heavy axe, and swung. Plaster sprayed in all directions. A chunk of clap board, the size of a doormat, outlined itself among jagged cracks. She removed the chunk easily, tore out a long strip of fiberglass insulation, and swung the axe again. The wood of the interior panel split, and she saw through a crack to a room with a desk, and a diploma on the wall.

After a succession of furious, labored blows, she climbed through a large opening, tribal mask in hand.

Instantly, there was a sound. Out past the doorway, behind the spindles of a climbing stairway, a black shape crouched. It's rumbling, throaty growl was unmistakably that of a predatory feline. Between the spindles, a pair of emerald eyes dilated above bone-white fangs.

Alice put on her mask and with a breath, she felt her body shift naturally into the posture of her warrior persona.

The panther vaulted over the railing and sprung toward the office. With a muted thud it landed on its feet, powerful and alert.

She held the axe horizontally in front of her. Although she was prepared to fight, she spent little mental energy on the animal. She advanced, staring with the steady eyes of the warrior. With the eyes of Blood Moon, for that was her name, she stared into the space above the panther.

The cat prowled watchfully past her, and inspected the hole in the wall. She advanced to the stairs, invulnerable. Invisible.

…except to the Hollywood-styled, child vampire in the upper hall, who crouched in seething hatred, and vile hunger, in demonic rage, paste-skinned and white eyed, who lunged through the air the moment Alice was in sight.

White fangs sprayed saliva. Small features—a nose, an ear—implied sweet innocence and begged for her hesitation, as a child's high-pitched, anguished squeal deafened her.

Blood Moon decapitated the creature with a single swing of the axe-blade.

CHAPTER 63

Julia wanted her mother. This wasn't fair. She was tied up and no one was supposed to do that. She had to pee from being in that box so long. *God! Make him stop!*

When the tall man with her father's face pulled a razor out of his pocket, when he unfolded it, she knew what was about to happen. She knew what he was going to do. But she didn't want him to! She didn't want to be dead, and in a box forever, and never see her mother again.

She cried. Her mind wanted to make her think of something else—that field of daisies where she played with her friends. She wanted to go back to her mother, to that place by the ocean, to that fuzzy dream, no matter how much it hurt. She wanted her mother.

Her mother would be so sad if Julia died now.

"Leave me alone!" she cried. "Get out of my house!"

Some part of her mind thought, I'm not three years old, I'm not a baby. But she heard herself screaming, and it was just like being a little baby in the crib, crying for her mother in the middle of the night. Raging with fear.

Her arms and legs were trapped. Her forehead was strapped to the back of the chair. So when he drew back with the blade she couldn't even tuck her chin. It wasn't fair, it wasn't fair, that she couldn't even try to protect herself. She was just a little girl.

Her eyes closed tight. It would all be over, in a second. She wouldn't be a statue in a box, she'd be with God. She was sad about it, though.

"DON'T YOU DARE!" someone shouted.

Julia opened her eyes, and the tall man spun to face someone else in the room, someone whose face looked like it came from a bright, ancient painting in a museum, and who was bathed in light. She held an axe.

The tall man hollered. "What the Christ?!"

And a deep voice asked, "Do you remember me?"

There was a short silence.

"Who sent you?"

The woman laughed. "You're confused."

Someone else came into the room, then, but only Julia saw little Beth, at first.

No, it wasn't Beth, not really… was it?

It was. But she was different. She seemed older than before, and her skin was normal, not milky-clear. She crept from behind the man's desk, and she snuck along the edge of the room until she was near Julia. Behind the tall man, the girl turned, and faced the woman in the mask.

The tall man was saying something, but Julia couldn't listen. She was watching the way the girl, Beth, and the woman in the mask looked at one another.

Three bodies appeared on the floor, one by one. Bazil, Liza and Eli, all stiff-looking, like paste dolls.

The woman slowly reached up and lifted the edge of her mask. She removed the mask completely, but the light around her didn't change. She was a grey haired woman, and she looked very old, and sad. She held Beth's attention for a moment, with something strange in her eyes, something so kind, and loving. Then Beth turned and came to Julia.

"Ah," the tall man said. "Ha! I see. How old and ugly you've gotten."

"You should have stayed dead."

Beth whispered to Julia, "I'll get you out," and she began tugging at the straps.

"Your work is over," the woman said.

"I'm glad you've come," he said, "Hard as that may seem to believe." He turned and walked past her to a shelf. "I have something for you. From your mother."

He brought down some kind of pouch, which he fiddled with as he walked back to her. "I hope you like this," he said. "Wait..." He put his hands behind his back. "Do you remember our game? Which hand?"

Julia worried the tall man would see Beth, but the woman turned, and with animal strength, she flung the axe end-over-end through the air. It wedged into the wall with a bang, diverting his attention. "Your games were never fair, and you've already lost," she said.

"Ah, very well," he sighed. "Still, you must have this. Your mother always meant for you to have it."

As Beth tugged at the straps, Julia watched the tall man's hand dip into the pouch behind his back, and she saw what he pulled out: the same weapon he'd threatened her with seconds before. It was a trick—a magician's trick—and she wanted to cry out to the woman. But it was over before she could.

"Ahh, hell, I'll just give it to you," he said.

He swung his arm, and with a smooth stroke he waved the thin metal wand below the woman's chin.

The woman made a sound like a cat wretching. She gagged. The mask dropped from her hands with a clatter, and she clutched her neck. She stood silently, her mouth wide open.

The man wiped the razor blade off on a handkerchief.

Then Julia saw the red running down the woman's clothes.

The woman dropped to one knee, with a shocked expression. Blood spurted between her fingers, and gathered in a pool around her.

Chapter 64

Van Rensselaer wiped off the blade and stared at the body of his eldest daughter. The bitch. Why did so many betray him? His own daughter! No wonder he could expect nothing better from strangers.

This one could have had a place, had she approached him properly. He would have honored their former bond. She'd been an integral element of his work, in the early days. When he was just starting out.

Look at her now. Dead. When she could have been immortal.

But things were moving forward. The Great Laws demanded much from him, but clearly the message now was to move on.

His resolve was strengthened. Cut all ties. Cut the throats of those who meant to slow him.

He turned to face Julia Clausin, and to proceed.

She was strapped tight in his chair, below the princely veil of apparatus. Anne McGilvary.

The mother. Not the daughter.

It was the mother who was his prisoner. Yes. Had he been confused for a moment?

The mother, yes, that's right. What could confuse him, when everything was as he wanted it?

She stared at him.

"Anne! I'm so pleased." He walked up to her. "Ah, you see? It's what was meant, all along. Yours is the first adult spirit to merge with mine."

The psychotropic mixture was in the bowl on her lap. When he stirred it, with the small, silver spoon, he felt the warmth of her belly and loins, and realized the spoon had become electrically charged from his touch. He stirred the mixture slowly and playfully, to heighten her excitement.

"You see how it all falls into place?" he said. He glanced up. "The invention is finally ready."

The storm outside shook all the windows and walls in the house.

"It's for you, dear. This is how we become joined. Through the invention. We merge. With me. And every incarnation I give you with future impulses will really be you, my love. They will have that authenticity. You see?"

He brought the spoon to her lips, amazed by the steeliness of her blue eyes.

"Now, open up, dear," he said.

Her mouth opened wide.

Spooning the dark mixture into her was sexual—a form of intercourse new to him, but pleasurable as any he had known.

"There," he said. "Now, swallow. I know it tastes bad. But you must learn to love it!"

Yet, as she swallowed, there was no indication of displeasure—so enamored of his will had she at last become.

"That's a good girl," he said. "Now another. Yesss…"

The pleasure grew in him. The blood in his stomach and in his erect organ swirled with warm delight.

"You were such a fucking bitch, Anne." This time he jammed the heaping spoon into her mouth, until her lips pressed against his knuckles. "Before you learned the truth. Yess -" Her eyes rolled back, and a little sound curled in her throat.

He lifted the bowl, draped a leg across her lap and straddled her. He brought the bowl to her lips, and began feeding her with his fingers. "Oh, you like that, don't you. Come on, eat it. That's right." He pressed his crotch against her belly. "Yess, every last bite. Swallow. Good. Come on, more. Swallow. Here. Here. Here!"

He started to ejaculate in his clothing—against her—and he reached behind her and pulled the wire near the window casement to start the device working.

When the machine started humming, though, he was stunned. He straddled the chair, but no one was in it. His legs were threaded through the spirals formed by the child-sized armrests. But no warm female sat beneath him, just a hard chair, smeared with his valued mixture.

"Shit!!!"

His orgasm continued, uncomfortably. As he struggled awkwardly with his confined legs, and attempted to free them from their foolish position, he looked around. The woman stood behind her daughter, in the center of the room.

"What the fuck?!" he shouted.

Then the mother was gone, vanished. Some kind of trick. The brat alone was left.

Van Rensselaer climbed shakily out of the chair, his belly moist from ejaculate.

Julia crouched by the body of the daughter who had betrayed him, as if the lifeless woman could protect her. The child knew there was no one else to hide behind. She knew she was next.

CHAPTER 65

A fierce roar awakened Anne from a bottomless slumber. She opened her eyes and saw the baby monitor—it had dropped to the stone floor beside her and was cracked, and singed.

She had been with Julia. She couldn't remember it, exactly. But emotionally, she knew.

Somehow, she'd helped her daughter.

Light, like a shower from a torn feather pillow, tumbled into the crypt, and a man stood in the dim halo.

He spoke her name, and he came near her. His clothes were bloody, his face familiar. "Where's Julia?!" he said.

Anne sat up, and cradled herself. "I don't know," she said weakly. "I think she's gone. I think my baby's gone forever."

"Anne—"

She shook her head, and smiled at him. "No, I think it's alright. I think she's…somewhere peaceful now."

"I spoke to someone," he said. "She was supposed to come here—"

"It's alright," Anne said.

He sat down beside her, and warmed her with an embrace. Then he told her about Alice Van Rensselaer.

Anne could sympathize with Alice's shock and horror over forgetting her little sister's name. There was a time, though it seemed long ago, when Anne had forgotten Julia. But never again.

"It wasn't her fault," Anne said. "That she couldn't remember…"

"No," Ed said. "The father never used the girl's real name. He called his youngest daughter 'the quiet child.'"

Anne's chest tightened. A flood of poison raced through her.

"Oh God!" she said, rising unsteadily. "We have to get her out of there!"

"What?"

"She's in there! She's not dead!"

   * * * * * * * * * *

They hurried deeper into the crypt. At some point in the sloping corridor, ocean currents liberally penetrated the chinks in the walls. Cold water rose to their ankles, and higher. Then the floor leveled off, as they reached the next chamber.

It was a larger space. The opposite wall held a row of coffin sized enclosures, sealed off with marble slabs. Three of the slabs were engraved with names and dates. Ed shined the light on them. Two parents and their child. Victor Van Rensselaer, his wife Agnes, and their daughter, Elizabeth.

He unzipped his bag of tools, pulled out a hammer and a spike and started whacking away. Within ten minutes the grouted seal was shattered, and chunks of rock plunked into the water. Anne shivered, and held herself, as Ed removed the slab and tossed it aside with a splash, and a thud.

Despite numerous decades in this damp place, the coffin was solid, though grey mold coated it thickly. Together, they reached in and dragged the coffin toward them through a path of dust.

Cut into the left wall of the room was a table-high alcove, and they hoised the child-sized box to the shelf therein. Then they forced open the lid.

Anne uttered a horrified cry, and Ed held his breath.

She was so petite. Like a china doll. That was how her skin looked, too. Eggshell white, and brittle. And while she was as motionless as porcelain, the delicateness of her features made her alive-looking, and beautiful. Lying there in a ruffled dress, with her arms folded across her chest, she seemed like any moment she might begin to talk. Her open eyes stared, as if made from glass.

Almost imperceptibly, her lips parted.

A faint, green light seemed to shine from her mouth.

The crypt filled with a whispery sound like the sea. Unlike the sound of waves, though, this rush of air did not crescendo, but grew steadily for what seemed like minutes, until it was nearly deafening. Anne and Ed clung to one another. The light in the girl's mouth grew brighter, and there was the slightest rise in her belly.

Then the sound receded as slowly as it had come.

"Her breath?" Ed asked.

"Slowly," Anne whispered. "She breathes so slowly."

They listened for another breath, but none came.

Anne lifted the child in her arms. The grave marker had indicated that the girl was five years old when she was buried, and although she was much, much older now, she had the size and weight of a child of three. Her skin was softer than it looked, rubbery, cold to touch, and thin as the petal of a lily. Blood vessels forked and tapered just below the outmost layer. Her arms were crossed, and her fingers curled into tiny, tranquil fists. When her head tilted back against the crook of Anne's elbow, her jaw fell open, and the green light sharpened, changing her skin color into something sickly.

"Get that thing out of her mouth!" Anne said.

Ed gently reached in with a thumb and forefinger. There was a quiet rattle of stone against teeth as he rotated the gem. Then he removed the acorn-sized, emerald-green crystal.

"Her hands, too," Anne said. Ed helped to gently unfold Elizabeth's small fingers, no stiffer than wet clay. Each hand revealed a multi-faceted, polished crystal.

"Get rid of them," Anne said.

One by one, Ed whipped them at the far wall, where they exploded. Sparkling fragments and crystal dust plunked into the water.

She asked him to get the blanket, and when he returned with it balled in his arms, the child, Elizabeth, coughed a quick, quiet cough.

For some reason, to Anne that cough was an undeniable signal. It was so weak, and fatigued, yet within it was a cry of relief, a sigh of passage. The child's skin was changing before her eyes: the network of veins all turning dark black.

As Ed opened the blanket, an object, which had not been there earlier, tumbled into the coffin. Grateful, Anne scooped up Julia's pretty Marianne doll, and she tucked it in little Elizabeth's arms, and wrapped them together in the blanket. With her shoulder, she wiped a tear to keep it from falling on the girl's cheek, and she tucked Elizabeth and Marianne in together.

Ed put an arm around her.

"Don't worry, honey," Anne said. "No one will hurt you ever again."

CHAPTER 66

Van Rensselaer couldn't believe his eyes. Julia had just rolled the dead woman onto her back. Now a gaping wound opened in his aged daughter's chest, and Julia's hand sunk into it.

"All right, YOU!" he yelled. "Come here this instant!"

Julia turned, faced him, and her hand withdrew from the corpse's chest cavity with a sound of wet suction. She rose, clutching a clump of gore.

What the fuck was she doing?!

Not magic?!

"You heard me!" he shouted, in his loudest voice. But the child stood there silently, not moving. "One!" he counted. "Two! If you make me come get you, you'll be very sorry! Three!" He marched across the room until he stood two feet from the corpse.

That's when he saw the other bodies, strewn on each side of him. Children.

And he saw another little girl, beside Julia.

He screamed. "What?! I don't believe this! You are in for it now! You listen to me—!"

Julia passed the human heart to the other girl, his source, his strength… his quiet child. How could she have—? How could she be here?

The quiet child took the gory object. She held it in front of her and stared down at it. "Daddy?"

The sight paralyzed him. Impossible!

A burst of orange sparks exploded to his right. He turned. The heart in the chest of the older boy's corpse smoldered. Black clouds tumbled upward from it. Another blast, on the other side. Another smoldering heart, like melted tar, bubbled upward through the chubby one's motionless breastbone.

Then the heart from the dark-haired boy's corpse jumped from a depression in his sweater, and danced, like a jolted animal, over the floorboards. Black ash shot upward from it.

Van Rensselaer stepped back. She was trying to confuse him, she was—

He'd rip the bloody thing from the quiet child's hands, and smash it. Then he'd grab her, and Julia, and -

"Here, daddy…" The quiet child stared down at the heart in her hands like it was some kind of crystal ball. "You forgot my name. It's Eli, daddy. It's Liza. It's Beth. My name, daddy. My name is Elizabeth!"

The heart Elizabeth held glowed blue. An icy heat radiated from it. He felt it warming him from that distance. Then, in the liquid coating on the muscle she held, thousands of blue needles appeared, shining, with frenzied movement like electrified minnows. Their incandescence intensified, and they lifted into the air and streamed through space toward him.

He screamed, and waved his arms frantically, as the needles engulfed him, and struck him like sharp, electric stingers. A cosmic ribbon trailed through the air behind them.

The heart in his daughter's hands rose, as if borne on hurricane winds. It sailed upward, streamed through the sparkling trail, and struck Van Rensselaer with cannonball force. It jolted him, and knocked him through the air.

He sailed backward and crashed into the far wall, into the brassy mesh of filaments and gems above the little chair. A wire extending down from the widow's watch nearly sliced his ear off. Blue sparks rained upward and penetrated the ceiling.

The mechanism above began to grind. Damn it! Something had come unbalanced. The device was too fragile.

The splattered, phosphorescent heart clung to him, a gooey blob of pulsating gore. Blue light blinded him, and he smelled burning. Sparks showered from the ceiling; some plunged into the packing straw of the open crates. The room began to fill with smoke.

Through the thickening dark haze, he saw animal murals on the walls. The two girls knelt by a shiny coffin, hands folded. In bright, sing-song unison, they prayed to the old God.

CHAPTER 67

The house was a cathedral of flame, caged by brittle embers. Firemen ducked, and cowered from the heat as they skirted the property, hurrying in all directions. The flashing lights in front were dull compared to the blaze.

Anne clutched at a firefighter's thick sleeve. "Did anyone get out? Please!"

He glanced over his shoulder. "Just one, ma'am."

The man sat on the big rock in her front yard, her husband's face marred with soot. He was wrapped in a blanket, and he took occasional breaths from an oxygen tank. A fireman beside him wrote in a notebook.

The discomfort of the gun digging into the small of her back had all but escaped her notice. Now she reached behind her, and took a step.

He lowered the oxygen mask and glared at her with a blend of malice, disgust, and indifference. "My wife," he said to the fireman.

She drew the gun.

"What in hell?!" the fireman shouted.

Ed screamed her name.

She cocked the gun. Van Rensselaer stood up and glared. She aimed at his heart.

A symphonic maelstrom of raging wind, gushing hoses, popping and crashing embers, and men's voices, excited in battling the blaze, all receded beneath the peal of a single gunshot.

Van Rensselaer caved at the chest. His eyebrows registered disbelief as he gasped, and he clutched the wound. A splash of blood, like a small ocean wave, spilled from his mouth, and he fell.

CHAPTER 68

I'm amazed at my good fortune, to be chosen like this. To be singled out. Most everybody goes through life unaware of the awesome powers all around. I must be some kind of angel.

My ascent began with a special murder. At that moment the universe took notice of me, and it sent me a signal. By resurrecting the dead, the universe gave me a sign, and drew me into that special realm where everything is possible.

At first it was frightening. But no more. The great laws of physics and chemistry work together in my veins.

I remember a final turn in the maze of events, a turn that led along an upward sloping tunnel. I knew I was closer. I shimmied through a pipe which any normal man would have found too narrow. And when I saw the ladder, I recognized it for what it was: an invitation to heaven.

I pushed the manhole cover aside. That metal disk was like a cap to my consciousness. Awareness bloomed in the supercharged, open air.

The light of heaven blazed, a short distance from me, surrounded by the blackest darkness. It was a brilliant, amazing light, more fiery and intricate than any I'd seen before.

It led me to a gathering, held in my honor. The house I'd once so bravely entered, where I'd performed that valiant and noteworthy execution, had transformed into a luminescent shrine.

They were expecting me. I would know what to do.

I drew near an electric-red fire truck, excited about my grand entrance. That's when I saw him—the sacrificial victim. Wrapped in a blanket, a look of amazement on his face, he seemed spellbound by a vision of his own. He did not see me, this undead man whose purpose was to die once more, to be killed again, thus styling my entrance to eternity.

I set down my bag, knowing I would never need it again. The chemicals in there embodied an embryonic method of passage. The gun was the final key.

A man in yellow, sitting on the back of a truck, took a long drink from a bottle. The mood was festive. But I paid no attention. The fiend had become a lamb, who now uncloaked himself, and let the blanket fall in preparation. I took aim, and fired.

*   *   *   *   *   *   *   *   *   *

A firefighter leapt off the truck and knocked Willie Prager to the ground. There was shouting and commotion, and his face pressed against wet concrete. Two men held him, their knees injuring his back. But inside, he was serene. He knew he'd won his admission to everlasting bliss.

CHAPTER 69

It was past three in the morning by the time the flames were out. Heavy rains returned and extinguished the last, smoldering embers. They sat in Ed's car and watched in halogen light as a section of the skeletal third floor crashed tipped and fell to the earth. Half the house had caved in, right to the ground level. The front wall was mostly missing. Jagged cross-sections of floor opened onto a ten-foot pile of rubble.

When questioned by the police, Anne said she'd drawn the gun because her husband was a dangerous man who had tried to kill her. She said she believed that he had caused the blaze. She said she had no intention of shooting him. She only wanted him arrested.

She was asked to report to the police station at her earliest convenience, to have her statement taken. The police confiscated the gun, and told Ed he would have to sign a release for it. Willie Prager was placed under arrest.

Daylight began to break, and when Anne awakened in the car, most of the firefighers had gone. Police were still about, and she knew some were searching through the rubble for her daughter's remains. She told Ed she wanted to look, too.

"They won't want you to."

"I don't care."

As they stepped unseen into the mess, soot covered their clothes.

A broad section of the east wall was charred through, and the ocean swam beyond. Anne was like a snail, now. Her only home was on her back.

She picked through char, through fragments of a lost world, a long-ago life. It seemed pointless. When she found her once-prized, ruby bracelet, in need only of some cleaning, she held it briefly then returned it to the ruins. The only thing she hoped to find, was some bit of remembrance. Something of Julia's.

Everything Anne loved was gone. Even her heart seemed to have burned up and shriveled to nothing.

She closed her eyes, feeling her cheeks getting hot and wet. She'd suffered the agony of Julia's death repeatedly, so she knew what kind of torment to expect in the coming months and years. Though it wouldn't be like that, not like before. Because she knew what was real. She knew what was possible, and what was everlasting.

In the far-reaching black space behind her eye lids, she imagined her own heart ablaze with grief and love. She hoped its pale light would guide Julia to an eternal, perfect place.

When she opened her eyes, feeling exhausted, ready to go, fearing the days and months ahead, she saw a glint among the embers. The only shiny thing left, no doubt. She trudged over toward the faint glimmer, to investigate, and she climbed carefully onto a pile of burned, broken wood. She tossed a jutting board aside.

The metal thing was recognizable. It was one of two brass handles from Julia's toy chest.

Anne's weight shifted, and her leg slid down into a hole in the rubble. When she regained her balance, she determinedly threw boards aside until the toy chest was completely uncovered.

"God almighty!"

Anne's hands were black from the boards she'd removed, but no part of the toy chest was melted nor blistered. There was not a mark of soot on it. Not a single flake of ash had settled on top. The chest was brightly colored. It was intact, but it was altered. On all sides, images of forests, jungles, deserts and the sea, of life-like animals with unique personalities, were emblazoned, as if through some unknown printing process whereby the murals from Julia's playroom had been transferred. The chest was like something newly ready for purchase in an upscale specialty shop. And when Anne raised the lid, she saw a child curled in awkward rest. Her sweetheart's eyes fluttered open.

Julia spoke sleepily, with a sweet smile, as fresh as if she'd awakened from a peaceful night in her playroom. "Hi—"

"Julia!" Anne cried, seizing her daughter, pulling into her arms. "Sweetheart!" She saturated Julia with kisses, and held her closer than ever.

About the Author

John McKenna is a graduate of the Trinity Rep Conservatory theatrical training program in Providence. He holds a Bachelor's degree in education. He lives, writes, and teaches in New England, alongside his wife: artist and teacher, Eleanor McKenna.